RHIANNON

CAROLE LLEWELLYN

LARGE PRINT

Oxford

First published in Great Britain 2010
by
Robert Hale Limited

Published in Large Print 2010 by ISIS Publishing Ltd.,
7 Centremead, Osney Mead, Oxford OX2 0ES
by arrangement with
Robert Hale Limited

British Library Cataloguing in Publication Data
Llewellyn, Carole.
    Rhiannon.
    1. Abandoned children - - Wales - - Fiction.
    2. Wales - - History - - 20th century - - Fiction.
    3. Domestic fiction.
    4. Large type books.
    I. Title
    823.9'2–dc22

ISBN 978–0–7531–8698–5 (hb)
ISBN 978–0–7531–8699–2 (pb)

Printed and bound in Great Britain by
T. J. International Ltd., Padstow, Cornwall

For
Amy and Sophie
Robert and Clare
Paula and Paul
With all my love

Acknowledgements

My thanks to everyone at Robert Hale Ltd. My thanks also to my writing friends at Brixham Writers' Group, for their help and encouragement. Finally my love and thanks to Barrie for his love and support.

CHAPTER
ONE

November 1908

Rhiannon Hughes sat crouched in the darkness on the top stair. She shivered with cold and fear. Her winceyette nightgown pulled over her knees proved scant protection against the chill of the early November night. Her chest was tight, her mouth dry. What would the next few hours bring?

"What on earth are you doing sat out there? Come back to bed before you catch your death," Mair called out.

Rhiannon quickly turned to face the bedroom. "Shhhh! I don't want Dad to know I'm here," she whispered, her fingers brushing aside a few unruly chestnut curls that had fallen loose over her eyes. "As soon as I hear Nellie come in, I'm going to go down and try to keep the peace."

"You'll be lucky." Mair sniggered. "My mam's really gone and done it this time. God help her when she comes in, and I say, serve her right!"

"You know you don't mean that."

"I do too. Dai's been good to us. Why does she have to go and spoil it?" Mair asked. "Rhi? What if Dai throws us out?"

"Don't be daft! My dad would never throw you out. He loves you."

"But —"

"No buts. He loves you and that's all you need to believe. Now get to bed."

"All right, Miss Bossy-Boots, I'm going."

It surprised Rhiannon that Mair hadn't put up more of an objection but she needed to be on her own to listen intently for the sound of the back door opening: the signal that her stepmother had returned. Although part of her agreed with Mair, she felt she had at least to try to stop the row. She had never seen her father so angry. It was obvious to her that he had come home early from the pit especially to catch Nellie out.

These past weeks her father and Nellie had argued a lot — mainly about her stepmother's choice of friends. Thankfully, up to now her father had managed to hold on to his temper. Rhiannon sensed that he kept control mainly for her and Mair's benefit; while one of them was in the room things never got out of hand. As the elder of the girls she felt it was left to her to run downstairs the minute she heard Nellie's voice — even though she knew it was going against her father's earlier wishes.

"Rhiannon, it's time you and Mair were in bed. You'll have to take yourselves up tonight. And, whatever happens when Nellie gets back, you stay where you are, do you hear?" her father had ordered.

"Dad, I'll go with Mair, but, please, let me come back down. I could make you some supper."

2

"I'm not hungry," he snapped. "Just do as you're told. Get to bed!"

The tone of his voice convinced Rhiannon that she had better do as he asked; she didn't want to risk upsetting him further. She looked across to Mair. Mair, ever the pessimist, ran the edge of her hand swiftly across her throat as if it were a knife — that's how much trouble she thought Nellie was in.

"Come on, Mair, it's time for bed," Rhiannon said.

"Do I have to?"

"Yea, 'fraid so."

"Are you coming too?" Mair asked.

Even though Rhiannon was fifteen and a half — a good three years older than Mair, Mair still objected if Rhiannon stayed up later than she did.

"We're both going. Now come on."

Reluctantly Mair crossed the room to kiss her stepfather goodnight. As she placed a soft kiss on his cheek, there was no response. Other nights he would have insisted on taking them up the "wooden hill". Tonight he obviously had other things on his mind.

As Rhiannon stepped forward to place her own kiss on her father's gaunt, grey face, she made a last attempt to pacify him,

"I'm sure Nellie won't be long. I suppose she didn't expect you home so early."

"That's bloody obvious," he snapped. Then, checking himself, "Sorry, love. I shouldn't swear and definitely not at you. None of this is your fault. I still can't believe she left the two of you on your own."

"It doesn't happen that often, honest, Dad," Rhiannon lied, in an attempt to calm him, her fingers crossed in the hope that God would forgive her fibbing, and she threw Mair a look that told her her fate if she dared contradict her.

It worked. For once Mair said nothing.

"Rhiannon, love. You don't have to lie for her. For months I've ignored the whispered rumours of my butties down the pit. You see I thought they were just trying to goad me — they've done it to others before, 'just for a laugh'. But this time it seems they were speaking the truth and the laugh is on me." He put his head in his hands.

"Goodnight, Dad," Rhiannon said. Instantly followed by Mair's "Goodnight, Dai."

Dai lifted his face, his eyes full of sadness. "Goodnight and God bless the both of you. You really don't deserve this." He gave them a tender smile before adding, "Rhiannon, love, do your dad a big favour and turn that lamp down before you go up. I need to sit alone in the darkness for a while."

They left him sitting in his old rocker, staring into the fireplace. His silhouette was highlighted by the huge fire in the grate. His breathing was laboured, nostrils flared, fists clenched to his mouth. He bore no resemblance to her once mild-tempered father — this man looked as if he were possessed by the devil.

Mair Parsons was fuming. Who did Rhiannon Hughes think she was ordering her to bed like that? It probably looked as if Mair, for once, was doing as she was bid — but in truth Mair really couldn't see the

4

point of sitting on a draughty landing, especially on such a cold night, so *she* took herself off to bed.

As she snuggled under the bedclothes she prayed her mother would come home soon. Dai was a good man and didn't deserve the way her mother was behaving. She'd obviously gone back to the way she'd behaved when they lodged at the Tredegar — they'd shared a room there, and many a night Mair was left to fend for herself while her mother was down in the bar drinking. More than once she had to suffer being pushed from the bed to sleep on the floor when her mother brought a man back. When that happened Mair would spend most of the night with her fingers in her ears — it was at these times that she truly hated her mother.

Although Mair had only been eight years old at the time she clearly remembered the cold November day, four years ago, when she and her mother had made the mile walk from the Tredegar Pub to Dai's house in Ponty, one of the many small mining villages in the Nantgarw Valley.

"Now, you be on your best behaviour when we get to Dai Hughes's house. Don't say a word. And don't contradict anything I say, do you hear? I don't want you to bugger up my chances," her mother had said.

Mair nodded. That morning Nellie had insisted on them both making a special effort with their toilet and clothes. Nellie had dressed in a crisp white shirt, grey flannel long skirt, and shawl; her light-brown hair was gleaming with health and her blue eyes were so full of life. Mair had never seen her mother look prettier. She instinctively knew that this Dai Hughes, whoever he was, had something to do with their future well-being.

"Good morning, Mr Hughes," her mother had said as Dai answered the door of his terraced house. "I've heard that you're looking for someone to keep house and look after a young 'un."

"Yes. That's right. And who might you be?"

"I'm Nellie Parsons and I've come to offer myself for the position," she said with confidence.

Mair couldn't help but smile to herself. These were the exact words her mother had been repeating as they walked.

"Morning, Dai," a middle-aged woman called from next door.

Dai mumbled a quick, "Good morning." At this moment he could do without Ethel's idle chit-chat.

"You're up bright and early, Dai, but then you've got more sense than my Jack; he's still sleeping off the bellyful of ale he supped at the Tredegar last night." She turned to the good-looking, tousle-haired, young lad leaning against her doorframe, "I ask you, what sort of an example is that to be setting my Frank here, not to mention the young 'uns?"

Frank shook his head, "Come on, Mam. After working a full week down that stinking pit he deserves a few pints."

"I suppose you're right. Let's hope you don't go to work there, eh?"

As Ethel turned her attention to cleaning the door knocker, Dai breathed a sigh of relief — but he hadn't bargained on Frank.

6

"Mr Hughes, I was just thinking of calling on Rhiannon. Is she in?" Frank asked, his eyes darting from Nellie to Mair and then to Dai.

"No — no, she's gone on an errand for me — mind you she'll not be long. I'll have her give you a shout when she gets back, eh?"

Frank and Rhi had been friends since they were toddlers. If the truth be known, young Frank Lewis had more than a soft spot for Dai's daughter and, while Dai never objected to their friendship, he wanted more than an early marriage and a houseful of kids for *his* Rhiannon.

"I hope she's back before your visitors leave. If I know Rhiannon, she'd be that put out if she missed them — and who could blame her?" The lad flashed a cheeky wink at Nellie.

Dai threw him a disapproving look.

"I think you'd better come inside. Although I'm not promising anything, mind," he said, turning to Nellie. Then, by way of explanation, "Ethel Lewis, from next door, is a kind soul. But she can be nosy with it. I dread to think what she and her son will make out of you two turning up on my doorstep."

"It's all right; with a family like mine I've had to grow a thick skin where valley gossips are concerned."

Dai looked uncomfortable. "Please, take a seat in front of the fire."

Before taking her seat Mair couldn't help but notice the way her mother deliberately brushed herself against Dai.

For a moment he looked flustered.

"Are you all right, Mr Hughes?" her mother asked, in an unusually sweet voice.

Dai gave a nervous cough. "Yes-yes, I'm fine," he answered. "The thing is . . . I was really looking for someone older. It's a big responsibility tending house and looking after a ten-year-old child." Dai appeared to be trying to put her off.

But her mother was having none of it. "I'm twenty-five, so you needn't worry on that score. And I've had years of practice looking after all my mother's brood."

Mair and her mother had lived with Grandma Lily and Grandpa Jack in Carn Terrace at the top end of the valley, for as long as she remembered. With her grandpa in and out of prison and her gran always drunk it fell on her mother to run the house as best she could — often at Mair's expense.

"Look, Mr Hughes, I'll tell you the honest truth. I recently lost my job at the Home and Colonial — a job I really enjoyed until my dad had to go and spoil it by breaking into the shop and stealing the takings. I suppose you've heard he's back in gaol?"

"Yes, I've heard. But it's never fair. Surely you shouldn't be penalized for something your father did?"

"It's kind of you to say so, but it doesn't alter the fact that with my father in prison and me losing my job — it's thanks to him that we couldn't pay the rent and have been evicted from our house in Carn Terrace. My mother has buggered off to Nantymoel, taking my four sisters, to live with our gran. There's no room for Mair and me, so we're lodging with Dilys Morgan whose

8

parents keep the Tredegar public house. Mr Hughes, I desperately need this job if I'm to pay my way."

"It sounds to me as if we're as desperate as one another. Since my wife's death, almost a year ago, I've found it very difficult to juggle going to work and looking after Rhiannon."

"You work at Glengarw colliery, don't you?"

"Yes, at pit bottom. Up to now I've been lucky. If George Evans, the foreman, hadn't been so sympathetic since the loss of my wife, making sure I only work the day shift, I don't know what I'd have done. But recently a few troublemakers have made complaints; they say I've been given special treatment. So there's nothing for it, I'm going to have to work my share of the night shift every other week. Which is why I'm looking for someone to live in and be here for my Rhiannon."

"It must have been very difficult for you — left on your own to bring up a young daughter?"

"I suppose it has been. Mind you, Rhiannon can cook and sew as well as the next — my Rose made sure of that. And the neighbours have been good. Especially Ethel from next door — twice a week she brings us a large saucepan of cowl. I offer to pay but she won't hear of it, insisting that a bit of end of lamb and a few vegetables cost next to nought — she's a heart of gold that one. Anyways, I need to know that there's someone here to get Rhiannon to school and put a good hot meal on the table when she gets home."

"I've never had trouble getting up of a morning and as for my cooking, well, since I took over the cooking duties at home, there's been no complaint from my lot." Nellie flashed him a smile.

Dai scratched at the stubble on his chin. "Look, if I was willing to take you on for say . . . a month's trial, what about your own daughter?"

Mair held her breath.

"I did think to bring her with me. We could share a room. She's no trouble, honest."

Dai looked down at the young girl; with the same blue eyes and light brown hair, a miniature of her mother. "How old is Mair?" he asked.

"She's eight. Look, if you'd rather I didn't? I know Dilys's mam wouldn't mind her staying on at the pub, and for her trouble Mair could help her wash the pots of an evening."

Another lie; earlier that morning Mair had overheard Dilys tell Nellie, "Don't even think about leaving your brat with me. If you go then she's got to go too!" Mair was about to remind her mother, but thought better of it.

Dai looked concerned, "That won't be necessary," he said. "I'll not have my daughter being looked after at your daughter's expense. So, yes, you can bring her with you. She can go to school with Rhiannon; they'll be company for one another."

Mair breathed a sigh of relief.

Dai smiled. "What do you say? Shall we give it a go?"

"When do I start?"

As they headed back to the pub to pack their few belongings Mair couldn't contain herself any longer,

"I'm that excited about us lodging with Mr Hughes. I liked him a lot. Did you like him, Mam?"

"Like him? The main object of the exercise was to make him like me and it worked too. Didn't you notice how the silly old bugger couldn't take his eyes off me? It'll not take me long to have him wrapped around my little finger — although we may have to tread carefully around his precious Rhiannon for a while."

Mair hadn't fully understood what her mother meant. But knowing her mother as she did she could tell she was up to something.

Dai Hughes wondered how long he would have to wait before his young wife decided to return home — or maybe she was in the habit of staying out all night? With him working the night shift every other week, how would he know? He stared at the erratically dancing red flames; they seemed to reflect his mood. He was so angry, not just with Nellie but also with himself. It had been his weakness that had ultimately brought them to this. If only he had been strong enough to resist the temptation to take her to his bed, there would have been no need for him to do the "decent thing" and enter into this sham of a marriage.

At first he had kidded himself that it was for the best, telling himself Rhiannon needed a woman in the house. He even told himself that Rose, his dearly departed wife, would never have wanted him and Rhiannon to live alone. Anything, but admit his unnatural obsession with Nellie — a girl almost young enough to be his daughter. What a fool he had been.

The sound of the noisy back-door latch made Dai jump. After spending what seemed like hours sitting in front of the fire his eyes had become accustomed to the darkness. He watched in silence as his wife tiptoed across the stone floor, her arm outstretched, feeling for the oil lamp on the table. On finding it her fingers slowly turned up the wick — filling the room with a harsh yellow light.

"Decided to come home then, have you?"

"Bloody hell! Y-you frightened the life out of me."

He watched as she made an effort to straighten her dishevelled clothes.

"What're you doing home s'early anyway?" she asked, her speech slurred.

"I live here, remember? And from what I can see, it's a good job I came home when I did. God only knows what you get up to when I'm on nightshift."

"Spying on me, hoping to catch me out then, were you?"

"It wasn't my intention — but unfortunately, that's the way it's turned out. What do you think you were doing leaving the house?" Dai demanded.

"I wanted to have some fun. Where's the harm in that?"

"Where's the harm? Do you really think it's right to leave Rhiannon and Mair alone for God knows how long?"

"For God's sake, man. When are you going to realize that your precious Rhiannon's no longer a baby? She's nearly sixteen!"

At that very moment Rhiannon burst into the room, out of breath from running down two flights of stairs, annoyed at having nodded off on the stairs only to be woken up by their loud voices.

"And talk of the devil, here she is — Daddy's little girl."

Dai walked over to her and, placing his arm around her shoulders looked into his daughter's big brown eyes. "Rhiannon, I want you to do as I say and go back to bed. I need to speak to Nellie alone."

"Please, Dad. I don't like it when you two quarrel." Rhiannon turned to her stepmother. "Nellie, pl-ease. Just say you're sorry."

"Go on. Do as your wonderful daddy says. Bugger off back upstairs with the other brat," Nellie barked.

"Don't you dare speak to her like that," Dai spat. "And don't ever let me hear you call your Mair a brat."

"And what are you going to do about it?" She sniggered, her body swaying from side to side.

"You're drunk! You've been down the pub, haven't you? What kind of a mother would rather be out drinking with her cronies than stay at home caring for her children?"

"I'm not drunk. Just a bit tipsy. And yes, I have been with my friends. They understand me, they make me laugh and they let me have some fun. I'm twenty-nine, for Christ's sake! Four years is long enough. I'm too young to be stuck here with you . . . I hate you!"

She lunged toward him with fists held aloft, as if intending to hit out at him. Instead she lost her balance and only his quick reaction — reaching out to catch her

— saved her from falling face down onto the stone floor.

"Rhiannon. Go to bed. I'll not tell you again. Go now!" Dai shouted.

Dai watched her leave the room reluctantly, her eyes pleading with him not to lose his temper. God, how he wanted to control himself, if only for his daughter's sake, but this woman would test the patience of a saint.

With Rhiannon safely out of the way Dai made a grab for his wife's shoulders. "So, you hate me, you hate the kids, you hate living here? Well, that's too bad. You wanted this marriage, and while you're under my roof . . ." He stopped when he realized he'd been shaking her body like a rag doll.

"Let go of me," she screamed pulling away from him. "Your roof, my arse. It belongs to the colliery, not you. And as far as I'm concerned you can stick it where the sun doesn't shine."

"This is my home. And while you live here you'll behave yourself, is that clear?" He raised his hand to strike her, and then stopped himself. What was he doing? In all the years he'd lived with his Rose he'd never once laid a hand on her — not that he'd ever had cause. All his life he had abhorred the men who resorted to violence against women.

"You're such a big man, aren't you? Oh yes, you can shake me, manhandle me, and raise a hand to me — all very manly indeed. But it's a different story in the bedroom, now isn't it? There the only thing you can raise is a smile." She stopped and gave a loud, exaggerated laugh. Then, slowly moving her hands, she

14

began caressing her own body. "What I want is someone to lust after these breasts, these hips, these thighs —"

"Stop it. You're behaving like a harlot!"

"Typical! Well, what I need is a real man — not a bloody excuse for one. Your idea of having sex is the three 'W's' — whip it in, whip it out and wipe it."

"That's enough. Shut your filthy mouth. I'll not have the children subjected to such gutter talk, do you hear?"

"Your Rhiannon, you mean. Don't want her knowing 'bout you having a small one, eh?"

"Nellie, I'm warning you!"

"Go on. Hit me, why don't you? I can see it in your eyes, you'd just love to thump me one, wouldn't you?"

Dai stared at his clenched fists. She was right. At that precise moment he had an overwhelming urge to belt her. But instead he made a grab for the back of the chair.

"See, you're not even man enough to belt me. Well, I've had enough of this house, the kids and most of all you. I'm going. I only came back to pick up a few things and I'm off."

"What do you mean off? Off where?"

"I'm leaving you. In fact, I'm leaving the valley. The truth is, I've had a better offer from someone who really knows how to give a girl a good time!"

"Another man, you mean?"

"Give the man a prize. It's finally sunk in," she sniggered.

"What about your Mair? She's your own flesh and blood."

"She's all yours. From now on you and your wonderful Rhiannon can have her. I never wanted the brat in the first place. But I knew if I brought her with me you'd feel sorry for her. All that pretending — being nice to Rhiannon, cleaning house, cooking, going to bed with you. All a means to an end. I truly believed you were a 'good catch'. How wrong can a girl be? I don't want you and I don't want your name. I shall leave as I came — as Nellie Parsons!"

"Get out. Take what you want and go. We don't need the likes of you. Go before I do something I know I'll regret."

Rhiannon and Mair sat on the stairs; they'd heard everything right up to the back door being slammed as Nellie made her dramatic exit.

"Oh, Rhi. She's really gone and left me. What am I going to do?"

Rhiannon pulled Mair to her. "You're going to stay put with us. This is your home, Mair. I think of you as my little sister, so we must stick together, be strong and look after Dad."

It was true. The early resentment Rhiannon had felt when Mair and Nellie first arrived, at least where Mair was concerned, no longer existed. Over the past four years she and Mair had formed a genuine bond and Rhiannon couldn't imagine not having her with them. And while Rhiannon found it hard to sympathize with the loss of Mair's mother, she was concerned for her father's state of mind when the gossips got their teeth into Nellie's leaving. She could almost hear them now. "The poor man. His first wife died on him and this one's up and left him. Mind you it was doomed from the start, with her being young enough to be his daughter — there's no fool like an old one, eh?"

As Mair continued to cry on her shoulder Rhiannon felt a pang of guilt for her own true feelings: relief, that Nellie had gone. This meant that she, Rhiannon Hughes, was now the woman of the house.

CHAPTER
TWO

Nellie raced from the house carrying only a small suitcase — not much to show for four years, she thought. Still, at least she had a nice warm coat to shield her from the winter chill in the air. As she made her way down King Edward Street, thankful for the part moon lighting her way, she could hardly contain her excitement. She felt a sense of achievement. Soon she'd be on her way to Cardiff and a new life with Harry Stone.

Nellie had first met Harry a year ago when he called at the house touting for business. He was a travelling salesman knocking on doors throughout the valley, with a large suitcase full of everything from a pair of silk stockings to a scouring brush. He was so unlike any other man she'd ever met. With his swarthy good looks, he was so sure of himself, wearing a thick serge dark suit with a starched white shirt, a bowler hat perched jauntily on his mop of jet-black hair; it was obvious to all that he was no valley boy. Nellie was instantly taken with him, even before he began openly to flirt with her.

"Well, now. Aren't you the pretty one? I'm sure I must have something you'd like . . ." He paused to look her up and down before adding, with a wicked smile, "in the suitcase, of course."

She actually blushed.

"Come on, how about a nice pair of silk stockings? They're only a shilling — or just sixpence if you let me fit them for you."

Nellie giggled. "You saucy thing, you!"

"Well there's no harm in a bloke trying, now is there?"

He didn't have to try very hard. Nellie was so bored with her humdrum life, a fact not missed by the wily Harry Stone. He sensed she'd be like putty in his hands. And, after over an hour of trying to tempt her to buy something, he eventually offered her the one thing he was sure she wouldn't refuse.

"At least take pity on me and meet me for a drink one night."

At first she acted all coy. "What a cheek! What a thing to ask a respectable married woman. And don't pretend you didn't know. I've seen you looking at my wedding ring."

"Sure, I know. But where's the harm? And I promise, I won't tell if you don't."

Nellie laughed. Then she nodded. "You're right. Where's the harm? It'll beat staying in this dump."

"Then it's settled. How does next Friday night suit you?"

She smiled. Next Friday night Dai would be working the night shift. "Yeah, that suits me fine."

"Great! I'll pick you up at, say, seven-thirty. I'll wait at the end of the street. Don't be late!"

"What time's your train back to Cardiff?"

"The last one's 10.45p.m. Mind you, I could always book into the Royal Hotel for the night."

"That'll cost you a few bob."

"I can afford it. Mind you, don't you go telling everyone that. It wouldn't do to show my punters how well I'm doing off their backs, eh?" He touched the side of his nose and winked.

When Friday night came Nellie had no qualms about leaving Rhiannon looking after Mair. She'd never loved Dai. Up to now their sham of a marriage had suited her but the time had come for her to have some fun, starting with this travelling salesman.

From then on every time Dai did the night shift Nellie would sneak out of the house to meet Harry, sometimes staying out all night, always making sure to be indoors before Dai was due home.

Much to Nellie's surprise what started as just a bit of fun ended with Nellie becoming well and truly smitten with Harry Stone. Although, for all his flattery, she was never sure how he truly felt about *her*. Then one night, right out the blue, he asked her to go away with him.

"Come on, Nell. Why don't you up sticks and leave that miserable old bugger you're wed to? You could come stay with me in Cardiff — there's plenty of room where I'm lodging."

Her whole being wanted to scream out "Yes! Yes! Yes!" But she stopped herself. It was a big step. And, boring as life had become with Dai and the kids, she at least had security and a roof over her head.

"But how will I live? All I have to my name is the few bob I've managed to fiddle from the housekeeping each week."

"Don't you worry your sweet little head 'bout that. I'll be more than happy to sub you till you find a job. It's the least I can do for my girl."

Her heart fluttered. It was the first time he'd ever called her *his girl*. "But it may take me ages to find a job."

"I've already put some feelers around and believe me, Cardiff is calling out for a girl with your talents."

She wasn't at all sure. But he sounded so full of confidence.

"Do you really think so?"

"I know so. You stick with me, kid. And together we'll make a fortune."

As Nellie turned the corner she breathed a sigh of relief to see Harry waiting for her, his large suitcase, holding all of his goods for sale, at his side.

"At long last. Where the hell you been? The last train leaves Pontryl in twenty minutes. If you hadn't shown you wouldn't have seen my arse for dust and you'd have blown any chance of getting away from this dump of a place. I don't like to be kept waiting. You'll do well to remember that!"

His anger took her completely by surprise. She hadn't expected a reprimand. Up to now she had only known Harry Stone, the fun-loving joker; she hadn't seen this side of him before. She quickly decided to tread carefully until she had him completely under her spell — just like Dai.

"I-I'm sorry, Harry. Dai was there waiting for me, we had a terrible row. He was so nasty." Then she added, "Mind you, when he begged me not to leave him and the kids I almost felt sorry for him. I hadn't realized how much he loved me." She lied, not wanting Harry to know how much she now depended on him for a roof over her head.

"Well, if you want to change your mind?"

"No!" she blurted. Then, realizing how desperate she sounded, "No, of course not. I've made my choice. From now on my life is with you."

"Good. Now come on, get a move on. It's late and I can't wait to get you tucked up in my bed," he said, flashing a wicked smile, his anger having disappeared as quickly as it had come.

"Why, Mr Harry Stone, I could have sworn we made love not much more than an hour ago? It was great for me but if you can't remember then I'm not the woman I thought I was," she teased.

"If you think it was good in that squeaky single bed of your mate Dilys's, wait till I get you onto my own double bed!"

The train journey to Cardiff seemed to take for ever. From their carriage window, only the occasional flicker of the gas lamps as they passed through the sleepy villages en route, disturbed the blackness of the night. Excited as Nellie was, when Harry dozed off next to her, she struggled to keep her own eyes open.

"Come on, sleepy head, we've arrived," Harry said as he opened the carriage door.

As Nellie stepped from the train she felt a foreboding and made a grab for Harry's arm. With no home, no money and no job she realized how much she depended on his generosity. As she entwined her arm in his Harry pulled her to him and kissed her and all her fears subsided. She was his girl — he'd said so.

"It's quite a walk to my digs so, just this once, we'll get a cab. All right?"

"Anything you say, Harry."

"That's what I like to hear."

As Nellie stepped from the cab she was overcome by the pungent smell and automatically raised her hand to her nose.

"What's that horrible smell?" she asked.

"It's the Bay. It's low tide."

"The Bay? I didn't realize you lived near water. I thought you lived in the city."

"This is Tiger Bay and, in my mind, the life and soul of Cardiff. I'll show you around tomorrow. But for now, get up those stairs, woman!" He playfully tapped her bottom, edging her through the front door of a large terraced dwelling.

"It's too dark. I can't see where I'm going."

"Hang on while I get the box of matches out of my pocket." He lit a match. "Is that better? For weeks I've been asking the bloody landlord to fix the damn light on these stairs. He's an ignorant bastard. I can see I'm going to have to get rough with him."

Nellie gave a shiver. The stairwell felt damp and dirty. She hoped the rooms were better.

"Well, what do you think?" Harry asked, as he switched on the light.

Nellie looked around the dark and dingy bedsit. She didn't know what she'd expected but she definitely hadn't expected to live like this.

"It's a bit small, isn't it?" she said at last.

"Small but compact though, eh? And it's got everything we need. A wardrobe, a cooker, table and chairs and most important, a large feather bed." He pulled her to him, pushing her onto the bed. "What more do we need, eh? I know it's not as grand as you're used to," he sniggered sarcastically, "but, trust me, we'll soon be moving on to bigger and better premises." He tapped the bed. "This bed is going to make us a fortune."

"What do you mean? I don't understand."

"You'll know soon enough, darling. Now come here, you little sex-bomb, you." He roughly grabbed her hands, raised them above her head and spread-eagled her on the bed.

"Don't. You're hurting me!"

"I thought you liked a bit of rough."

Ignoring her pleas he climbed on top of her.

"Stop it! What's come over you? If this is how you're going behave I'm off!" He was frightening her.

"And where would you go? You've no money, remember. The sooner you come to terms with the fact that we need each other, we'll get along just fine. From the moment I clapped eyes on you I saw the potential

24

for you being my . . . our . . . ticket to a fortune. You've got what it takes." He released his grip on her hands, once again his mood had changed and he was gently kissing her lips, then her chin, then her neck.

She instantly forgot his previous roughness. This was more like it.

She loved it when he kissed her neck. But now wasn't the time; she needed some answers.

"Harry, love? I still don't understand. What can I possibly do to make a fortune?" She was both intrigued and excited at the prospect of making a load of money.

"You must know you've got what it takes — there must be loads of men crying out for a woman like you, men with money to burn."

She pushed him aside and sat bolt upright. "Are you suggesting what I think? You want me to seduce men for money!"

"Why not? You know you love it. I feel it. I sense it. You don't just want sex — you need it!"

Nellie couldn't deny the way she'd always felt. Most women only did it to please their men; she was different. But to charge money, become a prostitute?

"You must be mad?"

His hands grabbed her throat. "Mad! Don't you dare call me mad, you bloody slut!"

She felt his hand across her face. She screamed out. He slapped her again. She couldn't believe this was happening. This wasn't what she'd come to Cardiff for. Suddenly her boring life with Dai and the kids didn't look so bad after all. Maybe she could go back? The silly bugger would be sure to welcome her back — then she remembered how she'd slagged him off in front of his precious Rhiannon; she realized that going back was definitely not an option. From now on she was stuck with Harry Stone, so she'd better make the best of it. She stopped struggling.

"That's better. Come on, Nell, start seeing sense, think of the money!"

"How much money?" He had her interest.

"Loads and loads. With my contacts I'll get you the best punters in Cardiff. By the time I'm finished with you, you'll be the talk of the town. As I said before, stick with me, girl; I'll not steer you wrong."

She smiled, suddenly warming to the idea. Surely if Harry depended on her for his good fortune he'd be especially nice to her — no more slapping her about.

"I'll need some new clothes."

"Of course."

"And a fancy new hairdo."

"Anything you want, my sweet. Now come here, it's time to practise your new profession."

CHAPTER
THREE

March 1909

The pit bottom was 3,000 feet below ground at Glengarw Colliery; twenty-four men worked down there. And, even on this, an early spring day, underground felt airless and grimy. Through the darkness the signal went out to down tools — words whispered from man to man. It was time to take a break.

Dai Hughes flopped into the stall, his Davy lamp safely set beside him. Leaning forward in the darkness he checked down the line and, sure enough, the cap lamps of his fellow workers, which had, only seconds earlier, been thrashing about like fireflies, were now still. As was the row of sweaty, black faces and white teeth that caught the glimmer of light from lamps set low at each end of the coalface.

"You all right, Frank?"

"Yea, 'spec so. 'Ave to be, don't I? Can't say I'm looking forward to the rest of the shift, though. My arms already feel like lead weights, mun."

Dai Hughes opened his round-edged Tommy box and took out a thick slice of bread and dripping. After six hours of hard slog he felt he'd more than earned this meal break.

"It's been a tough first week for you, lad. Still, if it's any consolation, you're not on your own. Why, my shoulders ache like toothache!"

Dai hadn't been at all keen to take on Frank. He felt that a lad of sixteen would never replace John Jones — an eighteen-stone six-footer, built like a brick shithouse, who'd recently been given his own stall.

"Mr Hughes, if you'd just give me a chance to prove myself. You'll not regret it, I promise," Frank Lewis had pleaded.

For years Dai had worked and lived alongside Frank's father, but sadly Jack Lewis, a hardworking family man, had recently passed away — yet another victim to tuberculosis, leaving a distraught Ethel to care for her three children — sixteen-year-old Frank, eleven-year-old Sadie and six-year-old Martha. Jack Lewis had always wanted the best for his children. When Frank did well at school Jack worked every shift he could to allow his eldest to stay on at school and, he hoped, fulfil his ambition to join the ranks of the Welsh Regiment's Volunteer Battalion.

Jack had been so proud that he confided in Dai, "That's got to be better than a life down the pit, eh Dai?"

Dai had agreed.

But sadly it wasn't to be; Jack's untimely death changed everything. As the eldest, and only son, it fell to Frank to provide for his family and to keep a roof over their heads. To that end he needed to secure a position down the mine, so that the family wouldn't have to leave their tied colliery house.

"Well, all right. For your father's sake I'm prepared to take you on. I'm relying on you not to let either of us down, do you hear?"

All week they'd been working together on a low seam, which could only be reached on bended knees. This made every swing of the pick difficult for Dai. It was even worse for young Frank. He had to scramble around on all fours, gathering the freshly hewn coal off the floor to fill his "curling box" before lifting it shoulder high and emptying it into a waiting tram. When the tram was full a chalk mark on the side would tell the hauler, who came with a pony to take it away, that it came from Dai Hughes's stall. So far this week they'd managed to fill two trams. Each tram held a quarter of a ton, so this was no mean feat, ensuring they'd made their quota for the week. But, more to the point, today was pay-day — so no deductions from their wage packets.

"You've done well, lad. I'm sure if you carry on like this we'll soon be over our quota and making our bonus."

"Thanks, Mr Hughes. I'll try harder next week," Frank said.

In the darkness Dai sensed the lad's pride and was glad he hadn't mentioned that a bonus had been a regular occurrence with John Jones.

As Dai reached for his jack-tin full of cold sweet tea, he felt Frank settle down alongside.

"Dai?"

"Yes, lad."

"Tell me, do you ever get used to all the noises down here? I always imagined it quiet and peaceful, like. Of course, I'd heard talk of how cold, dark and damp it was. My dad, rest his soul, used to say it was as black as a cow's guts and twice as smelly."

Dai smiled to himself. "I know what you mean. The creaking timbers, the rumbling trams and the continuous banter between the men. I suppose you've also noticed how some can't swing a pick without grunting and groaning as if they're on the privy?"

"Yeah. And . . . well, to be honest, I find it all a bit scary," the lad whispered.

"You'll get used to it, I promise. Soon you'll know every noise as well as a good friend — even the creaking timbers — and that's no bad thing. For it means you'll be able to recognize any sudden changes. Believe me, lad, that's the time to really worry."

"Hey, Dai Hughes," a muffled voice called from down the line. "Seen anything of that wayward wife of yours?"

Dai gritted his teeth. "No, I bloody haven't. And I don't want to neither. Anyways, who's asking?"

"It's me, Selwyn Davies. I thought you'd like to know that I saw your Nellie down Butetown, Cardiff, last Saturday night."

"How come it's taken you all week to tell us then, butty?" another collier piped in.

"I've been off sick with a bad back, haven't I?"

"Bad back, my arse! If you ask me, it was too much of that ha'penny a pint Black beer they sell down Tiger Bay," Tom Morgan's voice bellowed. Everyone laughed.

Selwyn didn't bite, he was too keen to carry on goading Dai. "Anyways, there she was, your Nellie, done up to the nines. Dressed in a fur-trimmed coat and looking ever so prosperous."

"Ay, you know what they say? Fur coat and no knickers, and with her I can well believe it. I for one wouldn't mind paying sixpence for a feel of her whiskers, I can tell you." He sniggered as he added suggestively, "How's your young Rhiannon these days? It won't be long before you'll be beating the boys from your door — or maybe she's already been tested?"

Dai recognized Jack Dawkins's voice. He felt his temper rise. He knew he was being goaded. Over the past few months he'd grown used to it. Up to now, whenever they brought up the subject of Nellie he'd managed to hold his temper. Not so today. Today was different. Today they'd brought his Rhiannon into it. His temples were throbbing so hard that he felt that if he didn't speak out, he'd surely burst a blood vessel. Today they'd just gone too far.

"Jack Dawkins! If I were you, I'd shut your filthy mouth. Or I'll come and shut it for you!"

"And I'll help him," Frank said, only too ready to defend Rhiannon's good name.

Jack Dawkins, ignoring Frank, continued to goad Dai, "Come on, Dai — or should we start calling you Dewi, after our patron saint? Cause only a saint, or a fucking fool, would have put up with your strumpet of a wife for so long without giving her the beating she deserved."

Dai jumped up from his stall. "That's it. You've bloody asked for it this time —"

"Shhhh, all of you," Tom Morgan growled. "Something's not right."

Then there was silence.

The first thing Dai felt was the rush of warm air on his face. This was quickly followed by the sound of a distant rumble coming their way. As it came closer it grew louder and louder, and all around them pitprops began to shake, disturbing small pockets of earth from above.

"*Iusi Mawr!* What's happening?" young Frank yelled.

"Everyone take cover. It's a fall and it sounds like a big one!" Dai called out before diving back into his stall, landing on top of Frank. Only seconds later they heard the loud crack of the timber props snapping under pressure and the roar of roof caving in.

In the darkness someone shouted, "God help us."

"Dai, I can't die. I promised your Rhiannon I'd always be there for h-her." Frank's voice cracked.

"And you will, lad. You will," Dai whispered, just before a large boulder of rock crashed down on them and their Davy lamps went out.

"Mair, will you get a move on and lay the table?" Rhiannon called.

"What's the rush? Dad's not due home for another half hour or more."

Rhiannon smiled. She liked it better now that Mair called him Dad. It made it feel as though they truly were sisters.

32

It happened the day after Nellie left. Dai had arrived home from the pit a changed man. He looked older, his shoulders slouched, his head bowed. As he slowly took his place at the tea table he sighed. The girls noticed how red his eyes were but said nothing. For a while he just stared at his plate.

"Dad. Are you all right?" Rhiannon asked. Then she wanted to kick herself for asking such a stupid question.

He didn't answer. Instead he put his head in his hands and sobbed.

Rhiannon saw Mair's eyes fill up. "I could bloody kill my mother!" she shrieked.

Dai instantly stopped crying and looked up. "Mair, I'll not have such talk in this house, do you hear?" His voice was raised.

"Yes, Dai. I'm sorry," Mair half-whispered.

"I'm sorry too. Blubbering on like a babe in arms. It'll not happen again, I promise." He reached out and took both their hands in his. "I know what a shock Nellie's leaving is. But we have to get on and manage as best we can. From now on it'll be just the three of us, my two girls and me."

Mair jumped up and threw her arms around Dai and Rhiannon, and gave them such a hug. And from then on he was Dad to the two of them.

"Mair, I'll not ask you again," Rhiannon scolded.

"All right, Miss Bossy-Boots. Although I don't know why you're always in charge."

"Well, I am older than you."

"I'm nearly twelve," Mair protested.

"Yes, well I'm nearly fifteen, so there!"

Rhiannon had often thought how like Nellie Mair was — and not just in looks. Sometimes she could be really difficult, volatile even, with a vicious tongue and at other times she was gentle, loving and so considerate. Like two sides of a coin, one smooth, the other uneven. She was definitely her mother's daughter. It never mattered to Rhiannon how difficult Mair became, she always stuck with her and tried to understand. She tried to imagine how she would have felt if her own mother had walked out and abandoned her without so much as a second thought. At least Rhiannon knew that her mother had died loving her and, what was more, *she* had always known her father's love.

Rhiannon checked the evening meal. Tonight they were having boiled bacon and cabbage — one of Dad's favourites.

Mair, having given in at last and laid the table, called out, "Rhi, there's no salt."

"All right, I'll get some," Rhiannon answered. She was about to cut a slice of salt from the block in the larder when she heard the loud wailing sound of the colliery hooter blasting across the valley.

Rhiannon held her breath and listened as one . . . two . . . three long blasts echoed across the valley, informing everyone that there had been an accident at the mine and calling for volunteers.

"Oh please, God, no!" she cried, momentarily glued to the spot. She felt the salt dish slip from her hand and fall, as if in slow motion, onto the stone floor. The loud crash as it broke into tiny fragments made her jump, and she started to shake uncontrollably.

"What's wrong?" Mair asked.

"Three blasts of a siren? That's the signal for a fall at the mine."

"What, you mean an accident at Glengarw pit?"

"I think so. Mair, what time is it? Maybe Dad and Frank are already on their way home."

"I doubt it. It's only just after three. Dad and Frank aren't due up top until four o'clock. Oh Rhi, do you think they're all right?"

"Let's hope and pray."

And that's exactly what they did, they huddled together and prayed.

Outside they heard the familiar fast clicking sound of hobnail boots running past the front door. They rushed to the window only to find that what seemed like half the valley, ordinary folk, relatives, colliery officials, newspaper reporters, doctors, nurses, were hurrying behind a crowd of miners, they in turn were following behind the élite band of miners who doubled, when off-shift, as reserve rescuers. Everyone was heading towards the mine.

Rhiannon leaned closer to the window and felt the cold, wet condensation on the glass. A sure sign of how icy it was outside. She suppressed the urge to run from the house to join them, to make sure her dad was safe and well.

And what about Frank, kind, cheeky-faced, Frank? She just couldn't imagine a life without him. From as early as she could remember Frank had always been there for her. It was Frank who'd looked after her when she first started school, even shared his biscuits at playtime. It was Frank who tended her grazed knee when she fell down the mountain slope. It was Frank who'd been there to comfort her the day of her mother's funeral when she sat on the front doorstep, tears streaming down her face as she watched them carry her mam from the house in a box; a heart attack they'd said. But what did that mean exactly? And why did it have to be her mum?

She remembered how Frank had sat beside her and, as he put a clumsy arm around her shoulder, had assured her, "Whatever happens I'll always be here for you."

And now . . . was it possible that, in this one fragile moment, she could lose both him and her dad? It was too awful to imagine.

Then she heard the latch on the back door and, thinking it was her dad, she breathed a sigh of relief. "Thank God," she cried, as she turned to welcome him home. Only to find that Ethel Lewis from next door stood in the doorway. Rhiannon's heart sank.

"Oh, Rhiannon. Isn't it a worry?" Then seeing the disappointment on Rhiannon's face, "Sorry, love. Did you think I was your dad? I did knock, but —"

"That's all right. It wasn't your fault. Do you know what's happened? Is it a fall, an explosion or . . . what?"

"I don't know," Ethel replied. "Mind you, if the number of people going up there's anything to go by, it's pretty serious. I'd be up there myself if I didn't have

36

such a problem with my legs." She flopped into a fireside chair.

Rhiannon began pacing the floor. "I feel so helpless. Mrs Lewis, if anything happened to either of them, I don't think I could bear it."

"I know what you mean, if . . . Frank's only been working with your dad a week. With his dad not yet cold in his grave, surely God couldn't be so cruel to me?"

Rhiannon, seeing her neighbour struggle to fight back tears, reached out and gently touched her hand.

Ethel Lewis, after discreetly wiping her eyes with the hem of her apron, acknowledged Rhiannon's kindness with a nod of the head. "I'm all right, thanks. It's just . . . I feel so useless."

"I know what you mean," Rhiannon said, and, indicating to Mair she whispered, "I can't leave her." Rhiannon instinctively knew it would be no place for Mair.

"That's why I'm here. My Tom's looking after Martha next door. So, I thought, if I were to stay here with Mair, then you could go up there for the both of us."

"Oh no you don't," Mair piped in. "If you're going then so am I!"

"Mair, be reasonable. One of us has to stay here. Whatever would Dad think if he was to come home to an empty house?" Rhiannon knew her argument was strong, and it was partly true. She also knew it wouldn't do to tell Mair that she thought her too young to watch the injured, or worse, dead, men being brought up from pit bottom. It was only out of concern for her dad and Frank that she could face it herself.

"All right, I'll stay put. But if you're not back soon I'm coming up."

Rhiannon nodded; she was already grabbing for her shawl. "I'll go straight away and I promise, as soon as I've got some news, I'll be back."

"Now remember," said Ethel, "there'll be a lot of activity up there. Try not to get in anyone's way. You just watch and listen. There's bound to be a roll-call, that's how they tell who's . . ." She bit her lip. "Whatever happens, you best come back before it gets dark. Your dad would never forgive me if anything happened to either of you girls." Then she added, "don't you worry 'bout Mair and me. We'll keep each other company."

Rhiannon raced to the pithead, her mind in turmoil, her heart in her mouth. At the gates a throng of people, men, women and children stood in silence, listening as a colliery official read from a list of names. Their mood was like the weather, dark and gloomy, with heavy clouds threatening thunder.

"Selwyn Davies, Jack Dawkins, Robert Evans, Dai Hughes . . ."

"That's my dad! What does it mean? Does it mean he's safe?" she asked Dilys Morgan who was standing next to her.

"No, *cariad*, I'm afraid it means that, like the rest, he's missing."

"Oh, no! Please God . . ."

38

"Shhhh!" someone in the crowd shouted. "We can't hear the names."

And as the roll-call continued she heard him call: "Frank Lewis, Tom Morgan ..." Rhiannon put her hand over her mouth to suppress her sobs and control the urge to cry out again ... this time for Frank.

The names kept coming. Fifteen in all.

"Come on, love. All's not lost. At least they haven't found any bodies. As we speak, the rescue party is underground searching for them. My brother, William, is one of them," Dilys Morgan spoke proudly. "Our dad, Tom, is missing too. But I take comfort from knowing that the rescuers won't give up until every man is found ... dead or alive."

As if on cue, a mighty flash of lightning lit the sky overhead, closely followed by a loud crack of thunder. Suddenly the heavens opened and the rain lashed down. Still no one moved.

Rhiannon wondered if, like her, they all believed that the change in the weather signified God's anger. She hoped so.

The rain had stopped and it was getting dark when Rhiannon entered the back lane that led to her house. She was greeted by a sea of faces. Almost every man, woman and child, all her neighbours, were discussing what might or might not have happened up at the pit. When they saw her approach everyone stopped talking, the children even stopped playing and made a pathway clear to her front door, where Ethel and Mair stood, eagerly waiting for her return.

As soon as Mair caught sight of Rhiannon she ran to her side and, breaking the eerie silence, cried, "I thought you'd never get back. Tom Price has already told us that there are fifteen men missing and that Dad and Frank are among them. Have they found them yet?"

Rhiannon shook her head. She felt totally drained. It had been a long day.

"But you must have heard something? You've been gone ages," Mair moaned.

"I'm so sorry." Rhiannon fought back tears and pulled her wet shawl tight round her head. "I didn't want to come back until I had some positive news. But the colliery officials asked everyone not connected with the rescue to leave and let them get on with their job."

Suddenly Rhiannon's legs resembled lead weights, every step was an effort. Thankfully, by now she'd reached the front door.

"Thank God you're back." She felt Ethel's arms around her. "I've been worried sick. I suppose, if there's no news about your dad, there'll be none about my Frank either?"

"I'm sorry." Rhiannon felt so utterly useless. First Mair and now Mrs Lewis both depending on her for news and she'd let them down. All she could say was "sorry". How pathetic was that?

"It's not your fault, child. Come on, let's get you inside, you look done in. I've made a big saucepan of cowl. A bowl of lamb stew and you'll feel brand new." Rhiannon followed Mrs Lewis and the children into the kitchen.

"I suppose half the valley were up at the pithead?" Ethel asked as she dished up the stew.

"Oh, Mrs Lewis, it was awful. Mair, love, I'm so glad you didn't come. When I heard Dad's and then Frank's name on the roll-call it was the worst . . ."

A loud knock on the door silenced her. Around the table you could almost hear their hearts beating in anticipation of bad news.

Ethel slowly opened the front door to find Sergeant Morris, the local bobby, standing on the doorstep.

"Good news, Mrs Lewis. The rescuers have found your Frank safe and well —"

"Thank God — thank God," Ethel cried. "Rhi, Frank's safe!"

Rhiannon caught Ethel in her arms. "What a relief. See, there is a God."

Then she looked to Sergeant Morris, "Any news of my dad?" she asked.

"I'm sorry, *cariad*. Nothing as yet, but don't give up hope, the rescuers are still hard at it."

"Where have they taken my Frank? Is he injured? Can I see him?" Ethel asked frantically.

"He's at the pithead, being given the once-over by Doctor Lewis. He's a bit battered and bruised and obviously in shock. As soon as the doctor gives him the all clear I'll escort him back home."

"I'd appreciate that, Sergeant Morris. I don't want to leave the children."

"One other thing; as I said, he's suffering from shock. If I were you I'd let him rest up a bit before asking too many questions about the accident."

"Don't worry. We'll just be glad to get him back home."

At 9.30 that evening, with still no sign of Frank, Rhiannon and Mair decided to return home. Thankfully, now that he'd been found safe and well, they could see him tomorrow, the next day, the day after, and . . .

"Aren't you coming to bed, Rhi?" Mair asked, as Rhiannon tucked her in.

"I'll not be long, I promise," Rhiannon lied. Although genuinely euphoric that Frank was safe and well, she knew there was no way she could sleep while her dad was still missing.

Rhiannon glanced around the empty room. The room she'd previously thought of as warm, safe, homely, suddenly felt so cold and unwelcoming. Why had it taken her until now to realize that without the presence of her larger-than-life dad, it could never feel like home? How she wished she could throw her arms around him and tell him how much she loved him. Tears filled her eyes, she so wanted him — no, *needed* him to know how much he was truly loved. She vowed that the next time she saw him she'd do just that. Surely he'd be home soon? She'd decided to wait up, be there to welcome him when he walked through the door. And while she waited she'd sit in his armchair by the fireplace. On the chair she found her dad's old woollen jumper; she picked it up and snuggled it to her face, breathing in a mix of familiar smells: traces of firewood, coal, woodbines, camphor oil, and her dad's shaving soap. As she settled herself into the chair she wrapped the jumper round her shoulders and, closing her eyes, imagined it was her father cuddling her.

CHAPTER
FOUR

Rhiannon awoke with a start; it was morning and someone was knocking at the front door. She rubbed her eyes and instantly felt guilty. How could she have slept not knowing whether her father was alive or dead? What if the person at the door had come with bad news? What if . . .? She stopped herself. Such thoughts just wouldn't do.

She opened the door. It was a fine day. Thank God there'd been no more rain; another storm might hamper the rescue.

"Hello, Rhi. Any news 'bout your dad?" Jones the post asked.

Rhiannon shook her head. "No. Not yet. But we've heard that Frank's safe and well."

Eric Jones had only recently left school. His parents ran the local grocery shop and post office. His father, John Jones, the post, had been delivering the mail for years, and had only stepped down to make way for his son, so that Eric was one of the lucky few who had a readymade job waiting for him — there'd be no going down the pit for him.

"That's good news. Don't worry. Your dad's a strong man, I'm sure he'll be fine . . . anyway, this should cheer you up." He handed her a blue-grey envelope. "It's a letter from Paris, France. No doubt it'll be from your Auntie Florrie. It must be grand having someone famous in the family, eh?"

His attempt at cheering her up was touching, so, taking the envelope she managed to force a smile before returning indoors clutching the letter to her breast. It was as if, by holding it close, she could pretend her Aunt Florrie was actually there, hugging her, comforting her, willing her to be strong.

For a while she stared at the pale-coloured envelope. How she wished her aunt was there in person. Clutching the letter to her breast at least made her feel closer to her aunt and brought her, albeit momentarily, a little comfort.

Aunt Florrie had always had a soft spot for her. On one visit, long before Rhiannon's mother's death, she'd bought Rhiannon a china doll dressed in a brightly coloured frilly satin frock. Aunt Florrie told her it was called a can-can dress and proceeded to demonstrate the lively dance with its high-kicking steps, insisting that Rhiannon, Rose and Dai should join in. Oh, what fun they'd had. Rhiannon wondered whether she'd ever be that happy again.

"Who was that at the door? Was it news 'bout Dad?" Mair called out. She stood, still wearing her nightdress, huddled in front of the fire.

"It was Jones the post. And no, there's still no news."

"Why didn't you come to bed last night? You promised you wouldn't be long. Just you wait until I tell Dad that you've been telling lies."

"I really don't care." For once Rhiannon hoped Mair would have the opportunity to carry "clecks" to her dad. "Anyway, I knew I'd not be able to sleep and didn't want my tossing and turning to keep you awake. I was determined one of us would be waiting up when Dad came home."

"Oh, Rhi. Do you think we'll hear something soon?"

"I hope so, but I've decided that if there's no news by teatime I'm going to take another walk up to the pithead."

"Well, this time I'm coming with you!"

Rhiannon nodded her agreement.

Brushing past Mair, Rhiannon walked to the mantelpiece upon which, although reluctant to let go of it, she placed the newly arrived letter.

"Who's the letter from?"

"Aunt Florrie."

"What! All the way from Paris, France?"

"Yes."

Over the years Florrie had regularly kept in touch by letter, making sure they always knew where she was, and that she could keep up to date with all the family changes; including the arrival of Nellie and Mair and Dad's subsequent marriage.

"What does she say? Is she coming to visit?" Mair asked halfheartedly. Her thoughts elsewhere.

"I don't know. The letter's addressed to Dad. He can open it when he comes in."

"But what if . . .?"

"He'll open it when he comes in, all right?" Rhiannon repeated, throwing Mair a look warning her not to push it. Rhiannon wouldn't let herself even think about the "what if's?"

For the rest of the morning Rhiannon and Mair were determined to stay busy. They went through the motions of keeping house, neither of them saying very much, both lost in their own thoughts, both desperate for news of their dad while at the same dreading it.

It was mid-morning when Sergeant Morris and Jack Evans, an official representative for the colliery, came to the house.

"Hello, Rhi, Mair. May we come in?"

As the two men entered the kitchen Mair clung desperately to Rhiannon's arm.

"Have they found Dad? Is he all right?" Rhiannon blurted.

"Rhi?" Mair looked pleadingly at her sister.

"The rescuers found your dad about an hour ago," Sergeant Morris said, gently taking Rhiannon by the hand.

She snatched her hand back and moved closer to Mair. "Tell us, quickly, tell us. Is he . . . hurt?" Her eyes fixed on the sergeant's face.

"I'm afraid it's bad news."

"No! Please God! Does this mean . . .?" Rhiannon cried out.

The policeman slowly nodded his head.

"Rhi, what's wrong. What's happened to Dad?"

With tears burning her eyes Rhiannon threw her arms around Mair. "Mair, Dad's not coming back. He's dead!"

"N-no! N-no!" Mair cried out. "Rhi, tell them it can't be true."

Rhiannon, with tears flowing down her cheeks, hugged her stepsister so tightly that she could hardly breathe. "*Cariad*," she whispered. As she tried to comfort Mair, a realization hit her. Without Dad, there was no one to do the same for her.

As the girls clung to each other Rhiannon noticed the look of desperation that Sergeant Morris gave Jack Evans.

"Rhiannon, Mair, we are so very sorry," the sergeant said.

Rhiannon stopped crying. "But what happened? We've a right to know!" she demanded.

The sergeant sighed. Then, taking a deep breath, "There was a fall down the mine," he said. "The nature of business makes it inevitable for these things to happen from time to time —"

"Fortunately, with the new safety measures, it'll happen less and less," Jack Evans interrupted.

"Anyway, for whatever reason there was a fall and it was a big one. It may not be much consolation to you now . . . but you have to know that your father was a very brave man. Word is going around that your dad's quick action — alerting the men to the immediate danger — saved at least five of his butties."

"Including young Frank Lewis from next door," Jack Evans interjected.

Rhiannon and Mair looked surprised.

"Yes, it appears that your dad threw himself on top of him and in so doing took the main burden of the fall.

48

There can be no doubt that his quick action saved the lad's life."

The look on the girls' faces told him that this was too much to take in. It didn't alter the fact that their father was dead and, from now on, they were on their own.

"Jack, maybe it would be a good idea to ask Ethel Lewis from next door to come and sit with the girls for a while," Sergeant Morris whispered.

Jack Evans nodded his agreement and made his way to the back door. A few minutes later he returned followed by an ashen-faced Ethel.

"Oh Rhi, Mair, what can I say? It's such terrible news."

The girls didn't answer.

"You'll be in shock. I'll make us all a nice pot of tea, eh?" Ethel forced a smile.

"I think that's a grand idea, Mrs Lewis. Not for us though," Sgt. Morris said. "I'm afraid we've other families to see — it's a rum job — but it has to be done. Folk need to know." With a nod to Jack he headed for the back door. Jack followed.

"I don't envy you, and that's for sure. Do you know how many were lost?" Ethel whispered as she let them out.

"Yes. This morning the mine rescue team gave us the names of the sixteen men who sadly perished in the fall — all hard-working family men." The sergeant shook his head.

"What a bloody waste!" Jack muttered under his breath.

Ethel returned to the girls. She was filling the kettle when the back door opened. A hunch-shouldered

Frank stood in the doorway. His face looked thin and gaunt, his dark hair was less unruly than usual and, dressed in a collarless shirt and thick serge trousers, he looked like an old man. Slowly he entered.

"Frank. Now what are you doing out of bed? The doctor at the pithead said you needed complete rest —"

"I had to come, Mam." He turned to face the girls, "Rhi, Mair, I feel so awful about your dad."

Ethel quickly interrupted him. "Mair, love. Would you like to give me a hand with the tea?"

Rhiannon rightly guessed that Ethel's intention was to distract Mair and thus give her and Frank some time alone, and it worked.

As Mair helped Ethel with the tea tray Frank edged closer to Rhiannon. His clear grey eyes were soft as he looked at her.

"Rhi, you have to believe me. If I could change places with your dad I would . . ."

Rhiannon looked up at him. He was at least four inches taller than she. "You mustn't feel guilty."

"But —"

"Frank. You didn't cause the fall. I'm so glad you're safe. If I'd lost you too . . . I don't know what I'd have done."

He bit his lip.

Aware of his silent anguish Rhiannon caught around him. She felt him cling, as if for dear life. It felt strange to have a young man's arms hold her tiny frame so tightly . . . strange and yet, at the same time . . . comforting.

The truth was that no one could change what had happened or bring her dad back. Her father had died bravely. She owed it to his memory to care for the living.

Four days later a joint funeral was held for Dai Hughes and the other fifteen men who had lost their lives in the fall down the mine. It brought the valley to a standstill — everyone was eager to pay their respects to the dead miners and their families. Rhiannon and Mair went through it all in a daze almost detached from the proceedings. Since they'd been given the tragic news Ethel Lewis had insisted on looking after them, and not just out of gratitude to their father but because she actually cared.

A week after the funeral, and with the girls still struggling to come to terms with the loss of their dad, Ethel Lewis felt it her duty to speak out about the accident.

"Rhiannon, Mair — I have something I want to say to you both. It's common knowledge that your dad lost his life saving my Frank and I shall be forever in his debt. It's little comfort to you, I know, but I don't want you hating my Frank."

"Mrs Lewis, we don't hate Frank! In fact knowing he was saved helps make some sense of it all. At least Dad didn't die for nothing."

"Well, you may think that talk is cheap, but I want you to know that I shall never forget his sacrifice. Unfortunately there's nothing I can do for him, God rest his soul, but I'd like to repay him by taking you both in."

"What's she on about, Rhi?" Mair whispered.

Rhiannon shrugged her shoulders. "Mrs Lewis, I don't understand. Take us in — in where?"

"I'm not making myself very clear, am I? I want — no, I'd like you and Mair to move in next door with me, Frank and the little ones."

Rhiannon suddenly felt awkward. "Look, we do appreciate you thinking of us, don't we, Mair?" Mair didn't answer. "Don't we, Mair!" Rhiannon prompted.

"Yes — yes, of course," Mair said, getting the message at last.

"But this is our home," said Rhiannon. "I'm sure our dad would have wanted us to stay here."

"Of course, and I do understand, in an ideal world but . . . oh dear, you don't know, do you?"

"Know what, for goodness sake?" Rhiannon was getting a little fed up with Ethel Lewis's unanswerable questions.

"Know . . . that you're going to have to leave this house. You see, it's the rules. This house, like mine, is tied to the colliery. When a collier leaves or . . . dies, there has to be another collier in the house for the family to stay. That's why I was so glad when your dad took on my Frank after his father passed away."

"You mean they're going to kick us out?" cried Mair. "Rhi, can they do this?"

"Yes, I'm afraid so. I just didn't think." Rhiannon felt such a fool. Why hadn't she remembered the plight of many of their neighbours? Over the years her father had helped where he could, either in giving them a hand to move or putting them in touch with the Salvation Army who frequently found shelter for the homeless.

"They'll not ask you to move straight away. They usually give you a week or two before they send an official from the colliery to give you a nudge."

"Oh, Rhi! Where will we go? What will we do?"

"I've already told you. There's no cause to worry; you can move in with me," Ethel said, as if that was the end of it.

It was gone eight o'clock when Ethel Lewis eventually left them.

"What are we going to do, Rhi?"

"I don't know. First Dad's death and now this. It's so unfair. After all the years of Dad working so hard for them down the pit, I can't believe that they're just going to throw us out! How dare they?"

"It was kind of Ethel Lewis to offer us a roof over our heads, wasn't it?" Mair said, trying to calm Rhiannon down.

"Yes, I suppose it was. But, Mair, Ethel Lewis isn't family. We'd just be like lodgers."

"So? What are we going to do?"

"I don't know! Why do you always expect me to have all the answers?" Rhiannon fell into her father's chair. She wanted to cry but it was as if there were no tears left. How she wished she could set the clock back to when it was just herself and her dad; she'd been so happy then.

Then she remembered the money her dad had saved each week in the old tea caddy on the dresser. "For a rainy day," he had said.

"I'm sorry, Rhi. Please don't be cross with me. I promise not to ask any more questions. It's just . . . well . . . I miss him so much."

"Mair, I know. I miss him too. I didn't mean to shout at you, honest. Now, be a love and pass me the tea caddy off the dresser."

"What? Dad's savings?"

"Yes. He'd want us to have it. Let's see how much is in there."

Mair walked over to the dresser and gingerly reached for the caddy.

"For goodness sake, Mair, it won't bite you!"

Mair handed the caddy to Rhiannon as if it was a lump of hot coal from the fire and she was glad to be rid of it.

"It just doesn't seem right, taking Dad's money," Mair said.

Rhiannon shook her head. "Sometimes I really don't understand you," she said. Slowly she removed the lid, emptied the contents onto the table and proceeded to count them. We've the grand total of one pound ten shillings and sixpence. That should see us all right for a while." She raised her head to the ceiling and whispered, "Thanks, Dad."

Mair gave a deep sigh. "He didn't even get to read Aunt Florrie's letter."

Rhiannon looked towards the mantelpiece and Aunt Florrie's unopened letter. She raised herself from the chair and, as if in slow motion, made her way to the fireplace.

CHAPTER
FIVE

Florrie Grayson was pleased to be back in Wales; this Cardiff theatre booking had been long time coming. The last time she'd visited Wales it had been a short, painful visit — to attend her sister Rose's funeral. She still missed her sister, although Florrie had made a successful life for herself in France. Knowing that her younger sister was happy with a loving husband and child in the Nantgarw Valley had somehow meant she still had a strong foothold in Wales. Now, with Rose gone and Dai remarried, it seemed her links with the valley had greatly diminished. She shrugged off her feeling of foreboding telling herself she was being daft.

She couldn't wait to see Dai and Rhiannon again and, after the initial shock of hearing that Dai had remarried, she now relished the chance to meet Nellie, the lucky lady who had stolen his heart as well as her young offspring. Florrie had always had a soft spot for Dai, and secretly envied her sister, Rose, for having landed such a good, kind, hardworking man, a man whose love was so sincere. Florrie sighed; in another life maybe . . . One thing was for sure: she knew he would always regard her as part of the family, as would Rhiannon who reminded her so much of herself.

As she stepped off the train that had brought her from Dover, after she had already endured the choppy sea of the ferry crossing, she was glad to have arrived safely at last in Cardiff. Amid the hustle and bustle that inevitably followed — especially after such a long trip — she became aware of the familiar loud call from a newspaper seller, "*Echo, South Wales Echo*! Read all about it! Get your ev'ning *Echo* 'ere!" It made her smile and gave her a warm glow — it was good to know that some things never changed. It made her feel she was home.

Only as she got nearer to the newspaper kiosk did she see the tall, black-printed billboard and read: TRAGEDY AT NANTGARW COLLIERY: MOURNERS HONOUR THE DEAD. At first it didn't register, not until she heard the caller shout, "Nantgarw Colliery Accident! Read the official list of the sixteen men who perished." Then she stopped in her tracks.

"Florrie, what's wrong?" Walter Cahill asked. "You've gone as white as a sheet."

Walter Cahill, an American of Irish decent, had been her theatrical agent and manager for the past fifteen years. He had offered to represent her after a performance at the Théâtre Marigny on the Champs-Elysées, Paris. She had jumped at the chance of having an American as her agent. Florrie dreamt of making an American début; maybe Walter Cahill could make it happen.

A month previously, when he had announced that he'd landed her a prestigious Welsh theatre booking, she'd been very excited, especially when he insisted on accompanying her. Over the years they had become very close. He was good company, an incorrigible flirt who could always make her laugh. Florrie knew she was sometimes difficult to work with, but he never reproached her. She liked him. He seemed to understand her. At one time she thought they could maybe become more than friends but he was too professional ever to mix business with pleasure. Florrie had been grateful for that. She regarded him as a true friend.

Florrie had no regrets. The stage had always taken first place in her life. She breathed it, loved it, and lived for it. What man could ever compete with that? Mind you, she was no angel, far from it. There had been many men in her life, but they never lasted. She blamed herself. She'd come to terms with the fact that there wasn't a man alive who would be happy playing second fiddle to her work.

"Walter, would you be a dear and pick me up a *South Wales Echo* from the kiosk?"

"No bother. You just wait there a Goddarn minute."

She watched him walk to the kiosk, reach for some coins in his pocket and pick up a paper. It seemed an age, but in reality was only a few seconds. He placed the newspaper in her hand and she quickly scanned the story of the fall in the colliery and, more important, a list of the sixteen dead men in bold print underneath. When she spotted the name of **David (Dai) Hughes** she shook her head in disbelief. Then, she tried to convince herself that it might not be her brother-in-law. Surely there were many men in the valley with the same name. But when she read on and saw his address she knew there was no mistake. Again and again she read the words. She felt light-headed, nauseated and her legs felt like jelly.

"Florrie, are you all right?" Walter made grab for her. "Whoa, gal, I think you need some support." He smiled. "I know what you're thinking: any excuse to get his arm around me, but you looked as if you were about to pass out on me."

"S-sorry, thank you, I'll be fine."

"Come on; let's get you to the cab."

Florrie couldn't remember the car journey to the Angel Hotel or, for that matter, how she got to her room.

"There, you go, gal. Home sweet home — at least for the length of the tour," said Walter after the porter had offloaded her many suitcases and left the room.

Although still in a daze, Florrie had managed something garbled about the headlines and her family connection with one of the dead men.

"Look, you really should rest up. Arriving back after a long trip to such damn awful news, anyone's bound to feel like shit. I'll leave you for a while. If there's anything I can do just call. My room's just across the hall."

"Walter? Don't go. I feel so helpless. I need to get in touch with Dai's new wife and family. I feel so guilty that I wasn't there for them, especially Rhiannon. I should have attended poor Dai's funeral. My sister, Rose, would have wanted me to be there! I wanted to be there! Perhaps I should go to them — take a trip to the valley? What do you think?" She knew she was rambling but couldn't stop herself.

"Florrie, I know you're in a state of shock, but you dashing off to your family could cause big problems. I'm speaking as your agent now. I think it might have temporarily slipped your mind that your début at the Empire Theatre is scheduled for the day after tomorrow. Tonight you've a meeting with the musical director and costume fitter, and tomorrow you've a day's rehearsal and —"

"Don't you think I know all that? But this is my family."

"I do understand, but have you considered what'll happen if you break your contract? It'll not only hit you financially but think of all the loyal fans who have already paid up front for tickets to see you. Why not wait a few days? We've a day off on Sunday. I promise I'll drive you anywhere you want to go. What do you say?"

Florrie nodded her agreement. Much as she wanted to be with Rhiannon, she knew that what Walter said made sense.

Then she remembered. "Walter I sent them tickets to come and see the matinée show on Saturday. Do you think they'll come?"

"It's possible, I suppose. Now come on, you must rest up. I can't have my main gal turning up for rehearsals with dark rings under her eyes."

CHAPTER
SIX

"Mrs Lewis, may we come in?" Rhiannon called out as she let herself in to her neighbour's house.

"Yes, of course, love. I've told you before that there's no need to stand on ceremony. My door's always open to you two."

Ethel Lewis was sitting in front of a huge coal fire, her skirt hitched up over her knees, her bare legs mottled with red marks from the intense heat. Young Martha was sitting on the hearthrug, quietly playing with her building bricks.

"Come on in and pull up a seat. Don't let the pale sun fool you into thinking spring is just around the corner. There's a dangerous cold wind today and I for one shan't be moving far from this hearth, I can tell you."

"We've got some news for you," Mair blurted.

Rhiannon threw her a look. They'd agreed that Rhiannon would be the one to tell Ethel Lewis.

"And what news would that be then? Hang on. Let me guess. You've finally decided on a moving day. I was only saying to my Frank earlier today that you'd better do it soon, before you have the colliery bailiffs at your door. Am I right?" Her smile was warm and welcoming.

"Well . . . yes, we have decided on a moving day but —" Rhiannon was finding it hard to carry on.

"Come on, girl. Don't talk in riddles. Spit it out. Whatever it is, it looks as if your Mair is fit to burst from excitement."

"It's Aunt Florrie." Rhiannon held the letter. "With all that's been happening I forgot about this letter. It arrived the day after the accident. I left it on the mantelpiece for Dad . . . Well, anyway, last night I opened it and you'll never guess what. Aunt Florrie's appearing at the Cardiff Empire and look, she's sent us money and tickets for us to go and see the show!"

"Well I never!" Ethel shook her head in disbelief. "The last time I saw Florrie was at your dear mother's funeral. The three of us used to be such friends; we grew up together in this very street, you know? Mind you, I never saw two sisters so different." She rubbed her knees, as though rubbing the memories to life. "Your mother, Rose, such a sweet girl, content to stay close to home — you and your dad were her life, Rhiannon. While Florrie, well, she couldn't wait to leave the valley. She was a born show-off, loved to perform, loved to sing. Everyone believed that she was destined for great things — she had the voice of an angel . . ." Ethel sighed. "She'll not know anything 'bout your dad, then?"

"No. I don't suppose so. The letter says she was only due to arrive back in the country on March the eighteenth — the day of dad's fun —"

"We'll explain everything when we see her. Won't we, Rhi?" Mair interrupted.

"You're planning on going to Cardiff?"

"Yes. The theatre tickets are for tomorrow's matinée performance. We thought we could go by train and, well, Mrs Lewis, the thing is, we intend to stay with Aunt Florrie . . . if she'll have us."

"Oh, I see," Ethel said quietly. Then, turning to Rhiannon, "Have you told my Frank about this?"

Rhiannon shook her head, "No — not yet."

"Have you told Frank what?" Frank asked as he entered the kitchen closely followed by his sister, Sadie.

For a while no one spoke. Rhiannon flashed Ethel a pleading look.

"The girls are off to Cardiff to see their Aunt Florrie," Ethel offered.

"Cardiff? When? How? And when do you intend getting back?"

Rhiannon caught his hand, "Frank?" Her eyes filled with tears.

He put his arm around her, "Rhi what is it? What's wrong?"

"We're not coming back!" Mair blurted out.

"Don't be daft, Mair. This is your home." Frank looked to his mother for reassurance but there was none. He turned to Rhiannon. "Rhi what's going on?"

Ethel stood up, took a large woollen shawl from the back of the chair and wrapped it around her shoulders. Then she picked Martha up off the rug and wrapped it around the child.

"Mair, Sadie, would you both help me to get the washing in from the line? I think it's time to give Frank and Rhi a few minutes alone."

Reluctantly Mair followed Ethel, Martha and Sadie into the garden.

Frank turned to Rhiannon. "I can't believe you're planning to leave tomorrow," he snapped.

Rhiannon had been so dreading this moment. "Frank please . . . you must see it makes sense? We're soon to be given notice to leave our home. Aunt Florrie is the only family I have left. She'll know what to do. She'll take us in, I'm sure."

"But it all seems so rushed."

"This way, there's a chance for Mair and me to begin a new life. I really don't want to stay around here. Without Dad . . . it would be too painful.

Seeing the hurt look on his face Rhiannon reached out and touched his arm. He pulled away. "And what about me? I thought —"

Rhiannon quickly interrupted. "Cardiff's not that far away." Since the accident Frank had changed. Her father had always teased her that Frank was sweet on her. If that was true then she didn't want to hear it. "I'll come to visit often, I promise," she smiled at him.

"It won't be the same as seeing you every day."

"It may be even better. You know what they say: 'absence makes the heart grow fonder'. As soon as she said it she wished she hadn't. It was wrong to give him false hope. He was her friend and that was how she wanted it to stay. But the damage was already done.

He beamed a broad smile, "Well, I'm definitely coming to see you off at the railway station."

"I'd like that," Rhiannon said, and meant it.

Minutes later Ethel and everyone returned from the garden, Mair dutifully carrying the folded washing.

"Glad to see you two smiling. All sorted out then, eh?"

Rhiannon nodded. Although she wasn't at all sure that it was.

"Good. Now, if you plan to leave tomorrow, it's time we got you both sorted out. Have you packed? Can I help?"

"We're not taking much — only the bare essentials. We were hoping you could store some of our things, furniture and stuff?" Rhiannon asked.

"Of course, my parlour's almost empty. Frank? How about you get some of your butties to move it in tonight. Rhiannon, Mair, you two come for supper with us tonight."

"N —" Rhiannon was about to protest.

"I'll not take no for an answer."

"Thank you," Rhiannon said, genuinely touched by her neighbour's help. "We'd like that. And Mrs Lewis, I just want to say how grateful we are for all that you did for Dad and us over the years."

"Get away with you. What are neighbours for, eh? Now off you go, you've a lot to do. Frank, what are you waiting for?"

"Has anyone ever told you what a good sergeant major you'd make, Mam?"

They all laughed.

"I'm so glad you both like beef stew and dumplings." Ethel Lewis smiled as she watched the two girls tuck into their meal. "Can't beat a nice piece of brisket, that's what I say. It's my Frank's favourite and his father's before him. Any girl setting her sights on my boy would do well to remember that a way to a man's heart is through his stomach."

Frank looked across the table at the two girls and blushed. Sadie and Martha giggled.

Rhiannon, sensing his embarrassment, made to change the subject. "Thanks for moving our stuff, Frank. We really appreciate it."

"That's all right, Rhi. It was nothing"

"No! Not for a strapping lad like him and he's so handsome with it. He'll be a good catch for the right young girl and that's for sure." Ethel bristled with pride.

Shaking his head in despair at his mother's blatant attempt at matchmaking Frank looked towards the girls. "What time were you thinking of leaving tomorrow?"

"We thought we'd catch the eleven-fifteen train in the morning. Your mother said that it's a bit of a walk to the Empire Theatre from Cardiff station and we'd like to get there in good time for the matinée performance." Rhiannon stood up from the table. "Come on, Mair. If it's all right with you, Mrs Lewis, we'll head next door? We've a long day ahead of us tomorrow."

"Do we have to? I'm that excited. I know I'll not sleep a wink tonight," Mair begged; then, looking dreamily across the table, "I'd much rather stay here with Frank."

Mair's forward comments won her a glare of disapproval from Rhiannon.

Frank pretended he hadn't noticed the look of adoration from the twelve-year-old. "Rhiannon's right. An early night would do us all the world of good. If it's all right with you we'll aim to leave at around half past ten in the morning?"

"That'll be fine. As long as you're sure about coming to see us off?" Rhiannon asked.

He flashed a smile. "Honestly, Rhi, I'd not have it any other way."

"Well, this is it." Frank said, as he led the way onto the platform at Pontrhyl railway station. Rhiannon sensed he was putting on a brave face for her benefit.

"I've never been on a train before," Mair squealed.

"Quite an adventure. I envy you both." Frank spoke quietly.

"As soon as we're settled you must come to see us," Rhiannon enthused. She meant it.

"I'd like that." He bent down to place a gentle kiss on her cheek, "And you'd better remember your promise to come and visit, often," he whispered in her ear.

Mair, not wishing to be left out, offered up her cheek for a kiss.

Frank obliged with a smile.

As the train slowly moved out Frank raised his hand in a wave. Rhiannon and Mair waved back.

CHAPTER
SEVEN

Cardiff railway station was a dark and gloomy place, crowded with people all ignoring each other — not a bit like valley folk.

Mair reached for Rhiannon's hand. "Do you know the way to the theatre, Rhi?" She sounded frightened.

"No. But don't worry. I'm sure if we ask that station guard over there he'll direct us."

The guard was polite but brusque and left them in no doubt that the Empire Theatre on Queen Street was a good distance away. Without further delay Rhiannon, with their shared suitcase in her hand, led the way out of the station and, as directed, onto St Mary Street. Rhiannon sucked in a breath of cold, damp air. She hoped it wouldn't rain. Dressed in their Sunday best — grey woollen long-length skirts, high-necked blouses and grey over-jackets — the last thing they needed was to get wet through.

St Mary Street was wide, straight and very long, flanked either side by impressive large buildings. It was a hub of activity: pavements bustling with shoppers and hawkers, while open-topped trams, horse-drawn carriages and bicycles all vied for position on the road.

Under normal circumstances they would love to have stopped to take it all in, the wonderful window display of Howells & Co, the entrance to Cardiff market with its impressive stone arch, the old-fashioned tobacconist, with a stuffed grizzly bear just inside the door, would all have to wait for another day.

They headed north. The road stretched as far as the eye could see. After about a five-minute walk a wide-eyed Mair tugged on Rhiannon's sleeve. "Look, Rhi, there's Cardiff Castle. It's so big, so grand and so . . . beautiful?"

Rhiannon nodded her agreement. "Ethel said it was a sight to behold, and she was right."

"Do you think we might visit it one day? Ethel said it was open to the public on certain days."

"We'll see. Now, come on. I don't want to be late," Rhiannon urged as she led the way across Castle Street, which led to Queen Street — their destination.

Rhiannon decided it was too much to ask for her sister to maintain her silence of the train journey. Most of the time Mair had sat with her nose pressed against the window enthralled. Rhiannon had welcomed a respite from the twelve-year-old's inquisitiveness of the night before.

"What will we do when we get to Cardiff? Are you sure your auntie will take us in? If not, where shall we stay?" The very same questions Rhiannon had asked herself and more. Was she being foolhardy, leaving her beloved valley on a whim? What would Dad have said?

Last night she'd avoided having to answer Mair, and had simply said, "The sooner you get to sleep the sooner you'll find out."

Five minutes later they had their first glimpse of the Empire Theatre. The night before, Ethel Lewis had explained how the original theatre had been destroyed by fire in 1899, to be replaced in 1900 by a bigger and better one which was rightfully the pride of Cardiff.

Set in the middle of a row of shops, with the Molyneux Shoe Company to its right and a small sweetshop on its left, the theatre looked decidedly out of place.

It was remarkable how the sight of the theatre with its impressive gold-and-red frontage, marble entrance and two large shields cast in bronze standing proudly above the main doors, representing the county and the city, instantly lifted their spirits.

"Rhi, are we going to visit your Aunt Florrie before the show?"

"I don't think we should bother Aunt Florrie just yet. I'm sure she'll have more time for us after the show." If the truth were known Rhiannon wanted to put off her aunt's inevitable questions concerning the accident down the mine and the death of her father for as long as she could.

"Rhi, is there time for us to find something to eat? I'm starving."

"Your stomach will have to wait. By the look of the queues outside the theatre I think we'd best get in line. I don't want to miss the matinée."

The girls took their place behind a mixed theatre crowd: men wearing bowler hats, straw boaters and cloth caps; women, with flowered hats and feathered bonnets. Some wore elegant dresses, others were in shawls, blouses and long serge skirts.

"There's a sweetshop next door selling toffee apples. Can I have one, Rhi? Pl-ease."

Rhiannon reached into her purse and took out a shiny new sixpence. "I'm afraid it'll have to do you until we can arrange a proper meal."

"Thanks, Rhi. Shall I get one for you too?"

Rhiannon shook her head. Her stomach was doing somersaults.

"No thanks. I'm not hungry."

As their queue edged closer to the foyer they spotted the large poster over the door advertising "*All The Way from Paris — The Great Florrie Grayson!*" underneath a photo of her aunt in all her finery. Rhiannon stared at the photo. It had been nearly six years since Rhiannon had last seen her aunt. She looked exactly the same now — she hadn't changed a bit.

"Gosh, Rhi, I didn't realize she was such a beauty. You look just like her."

A man, dressed in a smart evening suit with crisp white high-necked shirt and bow tie, appeared on the top step in front of the theatre. He beamed at them as he raised a white-gloved hand in an exaggerated theatrical way. "Ladies and gentlemen, the box-office doors are now open. Those with tickets please form two separate queues. Stalls and circle to the right, upper circle and gods to the left.

"Which one are we in, Rhi?" Mair urged.

"I'm not sure. I'd better check."

70

Rhiannon reached into her pocket and pulled out the letter from Aunt Florrie containing the four theatre tickets meant for Dad, Nellie, Mair and herself. She removed two of the tickets and inspected them. "It just says BOX ONE. We'll have to ask someone. "Come on," she urged as she bent down to pick up her suitcase. "Let's join the queue."

"Not long, now, Rhi. I'm that excited I could wet myself!"

"Mair, will you behave?"

"Rhi, you're always so stuffy."

Soon the queue began to move faster. As it neared the large entrance they found themselves being pushed along by the crowd.

"Make sure you stay close, Mair, I don't want to lose you."

"No chance of that. I'm holding on to your coat as tight as I would a ten-bob note."

As they passed through the large glass double doors, with THE EMPIRE THEATRE etched in bold gold-leaf letters, they caught their first glimpse of the opulent theatre foyer; with its grand marble entrance, gilded doors festooned with plush red-velvet drapes, a high ceiling ornately decorated with blue flowers and gold cherubs and a sweeping brass-railed staircase covered in thick red carpet. It was so grand it took their breath away.

"Will you two stop dawdling and get a bloody move on? You're holding us all up," a woman complained from behind.

"Sorry. Come on, Mair," Rhiannon said.

A young girl not much older than Rhiannon held out her hand. "Tickets, please." On taking the tickets she did an immediate double take, her eyes darting from them to Rhiannon and then to Mair. Then, as she flashed them a friendly smile, she said, "Please follow me."

The young girl led them through a doorway, then up a few stairs to a small private seating area at the side of the stage.

"Here we are, then. Please . . . take your seats," the young girl said.

Inside the box there were four gilt chairs with red-plush seats, each facing the stage; so close Rhiannon could almost touch the elaborate gold-fringed red curtain that hung across it from the high proscenium arch.

She caught her breath and could almost taste the scent of wood, tobacco, stale beer and hair-oil, all combined — pungent and yet strangely pleasurable.

"Rhi, did you know it was going to be as lovely as this?" Mair whispered as the girl in her neat black-and-white dress waited for them to take their seats.

"No. I'm as surprised as you, but isn't it great? It's another world," Rhiannon said.

"Are you sure these are *our* seats?" Rhiannon enquired.

The girl smiled. "Miss Grayson booked this box for her 'special guests'."

Rhiannon nodded. "Oh I see." She didn't really. If it were true then it meant she and Mair were somehow special; surely that couldn't be?

72

Mair was first to take her seat, leaving Rhiannon to sit next to her.

"You might like to place your suitcase under the seat, miss, there's plenty of room."

"Thank you, I will. You're very kind."

"Miss Grayson gave strict instructions to look after you. So enjoy the show. I'll come and see you at the interval." Then handing Rhiannon a free programme she turned and left. Like Rhiannon's, Mair's head was on a swivel in an attempt to take in the vastness of the auditorium, the flurry of flowered hats, feather bonnets, straw boaters and bowler hats, so many beautiful people, all dressed up to the nines, filling every seat of the stalls and all three tiers above.

"Look at the top balcony, Rhi. It's packed with ordinary folk like us — you can tell they're not toffs. Are you sure we shouldn't be up with them? Mind you, I don't know that I'd fancy being that far up. Why, it's as high as the sky!"

"You heard what the girl said; we're definitely in the right seats. Maybe that floor's the one the man on the door called the gods? It makes sense when you think about it."

"Rhi, do you think my mother could be here?"

Mair hadn't mentioned Nellie for a long while, most of the time she made out she couldn't care less, but Rhiannon knew it must have really hurt when Nellie had upped and left.

"It's possible, I suppose. But you have to remember Cardiff is a very big place, she could be anywhere."

73

"Good riddance, that's what I say. It wouldn't worry me if I never saw her again!"

While Rhiannon doubted this to be the truth, she let it pass, sensing that it was probably Mair's way of coping.

Mair Parsons searched the auditorium, looking for her mother, while at the same time wondering what she would do if she found her. It was obvious that her mother wanted nothing to do with her. Why else would she have abandoned her? And it didn't stop with her mother. When her father had been due to be released from prison she had written to her grandmother in Nantymoel; it had done no good, not one of her family had ever attempted to make contact.

For a long while she had no idea where her mother had gone. Then, by chance, one of the valley gossips bumped into Nellie in Cardiff and couldn't wait to tell Mair how well she looked and how she'd never even asked after her daughter.

Mair swallowed hard, she'd made a vow not to cry. As far as she was concerned her mother was, like Rhiannon's, dead and buried. They were a pair of orphans. All they had was each other. But who was she trying to kid? They were nothing alike; Rhiannon never spent *her* childhood being pushed from pillar to post. *She* had a father who worshipped her and even though she'd suffered the loss of her mother, she could take comfort in knowing she had been deeply loved.

Now Rhiannon had her precious Aunt Florrie and, no matter how much they pretended, Florrie Grayson was nothing to Mair; they had never even met. Mair decided there and then to be on her best behaviour when they did — at least until she was sure that Florrie Grayson accepted her along with Rhiannon.

At the back of the upper circle was the Theatre Bar and behind this a place known to all as the promenade, frequented mostly by men and a regular haunt for prostitutes and rent boys.

Nellie hated the seedy Theatre Bar, full of unattractive low-life men. She much preferred it when Harry used to take her to the high-class Lounge Bar behind the circle with waiter service. It was here that she mixed with the élite and she and Harry were often invited to high society parties. Of course, the men still wanted the same thing — Harry made sure of that.

In the beginning Harry hadn't put any pressure on her. He had even encouraged her to be choosy.

"Don't you go bothering with any ruffians; you're worth more than that," he'd said. "You're more suited to the younger well-to-do men or, better still, the grateful, older gentlemen. There's no rush. I want you to be happy about it."

Nellie so wanted to please Harry.

It all started with one or two well-to-do punters, carefully chosen by Harry to ease her in gently. Part of her had been flattered that such well-heeled gentlemen were willing to pay for her body. What a fool she'd been. It wasn't long before she found out that Harry had actually paid two out-of-work actors to pose as gentlemen to ease her into her new profession.

"Come on, Nellie, love, give us a kiss," Jake Brewer pleaded.

Jake was one of her regulars, an ex-boxer with a broken nose and a cauliflower ear to prove it. He was in his late forties with a paunch the size of a punchbag. Mind you if his appetite for sex was anything to go by, no one could accuse him of not being fit.

"It'll cost you. You get nothing for nothing." Nellie sniggered.

"Not even for a friend of Harry's?" The man moved closer.

Nellie suppressed a shiver. Why was it that, these days, most of Harry's "friends" were fat, balding and reeked of stale beer and cigarettes?

"I thought Harry told you to be nice to me."

"Yes, he did. But he'll also expect me to have at least ten guineas in my purse at the end of the night. So take heed. If you want me you're going to have to pay!"

"Hey, where are you going?" the fat man called. "I was only joking. I've got money, lots of it. Come on, let's go to your digs."

As the lights dimmed, the orchestra, in a pit beneath the stage, started to play the overture. The programme said it would be a selection of music from the forthcoming performance.

Rhiannon felt a buzz of excitement causing the hairs on the back of her neck to stand up. It was so . . . magical.

As the audience quietened, the stage curtain slowly went up and through the shimmering heat haze above the footlights appeared a handsome young man dressed in full evening dress seated at a small table positioned at the side of the stage.

He stood up and banged on the table with a gavel that he held in his hand. The crowd cheered. He banged the table again. The crowd silenced.

"My lords, ladies and gentlemen, welcome to the Empire Theatre! It is with great honour that I, your chairman for the evening, call you to order. For the next few hours prepare to be amazed, astonished and, above all, entertained as you've never been entertained before." Once again he banged the gavel on the table. "With no further ado, please put your hands together for our very own . . . excitingly exquisite . . . Empire Belles!"

His voice was captivating. Rhiannon hung on his every word. She had never seen a man, possibly in his early twenties, so gorgeous; he was tall and well built, with dark-brown well-groomed hair and sparkling blue eyes. He oozed what could only be described as a sexual presence. Overcome by a strange feeling of excitement deep within, her body heat increased and from the way her face was burning she knew it was bright red. She was glad of the darkness.

She felt Mair tug her arm. "Cor, Rhi, he's a bit of all right, don't you think?"

Rhiannon was grateful for the loud applause from the audience making it impossible for Mair to hear, even if she'd deigned to answer her sister.

As the chairman took his seat at the table, a chorus-line of dancers dressed as bathing-belles tap-danced in unison across the stage. Rhiannon had never seen dancing like it, and longed to be one of them.

For the next hour Rhiannon sat spellbound. Mair must have felt the same because for once she stayed silent as one act followed another: dancers, jugglers, and a soprano who sang "I'm only a bird in a gilded cage" to perfection.

Rhiannon particularly enjoyed the performance of a young girl called Sally Webber, who came on dressed as a street urchin and sang: "All my life I wanted to be a barrow-boy", encouraging the audience to sing along with the chorus, which everyone, including Rhi and Mair, did with gusto.

Every now and then Rhiannon's eyes wandered to the table and, in particular, to the chairman sitting at the side of the stage.

To end the first half a comedian called Tom O'Reilly brought the house down with his constant mistakes and daft antics that had both girls laughing so much their sides hurt.

"I don't know about you, Mair. But if I laugh much more I'll end up peeing *my* knickers!" Rhiannon whispered. Of course she never would. She just wanted to show Mair that she wasn't really stuffy.

The first half ended to great applause and as the curtains fell and the house-lights came up on the auditorium there was a chance for the audience to shuffle in their seats or, if inclined, take some refreshment.

"Thanks for bringing me, Rhi. I wouldn't have missed it for the world. This is the life, eh? Do you think when we're living with Aunt Florrie we'll be able to do this every day?"

"I don't know; maybe. Anyway, for the time being I'll just be glad if she takes us in." Rhiannon didn't want to spoil things but she needed Mair to share her concerns.

"Don't be daft. Of course she'll take us in. Won't she?"

Concerned as Rhiannon was, she couldn't get the chairman out of her mind. She wondered whether he was a regular attached to the theatre or, like Aunt Florrie, a visiting artist. She looked in the programme and found his photograph. Underneath the name Gerald "Gus" Davenport. If she asked, maybe her aunt could introduce them. She scolded herself for being so silly. Why would a man like that want to be bothered with the likes of her?

Rhiannon felt a tap on her shoulder.

"Hello, miss, I've brought you a tray of sandwiches and a drink each." It was the young girl who'd showed them to their box. Leaning past Rhiannon she clipped the tray onto a convenient little bracket on the arm of her seat, obviously made for the purpose.

"Thank you," Rhiannon said. She nudged Mair, prompting her to do the same.

"Oh, yes. Thank you very much."

"Miss Grayson thought you might be hungry and didn't want your tummies rumbling during her performance." The girl laughed. "Now then, after the show someone will come to take you backstage, so just stay put and enjoy the rest of the show."

As the girls tucked into their cheese sandwiches they noticed that most of the men had vacated their seats, while the ladies remained with trays in place, enjoying some snack or other. A loud bell signalled five minutes to curtain up and at the same time an army of usherettes proceeded to remove the trays and discarded rubbish.

The Empire Belles opened the second half with an energetic dance with tap routine and elaborate twirls to the fast-tempo music. It was very exciting to watch and ended with each girl falling to the floor in the splits.

Gus Davenport strode on to the stage clapping his hands, encouraging the audience to give even more applause. "Ladies and gentlemen, our very own Empire Belles!"

As the dancers bowed and left the stage the audience became silent.

"At last ladies and gentleman, the moment you've all been waiting for. Like the can-can, this lady has travelled "All the way from Paris, France". Please give a big Cardiff welcome home to the delightful and delectable Miss Florrie Grayson!" As he returned to his place at the side of the stage he blew a kiss to the audience and for a moment Rhiannon could pretend it was just for her.

Florrie Grayson glided onto the stage to great applause, many in the audience leapt to their feet, clapping and cheering. She was dressed in a pale gold-and-blue elegant silk gown, nipped tightly at the waist with a long straight skirt that fishtailed at the bottom. There could be no mistaking what a striking-looking woman she was: a bit plumper in the face than Rhiannon remembered, but with a stage presence to be admired.

With an appreciative smile and a gesture of her hands, like a true professional, she quietened the audience. Then she gave a nod to the conductor, the orchestra began and Florrie burst into song.

Her rendition of "I'll be your sweetheart" had all the men in the audience swooning and every woman wanting to be her. She sang four songs ending with "My mother's eyes" which brought the house down. She had encore after encore, which only stopped when the curtain fell for the last time and the house lights went up.

"Wasn't she great, Rhi? Don't you wish you could sing like that?"

"Yes, if only," Rhi answered. The way she felt, just seeing her aunt and all the other acts, she knew she'd found her dream: one day to be on stage herself, wooing the audience.

As the audience shuffled out of the auditorium Rhiannon and Mair stayed in their seats.

"Excuse me, miss." A young fair-haired lad addressed Rhiannon. "Would I be right in thinking that you're Miss Hughes?"

"Yes, that's right," she answered warily.

"I'm Percy. I work as call-boy backstage. Miss Grayson requested that I should come to escort you to her dressing-room."

"Hello, Percy. I'm Mair. We're sisters," Mair offered.

"Hello, miss."

As Rhiannon bent down to retrieve her suitcase she tried to stay positive. Whatever the outcome of the meeting with Aunt Florrie, it was going to be nice to see her mother's sister again.

"I'll take the suitcase, miss. Now if you'd both like to like to follow me."

They followed Percy up the aisle to the back of the stalls, across the glittering foyer and out onto the foggy streets and into the cold evening air. Then they sharply turned down a narrow alleyway. It was getting dark and Rhi wondered if she should so readily follow this stranger.

And, as if echoing her doubts, Mair asked, "Where's he taking us, Rhi?"

Percy must have heard her, for he answered, "This is the quickest way to the stage door. Look, it's dead ahead."

In front of them they saw a large door — desperately in need of a coat of paint. Alongside the door a porter stood, as if on sentry duty, in a small kiosk.

For some reason unknown to the girls a large group of men seemed to be bombarding the man in the kiosk with, "Come on, Fred. If you'll just take my card to the tall dark chorus girl second left, I'll make it worth your while." Or "Go tell Sally Webber that if she's not out in five minutes, I'm off, and I mean it." And, yet another, "What'll it cost me for you to put in a word for me with Miss Florrie Grayson."

The porter didn't seem at all ruffled; some pleas he answered and some he ignored. Then he spotted Percy and called out to the crowd.

"Come on. Make way. Let these people through. If you be patient I promise to deal with each of you in turn."

As the crowd obediently parted Rhiannon and Mair, with heads bowed, tucked in behind Percy as he made his way through the door.

"Are these new dancers for the chorus then, Fred? One of them looks a bit young, but the younger the meat the fresher the meal, that's what I say."

The crowd laughed.

"And I say, shut your filthy mouth. These young girls are related to Miss Grayson. So show some respect," the porter barked.

"Sorry, Fred, I didn't know. No hard feelings, eh?"

They entered the stage door, relieved to be away from such obnoxious men.

Percy mumbled something about "Bloody stage door Johnnies" and led the way down the passageway to the wings, through the backstage shadows with their maze of hanging ropes and various pieces of scenery propped against the rear wall.

"Up there's the flies." Percy pointed towards the high ceiling. "It's pretty safe now, but it's a dangerous place to be during the performance, unless you know what you're doing."

"Why is it so dangerous?" Rhiannon asked.

"From up there men . . . stage-hands, control every bit of scenery by hoisting it in the air and flying it into position on stage. In comparison my job as call-boy's easy, but no less important." His pride was obvious.

"Here we are, ladies." Percy came to an abrupt stop. The door in front of them was marked by a silver star with the name MISS FLORRIE GRAYSON in large letters above it.

Percy gave a light tap on the door.

"Come in," a lady's voice replied.

CHAPTER
EIGHT

As the door of her dressing-room slowly opened Florrie Grayson swallowed hard. Her mouth was dry and her head felt as if it would burst. She wished now that she hadn't agreed to send Walter away.

When Walter had come rushing back from the front of house with the news that two young girls had taken up the private box that she had booked for the family, her first reaction was of blind panic. Up to now the only youngsters she had had any dealings with were young chorus girls who, by nature of their profession, touring from town to town, fending for themselves and living in digs, seemed older than their years. But a couple of young valley girls who had just lost their father? She wasn't sure she knew how to cope.

Walter had offered to stay with her but she refused. If the girls in the box were Rhiannon and Nellie's daughter, Mair, she owed it to her sister and Dai to face them on her own. She still couldn't understand why Dai's widow hadn't accompanied them.

As the girls entered the room Florrie stood up from the dressing-table and took a deep breath. As she did, by force of habit, she automatically raised her hand to touch the back of her styled coiffure; her dark-auburn dyed hair was piled high under her straw hat with its wide turned-down brim and its shallow crown trimmed with a bundle of pheasant feathers. She checked her appearance in the well-lit mirror. Satisfied, she stood up and, as she turned to the girls, she slid her hand down the smooth contours of her pale olive green afternoon dress.

The girls stood with mouths open as they attempted to take in, first the dressing-room with its bright lights, colourful drapes, velvet *chaise-longue* and the heady scent of attar of roses that filled it. Then there stood Aunt Florrie, dressed in her fashionable silk-satin dress and wearing what had to be the biggest hat they had ever seen. It truly was a sight to behold. In contrast, they felt dowdy and so . . . out of place.

"Aunt Florrie, you were brilliant on stage. We both loved your singing, I so wish that Dad —"

Florrie held out her arms. "Rhiannon, my dear girl, I was so shocked to hear about your dear father's death."

Rhiannon rushed into her open arms.

"Oh, Aunt Florrie, these past few weeks have been awful. It's so good to see you. I've missed you so much."

"I know. It was such a dreadful thing to have happened. I'm so sorry that I wasn't with you . . . but I'm here now."

Mair stood with her back to the door, her eyes focused on the bright lights that surrounded Florrie's dressing-table mirror in an effort to keep her mind off the scene in front of her. The sight of Rhiannon and Florrie clinging to each other made her want to scream out. She felt left out, rejected, hurt and completely alone. Why must she always be made to feel so jealous of Rhiannon? She'd been fooling herself. The truth was that she was Nellie's brat, and who in their right mind would want her?

Florrie and Rhiannon's embrace seemed to last for ever. Eventually they separated. Florrie took a step back and took Rhiannon's hand. "It's been such a long time since I last saw you. My, you've become quite the young lady, so pretty, so grown up — and the image of your dear mother."

Rhiannon smiled, pleased to have the resemblance to her mother confirmed. It was funny, she never thought of herself as pretty, although her dad had always insisted she was, but he had been biased.

"And this must be Mair?" Florrie turned to the thin waiflike girl standing by the door.

"Yes. She's Nellie's daughter and my stepsister," Rhiannon gushed.

"What do you mean, stepsister? You said I was your sister. Make up your mind!" Mair glared at Rhiannon.

"I'm sure Rhiannon didn't mean to hurt your feelings, child. Now, come over and shake my hand. It's so good to meet you at last."

Mair reluctantly walked over and shook Florrie's hand.

"That's better. In a little while I'd like you both to meet my dear friend Mr Walter Cahill. We thought we'd take you out for tea, a chance for us all to get know one another. Would you like that?"

The girls nodded. Rhiannon smiled at Mair and was rewarded with another glare. Rhiannon couldn't understand why Mair was in such a bad mood. She seemed hell bent on playing up in front of Aunt Florrie. Rhiannon had to control the urge to shake the ungrateful little madam.

"Before Walter arrives maybe you could help me. You see, I'm a little puzzled as to why Nellie didn't accompany you today."

Rhiannon made to speak but Mair beat her to it.

"My Mam's buggered off with the tallyman. She left ages ago."

"Mair! What's come in to you? Watch your language," Rhiannon scolded.

Mair simply shrugged her shoulders.

"Is this true, Rhiannon? Has Nellie left?" Florrie asked.

"Yes. She left last November with a travelling salesman. Since then it's just been Dad, Mair and me. Now it's just —"

Mair interrupted. "See, I'm not a liar."

"Of course you're not, child. I didn't mean to imply . . . it was just such a shock to hear that your mother has up and left you." Florrie turned to Rhiannon. "Are you telling me you haven't heard from Nellie since then?" she asked.

"Not a word. Not even at Christmas. Mind you, Dad made sure we had a good time. Didn't he, Mair?"

Mair, her eyes staring at the floor, nodded her agreement. She hated being reminded of how her mother had abandoned her.

Florrie shook her head in disbelief. "How have you both been managing since . . . the accident?"

"Mrs Lewis and her son, Frank, from next door, have been ever so kind. Mrs Lewis even offered to take us in permanent like. You see, now that Dad's . . . gone we've got to leave the house. Another miner and his family are moving in."

"I see." Florrie pondered for a while. "Have you any idea where Nellie went?"

"No. Not really." Rhiannon's voice was quiet.

"She left us to start a new life with her fancy man, didn't she, Rhi?" Mair blurted out.

For the first time Florrie's eyes focused on the battered suitcase inside the door. Her shocked expression said it all. "So, tell me, Rhiannon, what's to become of you both?"

"That's why we're here. We thought we could move in with you."

As if saved by the bell, there was a knock on the door.

"Come in," Florrie called.

Walter entered the room.

"Girls, this Mr Walter Cahill, the good friend I told you about earlier."

"Well, what have we here? A real bevy of beauty, I'd say, and that's for sure."

Both girls blushed at the compliment.

"Hello, you must be Rhi," he said, vigorously shaking her hand, "I've heard so much about you from your Aunt Florrie. It's so good to meet you at last. I hope you don't mind me calling you Rhi? But I ain't even gonna attempt your full name."

Rhiannon smiled. "Rhi will do fine, Mr Cahill."

"Please, call me Walter."

"And this one's gotta be Mayre?

Mair giggled at the way he pronounced her name.

"I just knew I was gonna have a heap of trouble with these Welsh names." He smiled as he shook her hand. "This must be my lucky day. It's not often an old fella like me gets to take three beauties out for tea. I hope you gals have had enough time alone, I've booked us tea at the Angel Hotel and the cab is waiting. Are you ready Florrie?

Florrie nodded. "Yes. I think the sooner we go the better."

If Walter sensed her agitation he didn't show it.

As they left the theatre via the stage door they came face to face with Gus Davenport, the show's chairman.

Rhiannon held her breath. He was even more handsome close up. He was tall and well built, with a mop of dark-brown hair, and sporting a thin, neatly trimmed moustache.

"I thought you were great this afternoon, Miss Grayson. You had the audience eating out of the palm of your hand," he gushed.

"Why, thank you, and thank you for warming the audience for me."

"My pleasure," he said. Then turning his gaze to Rhiannon he beamed a smile and repeated softly, "Oh yes, it's always my pleasure."

Rhiannon felt her colour rise.

"Gus, this is my niece —"

Before Florrie could finish the introduction Walter, much to Rhiannon's annoyance, already out through the door, interrupted, "Get a move on, you gals. It's starting to rain," he urged. "Sorry, Gus, my man. Maybe we'll catch you later, eh?"

"That's all right. I can wait," Gus called, his clear blue eyes fixed on Rhiannon.

There was a small crowd, mostly young men, waiting at the stage door. They instantly recognized Florrie Grayson and quickly gathered around her and the girls.

One young man called out, "Miss Grayson. I think you're wonderful!" Another thrust a piece of paper in her hand, "Miss Grayson, my card. I'm at your disposal." Yet another, "Any chance of an introduction to the young girls with you?"

Without a word Walter quickly cleared a path to the waiting carriage. When they were settled he tapped the ceiling of the Brougham with the end of his walking-stick and they set off.

Rhiannon, unable to help herself, looked back towards the stage door, hoping for another glimpse of Gus Davenport. But, much to her disappointment, he was nowhere to be seen.

"I don't think I'll ever get used to those damn stage door Johnnies," Walter complained. "Florrie, do they really believe that a lady like you would ever consider entertaining the likes of them?"

"You'd be surprised, my dear. There's many a stage performer taken in by their sweet talk." Florrie turned to the girls. "Rhiannon, Mair, I hope they didn't upset you."

The girls shook their heads.

Rhiannon remembered how Percy had also referred to stage door Johnnies when he escorted them backstage; now Walter had done the same and she was still none the wiser. "Aunt Florrie, what exactly is a stage door Johnnie?" she asked.

Florrie looked stern-faced. "Well, they're men who wait at stage doors hoping to pick up . . . meet the artists . . . dancers, singers any performer, really. They're usually after one thing — to take advantage. Don't get me wrong, some girls are only too willing. But I strongly advise you and Mair to give them a wide berth."

Mair struggled to suppress a giggle.

Walter and Florrie sat alone in the restaurant of the Angel Hotel. Earlier Florrie had suggested the girls might like to take themselves off to the ladies' powder room to tidy up before tea was served.

"What's up, gal?" Walter asked, gently touching her small-gloved hand.

"Sometimes I think you know me too well." She patted his hand. "Oh Walter, Rhiannon has laid such a bombshell at my feet. It turns out that the girls didn't come just to see the show. The truth is they expect me to take them in permanently!"

"You're not serious?" But looking into her eyes he knew she was. "With your tight schedule you couldn't possibly take on two young girls? You've far too many commitments."

"You don't need to remind me. How could *I* be expected to look after two young girls? We both know it's out of the question. It just wouldn't be practical . . . So why do I feel so bloody guilty? Walter, I'm Rhiannon's only living relative. She truly believed I'd take her in. How am I going to tell her?"

Walter pondered for a moment. "I think, in the short term, that maybe a compromise could be the answer."

"What sort of compromise?"

"Well, we know that you're contracted for the duration of the show's run. We could let them stay with us for a while. I'm sure I could negotiate a deal for an extra room with the hotel manager."

"But what would I do with them while I'm at work?"

"They both seem quite capable to me. You could always have a word with the theatre's housekeeper. I'm sure it would do them both a power of good to be involved, maybe in the theatre's wardrobe, laundry or even selling programmes. I'm sure there's plenty they could apply themselves to."

"I don't know that I want to take them in, even for a short while." She gave a long sigh . . . "Whatever happens, we'll have to get them settled into the hotel with us tonight. And it'll give me time to think."

"Leave it with me." Walter looked up to see Rhiannon and Mair entering the restaurant. "Look, here they come. Will you be all right if I leave you for a few minutes? I need to speak to the hotel manager."

"Of course, and Walter . . . thank you. I don't know what I would have done without you."

"Hey chucks, I bet you say that to all us good-looking guys."

The girls arrived at the table in high spirits.

"Aunt Florrie, have you seen the powder room? It's enormous," Rhiannon enthused. "A lady took our coats and gave us each a clean white towel and a small bar of scented soap."

"I kept my soap; it's in my skirt pocket," Mair announced.

"So did I," Rhiannon admitted. "Sorry, Aunt Florrie, did we do wrong?"

Florrie smiled. She felt a lot more comfortable in their company now that she and Walter had found a solution — albeit in the short term. "No. Not at all. Everyone gets a fresh tablet of soap, so yours would only have ended up in the bin."

"I'm glad we took it, then. My dad hated waste." For a moment Rhiannon looked pensive.

Florrie could only imagine what hardship her young niece had suffered in her short life, but could it really concern her? It might have been easier if she had only Rhiannon to consider. Florrie wondered whether there might be a way to reach Mair's own mother.

A few minutes later Walter rejoined them. "All fixed up," was all he said, as he beamed a self-satisfied smile in Florrie's direction. Then, after he had given a nod to the head waiter, a smartly dressed waitress proceeded to fill their table with a selection of tiny sandwiches, fancy cakes and a large pot of tea.

The conversation over tea was light-hearted. Walter was a natural and found conversation easy with the two young girls. It pleased Florrie to see that both girls had taken to Walter — but then who wouldn't? He was such a love. Whereas Florrie relied on her talent as a performer to carry her through. Mind you, she did make them giggle when, both of them having eaten so heartily, she teased them saying, "I'd rather feed you two for a week than a fortnight."

It was only when they made to go that Rhiannon suddenly became tense. "Aunt Florrie, what's to become of us?"

Florrie hesitated. This was the moment she'd been dreading. "Well, the first thing we have to do is get you booked into the hotel."

Walter interjected. "I've already spoken to the manager and luckily there's a room right next to your aunt, ready and waiting for the two of you."

Florrie threw him a warm smile.

"Really? We've never stayed in a posh hotel before. There's lovely, isn't it, Mair?" Rhainnon gushed.

"Yeah, I suppose so," Mair said.

"Come on then. We'd better get a move on. Your aunt has another show to do tonight," Walter urged.

Florrie smiled. "There speaks the voice of an agent. But Walter's right. I've been having such a good time I almost forgot about tonight's show. Tomorrow is Sunday and my day off. What do you say to our discussing the future in the morning, over breakfast, after we've all had a good night's rest?"

Walter led the way from the tearoom to the lift situated on the other side of the impressive reception area. With its wall-to-wall red carpet and sparkling crystal chandelier hanging from the ceiling, so huge, it took the girls' breath away. Rhiannon and Mair held hands and looked up in amazement as Walter pressed the button to call the lift and, as if by magic, in what seemed like only seconds later, the metal doors opened to reveal a flimsy looking metal gate which the lift attendant, a young boy bell-boy, slid to one side.

As the lift started to ascend Mair closed her eyes. She felt lightheaded. She really didn't enjoy the feeling of being elevated at speed and was glad when the lift jolted to a stop on floor three.

Rhiannon on the other hand couldn't contain her excitement. "Ooh! What fun."

The bell-boy smiled.

As they left the lift the girls quietly followed Florrie and Walter down a long red-carpeted corridor, flanked by honey-coloured panelled walls and numerous brass wall-lights.

Halfway down the corridor the party slowed down.

Walter fumbled with the key. "This is your room right next to your aunt." He unlocked the door and handed Rhiannon the key. "I'm just across the hall from you all, so if there's anything you gals need, just knock on my door."

"Now girls, I'd like you to unpack your things and have an early night," Florrie instructed.

Walter gave them a reassuring look. "As soon as I drop Florrie off at the theatre I'll be back. I need to catch up with some correspondence so, if there's anything you need . . . just knock on my door."

With Walter gone, the girls were on their own. To their surprise their room was quite spacious, much bigger than the one they shared back home. There was a wardrobe, a dressing-table, a small writing-bureau and a closet hiding a washbasin and toilet facilities.

After quickly unpacking they washed themselves, slipped into their nightdresses and jumped into the luxurious double bed. They were too excited to sleep and spent most of the night recalling their time at the theatre. With their heads under the bedclothes, they attempted to sing from memory all the popular songs they'd heard during the show. When sleep came at last, Rhiannon dreamt she was dancing with Gus Davenport, his arms holding her, his warm lips brushing her cheek arousing her body with feelings she didn't understand.

Early next morning Rhiannon awoke, confused. She rubbed her eyes and began to take in the unfamiliar surroundings of the spacious room, which was now lit by the shafts of daylight that filtered through a gap in the heavy brocade curtains.

Leaving Mair still fast asleep in the bed Rhiannon quietly made her way over to the window. She pulled back the curtains to reveal a day of brilliant sunshine and a spectacular view of Cardiff Castle and the adjacent streets. She felt her spirit rise; since her father's death the weather, like her mood, had been black, depressing and cold.

Her thoughts turned to Frank. When they left him at the station he'd looked so forlorn. She missed him. She hoped he was well recovered after his ordeal underground. She felt suddenly homesick. Then she remembered the letterbox in the hotel's impressive reception area. She could write a letter. Yes . . . that was what she would do . . . she'd write to Frank.

> Room 62
> Angel Hotel,
> Castle Street,
> Cardiff.
> 20 March 1909

Dear Frank,
Just to let you know that we arrived safely and in good time for the matinée performance at the Empire Theatre.

I wish you could have been with us to see the grand entrance, the auditorium, the toffs in all their finery and all the wonderful stage performers. Aunt Florrie brought the house down — the audience wouldn't let her off the stage. I just loved it.

After the show we were taken backstage to meet her. She was so pleased to see us that she and her close friend Mr Walter Cahill took us out for tea. He's an American and I really like him.

You'll never believe it but we're all staying at the Angel Hotel — I'm not fibbing. Mair and me are sharing a room that overlooks Cardiff Castle, very posh, don't you think?

I hope you are feeling better.

I've been thinking of you all. Ponty seems so far away. With spring well and truly on its way, if I close my eyes I can imagine Carn mountain covered with daffodils. Unfortunately, this year, I'll not be there for the annual Whitsun Day parade in early May. I shall miss your mother's homemade Welsh-cakes. I bet you're thinking, all the more for you, eh!

Please write soon. I do miss our little chats or, better still, why don't you come to see us?

Give my love to your Mam, Sadie & Martha.

Love,

Rhi

As Rhiannon placed the carefully folded letter into the addressed envelope she hoped her light-hearted approach would work. She wondered whether Frank, knowing her as well as he did, would read between the lines. If he did he'd realize how homesick she truly felt. For all the excitement that Cardiff and the theatre had to offer, she would give anything to turn back the clock to her happy, uncomplicated and secure life, before the colliery accident. She gave a deep sigh . . .

"Morning, Rhi." Mair yawned, her hands rubbing the sleep from her eyes.

Rhiannon quickly slipped the letter into the pocket of her skirt. This letter was just between her and Frank; she didn't want it pawed over by Mair.

"I'm starving. What time's breakfast?" Mair asked.

Rhiannon thought, typical Mair, always thinking of her stomach. Mind you, it did seem a long time since tea yesterday. "I think we're expected to wait until we're called for."

Rhiannon walked to the closet in the corner of the room and poured water from the jug into the china bowl. After she'd washed and dressed she encouraged a sleepy Mair to do the same.

Once dressed Mair suggested they knock on Aunt Florrie's bedroom door to ask about breakfast.

"I don't think that's such a good idea. Aunt Florrie wouldn't have arrived back from the theatre until late last night. I'm sure she'd not thank us if we disturbed her this early. I wouldn't want to be the one to upset her but if you . . .?"

Mair shook her head and pulled a face. "No thanks! I know, what if I nip across the hall to Walter's room? He said we should knock on his door if we needed anything, and I need breakfast!"

"I suppose —" Rhiannon was interrupted by a timely knock on the door.

Rhiannon opened the door to a cheery-faced Walter. "Good morning, gals. I've called to escort you down to breakfast. It's just us three I'm afraid. Your Aunt Florrie always has her breakfast in her room. But she sends her regards and told me to tell you that she'll see you later."

As the girls entered the breakfast room their eyes focused on the long buffet table groaning with more food than they had ever seen.

"Our regular breakfast table is the one in the window. What say we settle ourselves down?"

Once they were seated a waiter, dressed in a crisp white shirt with a stiffly starched collar, black bow tie, waistcoat and trousers came to their table.

"Good morning, sir. Will it be the full breakfast for three?"

"No. It's a bit too early for me. I'll just have a pot of strong coffee. But these two gals are probably ravenous? Rhi, Mair, what do you fancy?" The girls stayed silent, not knowing how to order or what to say. Walter, sensing their growing panic, said, "How does bacon, scrambled egg and hot buttered toast sound?"

They nodded eagerly.

"Then that's settled."

"Will that be all, sir?" the waiter asked.

"I think two glasses of milk would make it just fine."

While Walter read the *Daily Telegraph* they ate heartily — the food tasted delicious.

Walter waited for them to finish, then lowered his newspaper. "Well, that's the quietest you two have been since I met you. No need to ask if you enjoyed it, eh?"

The girls smiled.

"Right. It's time to discuss the plan for this morning. Rhi, your aunt has requested you join her for a chat in her room as soon as you finish breakfast."

"What about me?" Mair asked petulantly.

Walter, ever the diplomat, ignored her tone and just smiled, "Well Mayre, I thought that you and I might take a stroll to Victoria Park. What do you say?"

Mair hesitated.

Walter pressed further. "I've been looking for an excuse to visit for days, they've had a delivery of new exotic animals . . . you really would be doing me a great favour."

Mair cursed him for putting her on the spot. If she refused him she would show herself up as a real brat. "Yes, all right," she mumbled, as she tried not to show how miffed she was at Florrie only asking to see Rhiannon. She wondered if this was the start of things to come?

Rhiannon gave a light tap on Florrie's bedroom door.

"Come in, child," Florrie called.

Rhiannon entered the light, spacious room and breathed in the heady scent of rose petals.

Florrie was lazing on top of the huge double bed, dressed in an elegant long cream-silk robe, heavily embroidered around the cuffs and collar and tied in the middle with a wide cummerbund. With her shoulder-length hair hanging loose and only a touch of face powder and lipstick she looked so much younger than the night before — more like the Aunt Florrie Rhiannon remembered.

"Rhiannon, dear, we need to talk." Florrie patted the bed, indicating that Rhiannon should sit facing her. When Rhiannon did as she was bid Florrie, looking decidedly uncomfortable, continued, "The thing is that since last night I've had more time to think about you and Mair coming to stay with me . . ."

"We'll be no trouble, you'll see," Rhiannon said eagerly.

"Yes, I'm sure. In a perfect world I would take you in and we'd all live happy ever after. But life is not that simple." Florrie looked away.

"Are you saying you don't want us?" Rhiannon asked.

"Rhiannon, you have to understand. It wouldn't be so bad if it was just you; after all, you're flesh and blood, but Mair? Look, what if we try to find Nellie? I'm sure, as her mother, she could be persuaded to take Mair in.

"No!"

"I beg your pardon."

"I'm sorry, Aunt Florrie. I didn't mean to shout. But I promised Mair we would stay together. It's what Dad would have wanted. Mair knows that neither her mother nor the rest of her family want her — I'm all she has. I'll not be parted from her. If you don't want us we'll "

Florrie raised the palm of her hand, "All right — all right. I don't know how we're going to manage it, but I'm willing to give it a try, on the understanding that it can only be short term, until my contract ends. Rhiannon, I do remember you were once good with a needle and thread."

"I still am."

"Good, I'll have a word with Mrs Gordon, the theatre's wardrobe mistress. I'm sure she would welcome an extra pair of hands. The trouble is, what to do with young Mair. By rights she should be at school. I shall make some enquiries. You do understand,

Rhiannon, this can only be a temporary arrangement; after all, my career must come first."

Although Rhiannon nodded her agreement, in truth she didn't understand how her Aunt Florrie could put her career before her family. But she instinctively knew not to voice her true feelings; instead she reach out to give Florrie a hug.

"Thank you, Aunt Florrie, you'll not regret it."

"Don't be so quick to thank me. While you're with me your lives will revolve around my work, the theatre and theatre folk. You'll soon discover that they're a breed of their own."

CHAPTER
NINE

It was late afternoon when Frank Lewis, having just finished his eight-hour shift down the pit, wearily followed the colliery railway line along the mountain path to his home a mile away in Ponty. Since that fateful day when the fall in the pit had taken Dai and fifteen other miner's lives, Frank had hated his job; so much so that at the start of every shift he dreaded the day ahead. A day spent listening for every sudden noise — and there were many, filled him with fear, anticipating another fall.

Frank would have done anything to change his job and leave the valley. But as the main provider for his family, he knew it was out of the question.

After his father's death, his mother had come very close to losing their tied colliery house. At first Frank had been very grateful to Dai Hughes for taking him on as his apprentice. Right up until the day of the accident Frank remembered how proud he'd felt to be Dai's butty. Now, while still struggling to come to terms with the recurring nightmares of that day, he would be eternally grateful to Dai for saving his life.

The day the accident victims were buried Frank had sobbed like a baby. He had been unable to come to terms with the fact that better men than he had lost their lives. The guilt he felt at seeing Dai's daughters, their father taken so suddenly, going through their grief. Never once had they questioned or blamed Frank for their father's death. While he understood the wrench it must have been for the girls, he couldn't help but envy the fact that Rhiannon and Mair had been given the opportunity to leave the valley and begin a new life.

Since their departure not a day had gone by when he didn't think of Rhiannon. How he missed her. The day she and Mair had left him standing on the station made him realize how deeply he felt for Rhiannon, and perhaps, if things had been different he and Rhiannon . . .? He stopped himself. Who was he fooling? With her exciting new life in Cardiff and him stuck here in the valley. They might almost be in different worlds.

"Hello son. Had a good day?" his mother asked.

"Tell me, Mam, how you think that working down that stinking hole for eight hours could ever be a good day?" he snapped. Then, seeing his mother's distress, he wished he hadn't vented his feelings on her.

Ethel nibbled her bottom lip, "I'm sorry, lad. I so wish —"

Frank caught his arms around her. "No Mam, I'm the one who should be sorry. I'm such an ungrateful, miserable bugger. I promise I'll buck up when I've had my bath and a bowl of that stew you're cooking on the stove."

His mother forced a smile. "That's all right, son. I know something that's going to cheer you up better than a bath or a bowl of stew. Look on the mantelpiece. There's a letter for you. Jones the post delivered it this morning. It's got a Cardiff postmark. It's from Rhiannon, I recognize her writing!"

Frank headed for the mantelpiece. He grabbed the letter, hastily opened it and proceeded to read its contents.

After a few minutes his mother's impatience got the better of her. "Well what's the news? How are they getting on?"

"Fine, I think. Only, reading between the lines like, to me Rhiannon sounds homesick. She sends her love to you, Sadie and Martha."

"Oh, that's kind of her," his mother said. "She always was a good girl. Mind you, I think she'll have her hands full with young Mair. Mair's mother was such a bad 'un, and you know what they say: 'an apple never falls far from the tree'."

"Don't say that, Mam. The way Dai took her in, insisting on treating her as his second daughter, especially after her own mother upped and left her, must have influenced her. She and Rhi are so close. I'm sure Mair looks up to Rhiannon."

"I do hope so. I still can't believe how Dai allowed that Nellie Parsons to use him. When his Rose, Rhiannon's mother, was alive he seemed such a sensible, level-headed fellow. I swear, if I hadn't seen it with my own eyes, I'd never have believed how a bit of skirt could've turned his head. So . . . you take heed, son."

Nellie Parsons stepped into her petticoats and pulled them up over her long stockings and drawers. She bent down to buckle her high ankle-boots before reaching for her new turquoise woollen dress with its tight, figure-hugging bodice. Nellie had been so pleased when Harry had arrived home one night with the dress.

"Harry, it's so lovely. I've never had such a beautiful dress. It must have cost you the earth." She was touched; surely only a man in love would spoil his woman so?

Nellie threw her arms around him and kissed him full on the mouth, a long lingering kiss, and all the while her firm breasts rubbed against him with the promise of a lot more. Harry was all hers and he truly loved her. She felt so happy . . . but her euphoria was to be short-lived.

As Harry lifted her up in his arms and carried her to the bed, he chuckled. "I'd say the dress will prove a shrewd investment. The better you look, the more punters and the more earnings, eh?"

Nellie stared at her reflection in the rust-speckled mirror above the marble-topped washstand. She liked what she saw. She drew a deep breath that caused her breasts to push against the fabric of the turquoise dress, the bright colour a perfect contrast to her pale-blue eyes. The bodice of the dress was a bit too low in the front, but what the hell: it was what the punters wanted.

Nellie smiled. Six months of working on the streets of Cardiff had changed her into a real glamour-puss. She brushed back her shoulder-length light-brown hair and retouched her red lipstick and rouge. Then she took her straw hat with its wide brim, its crown covered with silk flowers and placed it on her head.

Nellie glanced at the clock on the mantelpiece. It was almost seven o'clock, time she was on her way to the theatre. How she wished she didn't have to go. But she knew only too well what Harry would say and, more to the point, what he would do if she hadn't earned enough money. With this thought in mind Nellie picked up her fox-fur stole and kid gloves and headed through the door.

Nellie had hoped that Harry's display of temper on the first night would not be repeated — wishful thinking on her part. Where she was concerned he had become far too handy with his fists, and clever enough never to hit her where the bruises would show.

Since Nellie's hasty departure from Ponty, Harry had felt it prudent not to return there himself. "I think I'll try the Canton area here in Cardiff for a while. Everyone says that, for a salesman with my talent, with the steelworkers all earning such good money, there's rich pickings just for the taking." He threw Nellie a wry smile. "I think I'd really enjoy persuading their womenfolk to part with some of it."

She knew he was trying to make her jealous. But she ignored it. "Why try somewhere else? I thought you said you were doing well up the valley."

"Yeah, but you know what they say: a change is as good as a rest."

At first Nellie had suspected that the real reason for the change was that Harry didn't want to risk coming face to face with Dai or, for that matter, any of his mining butties, though she wouldn't dare say it to his face. Of course, since then, with the accident in the mine everything had changed. No Dai, and, up to now, thank God, no news from Mair. Nellie convinced herself that the girl must be all right; if it were otherwise surely she would have heard by now. It suited Nellie to pretend she'd never given birth.

As it turned out Harry's transfer of his work to Canton had been a good one. He was doing really well. In the last few months, as promised, they had moved to new and better digs in Westgate Street. This one had two bedrooms — which meant she didn't have to entertain the punters in her and Harry's bed. Like the curtains in the rooms, the Victorian furniture was dark and gloomy, but, for the time being, they would have to do.

Harry's working in Canton meant no more staying away or late-night train journeys. Most days he left around half past eight in the morning and arrived back in Cardiff around ten o'clock at night. Then, not wanting to risk disturbing her with a punter, he would go straight to the King's Head pub, on the corner of their street, and wait for her. Nellie usually arrived well before stop-tap to hand over her earnings.

Harry's mood depended on how many punters she'd had and how much they paid.

110

* * *

It was almost 10.30 when Nellie entered the King's Head. A drunk almost bowled her over as he made to leave; he reeked of stale smoke, beer and sweat. The noise coming from inside the tap room was deafening and through the haze of smoke the pale gas lights flickered. Once her eyes had become adjusted she saw the sea of bowler hats, cloth caps and flowered bonnets all milling around the piano: the usual Friday-night revellers out for a sing-song and a bloody good time.

Nellie spotted Harry, looking as dapper as ever, at the bar. He smiled and nodded, but it was only when she discreetly handed him four crisp white fivers, her earnings for the night, that he pulled her to him. Playfully slapping her arse he said, "That's my girl. I told you, you're sitting on a gold mine." She could tell he was pleased.

Nellie loved it when he called her "his girl". But if she was his girl how could he just stand by, and encourage her to sleep with other men?

Later that night Nellie, having downed a few ales and sensing Harry's continued good mood, plucked up the courage to ask, "Harry?"

"Yeah?"

"Now that you're doing so well in Port Talbot, couldn't I give up doing what I'm doing?"

"Want to be a kept woman then, do you? Well, think again!" Harry sniggered.

"I didn't mean that. I'd find another job, honest," Nellie pleaded.

111

"Don't make me bloody laugh. What else are you qualified for?" Harry scoffed.

"Maybe I could work in a shop, or a pub, or —"

Harry raised his hand in front of her face. Nellie ducked, expecting him to strike her, but instead he caught his arms around her.

"You daft ha'peth. When are you going realize that this is what you're good at?" He threw back his head and laughed loudly. "Thinking about it, you were probably born on your back with your legs in the air. That's why it comes so natural to you."

He was still laughing when Nellie shouted at him. "Are you saying that you expect me to sleep with anyone willing to pay for it for the rest of my life?" She felt her tears well up.

"Of course I don't! Now you're just being silly." He caught her up and gently kissed her forehead.

Nellie gave a sigh. For once her tantrum had paid off. Surely no man wanted the woman he loved to sleep around, not even for money?

"Now Nellie, you have to listen to me. It's not in my interest to steer you wrong. You've just got to bide your time. At the moment the reason you're doing so well is because you have age on your side."

She pulled away from him. "So, I've got to wait until I'm too bloody old, is that it? And pray tell me when that will be?"

"I'd say, at most, another year, maybe two."

"Bloody charming."

"I'm only being practical. It stands to reason that most men want their women young and firm; some say the younger the better. And that's where the big money's to be earned."

"And in two years' time what's going to happen to me?" What she really wanted to know was, would he want her, but she was afraid to hear his answer.

"By then, my sweet, if I have my way, we'll have a few young girls working for us."

She smiled. While she liked the sound of *for us*, indicating togetherness, his plan sounded too incredible for words. "Christ! Are you saying you want to run a brothel with me as the madam?"

"Now don't go jumping the gun. Let's take one step at a time. Our aim at the moment should be to recruit new blood. Someone to take over from you. Now, if we could find a pretty new youngster then . . . it would make sense for you to take a step back and just concentrate on showing her the ropes." He pulled her to him and kissed her mouth in a way he hadn't kissed her for a long time. It felt so good.

"What do you say, Nell, are we partners?"

"Oh yes — yes, whatever you say."

CHAPTER
TEN

April 1909.

Florrie Grayson felt pleased with herself. During the past weeks things had worked out far better than she could have hoped.

When Florrie had explained her predicament to Mrs Gordon, the theatre housekeeper, that lady had willingly offered to speak to each of the girls, to see where they could be best put to use. Mrs Gordon wasn't married but in the theatre housekeepers were always given the title of Mrs as a mark of respect.

From the very first it was obvious to all that Rhiannon was a natural. She proved to be a hard worker, willing to take on any job; no task was too large or small and, with her willingness to help, she soon became popular with every member of the company. Mair, on the other hand, had to be pushed. She hated being backstage. She much preferred being on show, in front of house, which made her well suited to sell programmes.

Florrie soon found out that Tom O'Reilly, the Irish comedian, was a former teacher. With the offer of a few guineas, she soon persuaded him help Mair with her reading, writing and arithmetic a few hours every weekday afternoon. Of course Mair protested. The very first afternoon, in an attempt to avoid the inevitable, she decided to go missing, only to be found hiding in a theatre skip, a large wicker basket where stage costumes were stored. When Florrie threatened to send her to Saint Joseph's, the local convent's boarding school, Mair soon saw sense and backed down.

Since the girls were both occupied for most of the day the only time Florrie saw either of them was when they occasionally popped into her dressing-room, or when they shared a carriage back to the Angel Hotel late at night. Yes, all in all it had worked out well.

Rhiannon had been working backstage for two weeks, helping out wherever she was needed. Some days she would work for the wardrobe, fitting and altering costumes; another day she might be working with props: helping with the furniture and scenery to ensure every prop was in place for each performance. More recently she had begun to run errands for Adam Fletcher, the show's producer and theatre company director. He was a man in his early fifties, highly respected for his experience and expertise by everyone in the theatre.

For some reason Rhiannon and Adam Fletcher instantly hit it off. Although he was a lot older than Rhiannon she liked and admired him; he was a perfectionist and she was sure that given the chance she could learn a lot from him.

"He may be a hard taskmaster, but he certainly knows his stuff. But then, having worked almost every theatre in the country and produced many successful shows, I'd expect nothing less," Dave, the stage manager had offered.

One day Adam Fletcher pulled her to one side. "Rhiannon, as we are about to begin rehearsals. I thought that if you can assure me you'll sit quietly I'd allow you to join me while I take each artist through their paces."

"Thank you, Mr Fletcher, I'd like that very much. I'll be as quiet as a chapel congregation in prayer, I promise."

"Good. You'll soon find out that I don't suffer fools gladly. But your obvious excitement at being involved with every aspect of the theatre shows a genuine eagerness to learn. I like that. And by the way, you can drop the Mr Fletcher, my name's Adam."

As she took her place next to him she couldn't help notice his growing agitation.

"Where's the bloody chairman? If he's not here in two minutes I'll have to start without him," he said, as he ran an impatient hand through his fair hair.

"I'm here," Gus called as he approached from the back of the stalls.

"Must you always cut it so fine?" Adam asked.

"Keep your hair on. I'm here now." Gus smiled.

Since that first night at the stage door Rhiannon had seen Gus Davenport many times backstage. She secretly longed to approach him, but knew that it wasn't her place. Sometimes he threw her a wink and a smile as he passed by. She did wonder whether he might be flirting with her but soon scolded herself for having such silly thoughts; it was, after all, just wishful thinking on her part. She still considered him to be the most handsome man she'd ever seen. Just standing this close to him made her heart beat faster and, as she met his stare, she hoped he couldn't read her thoughts.

"Come on, Adam, what's the delay? Are you going to officially introduce me to this young beauty, or maybe it's your intention to keep her all to yourself?"

Adam shook his head. "Gus, you really are such a predictable arsehole." He turned to Rhiannon. "Sorry for the language. This young lady is Rhiannon Hughes." He threw Gus a warning look. "Miss Florrie Grayson's —"

Gus interrupted him. "Niece, yes I know."

"Rhiannon, this is Gerald *Gus* Davenport, our chairman and general nuisance to every young girl or, for that matter, any woman with a pulse."

Gus Davenport held out his hand. "Don't you pay any attention to this slanderous old bugger. Jealousy can be such a terrible thing."

Rhiannon blushed and her hand visibly shook.

"Rhiannon, what sort of a name is that? It's a bit of a mouthful," Gus teased.

"It's an old Welsh name. It translates as 'divine' or 'princess'," Adam offered.

Gus smiled and made an elaborate bow, "Your Majesty, honoured to meet you, I'm sure."

Although she was still blushing, the way this man was making fun of her name annoyed her. "My name's Rhiannon Hughes and I'll trust you not to make fun of it!" she snapped.

"Gus, will you stop teasing her and take your place in the wings. If it's all right with you, I'd like to get this rehearsal under way."

"All right, let's do it . . . let's get this show under way," Gus said, as he marched off to take his place in the wings.

Within just a week of sitting with Adam during rehearsals and watching two shows every night from the back of the auditorium, Rhiannon, eager to prove the producer's faith in her, managed to learn each act word perfect — making her an obvious choice to stand in when the prompter fell ill.

"If you think you're up to it, then the job's yours, but you have to make sure to stand way back in the wings and stay out of sight of the audience at all times. And to be aware that, with the artists dashing on and off stage, the wings can be a hectic place," Adam said.

Rhiannon had jumped at the chance.

Rhiannon stood in the wings enthralled as she watched Dave, the stage manager, go through his checklist for the first show.

"Good luck, Rhi!" Percy called from backstage.

Rhiannon turned and smiled. "Thanks."

The SM raised his head from his desk situated in the wings at the end of the stage — out of view from the auditorium. "You've come highly recommended by the producer himself. So I'm sure you'll do fine."

Rhiannon took her place next to Dave. Her job as prompter was to hold cue cards and be ready to prompt the artists if they forgot their lines — be it a joke, a

118

conjuring trick or a song. She, rightly, felt pleased with herself at being trusted with such an important position. If she continued to work hard then maybe one day she would achieve her dream — to follow in her Aunt Florrie's footsteps.

On Dave's signal, Rhiannon saw Percy head for the dressing-rooms to inform the cast that it was just five minutes to curtain up. On cue the orchestra in the pit in front of the stage began to play the overture. As the music played and the auditorium lights began to dim, the intensity of Rhiannon's emotions caused her to catch her breath as goose bumps invaded her flesh.

The Empire Belles were lined up in the wings, ready to open the show.

"Percy, give the chairman another call, will you?"

Within minutes Rhiannon watched Gus Davenport squeeze past the dancers. As he did so he gave each girl a token peck on the cheek.

"It's about bloody time. Must you always cut it so fine?" Dave asked.

"I'd have come a lot sooner if I'd known this young beauty was here with you." He stared down at Rhiannon, his gaze burning her large brown eyes. "Greetings, Majesty." He gave another of his elaborate bows.

"My name's Rhiannon!" she snapped.

"Temper temper, Princess Rhi," he mocked.

"Rhi will do. And I'll thank you to not to make fun of me."

Behind him one of the Empire Belles called out, "You seem to have met your match with that one, Gus." The rest of the troupe laughed.

Gus moved closer to Rhiannon, his face almost touching hers. She could feel his warm breath. "I'm sorry. I really didn't mean to upset you," he whispered. "When you get to know me better, you'll realize I like to tease, it's what I do. Friends?" He took her hand in his and, raising it gently, kissed her palm.

She caught her breath. Luckily at that precise moment she heard the music reach a climax and, as the curtain rose to rapturous applause, he released her hand. He walked on to the stage to take his position at the chairman's table and proceeded to address the audience. "My lords, ladies and gentlemen . . ."

Rhiannon looked on in awe. This man oozed so much confidence; he was so elegant and so . . . handsome. She was overcome by the same feelings that had been stirred in her dreams. She felt her colour rise while at the same time, strangely, she broke out in a cold sweat.

Mair, with only a few programmes left and her moneybag practically bursting with coins, made her way across the foyer to the pass door that led backstage.

If Mair had to do a job, then she was quite happy selling programmes before the show. She liked being front of house, it gave her a chance to mingle with the audience, from *hoi polloi* in the stalls and dress circle to the ruffians in the gods. Most had a kind word for her and all were suitably impressed when she boasted that "The Great Florrie Grayson" was her aunt, telling herself that there was no harm in a little white lie.

Now that her job was done Mair eagerly made her way back to the chorus girls' dressing-room. She enjoyed helping them with their costumes and make-up, especially when they dressed her up and painted her face. They were all a lot older than she was and their chitchat was always lively, if somewhat near the knuckle.

"Mair, is that you?"

Somewhat startled, Mair turned sharply. She stared at the woman dressed in all her finery, her face partly obscured by her stylish, large-brimmed hat. She watched as the woman threw back her head and, flicking her hair away from her shoulders, smiled.

"Mair it's me, you daft ha'peth."

Mair's mouth gaped in astonishment. "Mam?" She couldn't believe her eyes. "What are you doing here?"

"I could ask you the same bloody question."

"I'm here with Rhiannon. D-Dai's d-dead," Mair stammered, still in shock at seeing her mother.

"I know. Poor sod." Nellie glanced down at the theatre programmes in Mair's hand. "That still don't explain how you come to be working in Cardiff."

"I'm not working really. I'm just helping out, like," Mair offered.

"Helping who? Some bloody fella, no doubt. Who've you picked up with?" Nellie snapped.

"No. It's nothing like that, Mam. I'm here with Rhi. Her aunt is Florrie Grayson, the star of the show."

Nellie pondered for a while. "Of course. Florrie was Dai's first wife's sister. Well I never. I can't believe, having seen her name up in lights for nights, that I didn't make the connection. Florrie Grayson, Dai's sister-in-law. Well I never," she repeated.

"How are you doing, Mam? Are you still with your fancy man?"

"Less of your cheek! Though, if you must know, Harry Stone and me are still together and doing very well, thank you." It would seem, not as good as you, eh? Nellie whispered under her breath, as she considered the options open to her regarding Florrie Grayson.

"Tell me, Mair. Where in Cardiff are you staying?"

"Walter, Florrie, Rhiannon and me, are all staying at the Angel Hotel. Rhi and me have got this huge room all to ourselves. It's lovely."

"The Angel is it . . .?" Nellie's mind was working overtime. "Look, I've got to get a move on. I've arranged to meet some 'friends' in the Theatre Bar."

"Will you come and see me again, Mam?"

"I might, you never know. Then again I might not." With that she was gone.

For a while Mair stood as if glued to the spot. Against all the odds she had come face to face with her mother. There had been no hugs, no tears, in fact no show of emotion at all. Although it saddened Mair to admit it, her mother obviously would rather be with her fancy man and his friends than with her own daughter. On the way backstage Mair struggled to hold back tears; she told herself she was better off without Nellie, but the hurt she felt just wouldn't go away. She decided not to mention meeting up with Nellie to anyone, especially not Rhiannon. She could do without Miss Popular's pity, thank you very much.

122

She made her way to the girls' dressing-room. She enjoyed being with them. They treated her as one of them and it was as good a place as any to keep out of the way of Rhiannon. The dressing-room was abuzz with activity. Fifteen girls shared the narrow room; along one side ran a mirrored wall complete with a fifteen-foot-long dressing-table and fifteen seats, thus allowing each girl her individual make-up area. On the opposite wall was fixed a long hanger rail to hold their costumes.

"Hello, Mair, you look as if you've seen a ghost. What's up, duck?" Sally Webber asked as she stepped out of her street-urchin costume and placed it on a hanger. She seemed unabashed to parade in her tight-fitting undergarments. Mair had never before seen such underwear. She felt her colour rise.

"I reckon some young ruffian in the gods has been taking liberties with her . . . the lucky cow!" Clara Boxall, one of the older dancers teased.

"What he do, shove his hand up your skirt or grab a feel of your tits?" Bella, a dancer at the other end of the dressing-room called, causing shrieks of laughter.

"Go on, you can tell us," Clara coaxed.

Mair didn't like being teased. "No! Shut up. Nothing's happened and there's nothing wrong with me, so there!" she shouted.

"We'll believe you, tho' thousands wouldn't," Clara goaded.

"On stage in three minutes," Percy called as he knocked on the door.

"Three minutes! Christ, we'd better get a move on or the SM will have our guts for garters."

The mood had changed and for now Mair was off the hook.

CHAPTER
ELEVEN

It was Sunday morning and, despite a sharp wind, had the making of a beautiful late-spring day. Nellie Parsons, having reverted to her maiden name, dressed in her new turquoise-blue dress and large straw hat quietly left the flat and, after closing the door, crept down the stairs and through the front door. She had left Harry sleeping off the effects of a late night down the pub. With a bit of luck she would be back before he woke up. If her idea went to plan, he was going to be so pleased with her.

Nellie walked briskly up the length of Westgate Street and within minutes had arrived at the Angel Hotel. Aware of the doorman's cursory glance, she immediately slid her gloved hands down to slightly raise her skirt before walking up the few steps to the grand entrance. With her head held high she waited for the doorman to open the large, heavy, brass-framed glass doors. She flashed the doorman a friendly smile. He nodded and, raising a hand, politely touched the brim of his red-and-gold top hat.

She entered the foyer and instantly caught her breath, overawed by its red-and-gold grandeur and the huge chandelier hanging from the high ceiling.

"Excuse me, miss. I'm the hotel manager. Can I help you?"

A smart middle-aged man, wearing a dark pinstriped suit, navy satin tie and a brilliant, crisply starched white shirt, stood in front of her.

Nellie didn't like the way he seemed to look down his nose at her.

She stood tall. She had been practising her lines for days. "I'm here to see Miss Florrie Grayson," she said confidently.

"May I ask if Miss Grayson is expecting you?"

"What's it to do with you?" she snapped. Then, seeing how taken aback he seemed, she gave a wry smile. "If you would be kind enough to just let Miss Grayson know that Miss Nellie Parsons is here, then I'm sure she'll want to see me." She threw him a look of defiance.

"Very well. If you would like to take a seat I will ring her room and let her know that you are here." With that, he turned abruptly and strutted off towards the reception area, his back so stiff and upright Nellie could have sworn he had a broomhandle stuck up his arse.

"First round to me I think, you pompous old bugger," Nellie mumbled under her breath as she sank into a deep dark-red leather chair situated in the lounge area.

Nellie sat fidgeting with her handkerchief for what seemed ages. She felt uncomfortably out of place, wide-eyed at the clientele as they passed by — totally ignoring her.

Eventually the manager returned. "Miss Parsons. Miss Grayson will be down to see you shortly."

126

Nellie threw him a look that said *I told you so.*

He kept his composure. "Miss Parsons, if you would please follow me. Miss Grayson has requested the use of my office to assure your privacy."

After escorting her to his office the manager took a quick departure. Apart from a huge mahogany desk, the manager's office was furnished and decorated in the same red and gold as the foyer and with similar leather chairs.

Within minutes there was a light tap on the door. The door opened and Florrie Desmond entered the room. She was wearing a dark-blue day suit with a figure-hugging bolero jacket and a long skirt, her high-piled auburn hair coiffed to perfection.

Nellie rose to her feet.

"Please, be seated," Florrie instructed as she settled herself in the seat opposite Nellie.

Nellie took a deep breath. "Miss Grayson, I'm Mair's —"

Florrie interrupted quickly, "Mair's mother. I know. Would this be the same mother who walked out on her when she abandoned my dear brother-in-law and young niece?"

Nellie was taken aback by the abruptness of Florrie's manner. This was not the reception she had expected.

"I had my reasons," Nellie said.

"All of them selfish, no doubt. Tell me, Miss Parsons, why are you here?"

Nellie decided it was time for a change of tactics. It was time to show this old music-hall star what a real performance was.

127

"Miss Grayson, it's true. I've not been the best mother in the world, but that doesn't mean that I don't love my Mair something dreadful. When I bumped into her the other day at the theatre, I realized how much I missed her. You see, Miss Grayson, for years, before I ever went to work for Dai Hughes, it was just Mair and me against the world . . . and now . . ." Nellie raised her handkerchief and pretended to wipe the tears from her eyes.

"So, you want her back, is that it?"

"In an ideal world, yes — oh yes. But no! Despite what you think, I couldn't be that selfish. It wouldn't be right for me to take her away from Rhiannon and you."

"Forgive me, I'm confused. If you don't want her back then what *do* you want?" Florrie sounded irritated.

"I thought maybe . . . some compensation? It's only fair that I be compensated for the loss of my child. Don't you agree?"

"And what do *you* think a fair compensation would be?"

Nellie found it hard to contain her excitement. She'd done it — She'd bloody well gone and done it! "I thought, say, two hundred pounds. Obviously, it would be a one-off payment. I'll not bother you again."

"All you want is two hundred pounds? I find that unbelievable." Florrie shook her head.

Nellie cursed herself — why hadn't she asked for more?

"Tell me, Miss Parsons, how low can you stoop? You would actually sell your daughter for a mere two hundred pounds?"

Suddenly Nellie knew it was all going wrong. "You can afford it!" she snapped.

"That's as maybe. I've got news for you. I'll not pay you a penny! In fact if, as you say, you miss Mair so much, I, for one, am all in favour of your being reunited with your daughter."

"But —"

"No! It's all arranged. As soon as I knew you were here, I assumed you had come to — rightly — claim your daughter. With this in mind, I arranged for my agent to inform Mair of the good news, and to ask Rhiannon to help pack her things."

At that precise moment there was a knock on the door.

Florrie stood up. "I'll wager that'll be her now." She faced Nellie and, sliding her hand into her jacket pocket, she produced a handful of crisp five-pound notes. "There's fifty pounds."

Nellie's eyes lit up as she made a grab for the money.

Florrie pulled her hand and the money to her chest. "Not so fast. You should know you get nothing for nothing."

"I thought there'd be a catch," Nellie spat.

"All I want you to do is continue your act — you know, the one where in an ideal world you'd love to have Mair back, and the money is yours. It's what Mair needs to believe."

"And if I don't?"

"I'm sure the police would be very interested in your plan to sell your daughter."

Nellie's head dropped.

"Is it a deal?" This time Florrie edged closer and placed the notes in Nellie's hand.

Nellie nodded. "It's a deal."

"Good. But remember this is a one-off payment; there'll be no more where that came from."

There was another tap on the door, this one more urgent. Florrie opened the door to reveal Mair and Rhiannon, both red-eyed from crying, escorted by a solemn-looking Walter, Mair's small suitcase at his side.

They entered the office and Rhiannon's eyes instantly pleaded with Florrie's but she was having none of it. The last thing she needed at this moment was an emotional scene.

"Walter, would you kindly escort Rhiannon back to her room."

"But Aunt Florrie, I don't understand . . . why are you sending Mair away?" Rhiannon pleaded.

"Rhiannon, don't be a silly girl, I'm not sending Mair away. Her mother has simply come for her. It is her right, after all. Miss Parsons desperately wants to be reunited with her daughter. And who are we to stand in her way?" Florrie threw Nellie a look, daring her to contradict her.

Nellie raised her handkerchief to her eyes and, once again, pretended to dab her tears. "Mair, love. I've missed you so much."

"I don't believe you!" Rhiannon shouted. "If you missed her so much how come you've never tried to get in touch?"

"Rhiannon, that's enough! Please do as I bid and go with Walter. I promise I'll come to see you soon to explain everything."

"But —"

"Rhiannon, I mean it!"

Rhiannon put an arm around Mair. "Mair, please, don't cry. I promise this is not the end of it."

"It's — all right, Rhi! I always — knew that — your — aunt — didn't want me," Mair sobbed. "I'll go with my mam — it's for the best, eh?"

Walter gently pulled Rhiannon away from Mair. "Come on, Rhi. I'm sure you'll see each other soon."

A reluctant Rhiannon did as she was bid. As she left the room she looked across at Florrie and Nellie and shouted, "I hate you for this."

Neither woman knew which one of them the outburst was directed at — maybe it was at both of them.

Florrie accompanied Nellie and Mair from the manager's office to the foyer in silence.

"Is everything all right, Miss Grayson?" the manager asked.

"Yes, everything is fine. Thank you for the use of your office. I'm pleased to say that our business has been satisfactorily completed and my guests are ready to leave." Florrie turned to Nellie. "I'll bid you goodbye now, Miss Parsons . . . Mair," she gave a false smile. "The hotel manager will show you out."

Mair glared at Florrie. Florrie dismissed it. She had always thought of Mair as a moody, petulant child. And one who needed strong parental control. As she watched Mair and her mother leave the Angel Hotel she congratulated herself on a good morning's work. It was now time to face Rhiannon.

★   ★   ★

Rhiannon paced the room. She was angry and upset. Not just with Nellie but also her Aunt Florrie. She totally blamed her Aunt Florrie for allowing this to happen. And when, as promised, Florrie came to her room, Rhiannon couldn't wait to vent her feelings.

"How could you have let this happen? Why did you just stand by and let Nellie take Mair away, away to God knows where?" Rhiannon was almost hysterical.

"Rhiannon, please calm down. It wasn't like that. My hands were tied. Nellie is Mair's mother. She was well within her rights. I'm afraid there was nothing I or anyone else could do to stop her. So the sooner you come to terms with it the better." With that her aunt left the room.

Rhiannon was fuming. It was obvious that as far as her aunt was concerned there was nothing anyone could do. But Rhiannon was having none of it. She didn't believe for one moment that Nellie wanted Mair back with her. This was not the Nellie she remembered. So what had really happened between Nellie and Aunt Florrie?

Rhiannon vowed to get to the truth. She had meant what she said when she promised Mair that this was not the end of it. She took her mind back to the events earlier in the day, when Walter had asked her to help Mair to pack her things. When she questioned why, he simply told her that Mair's mother had come for her.

"I don't want to go with her, Rhi," Mair had cried. "Please let me stay with you. I promise I'll be good."

Rhiannon felt powerless.

"I don't understand. Where has Nellie suddenly appeared from? How did she know where to find you?"

"It's my fault. I bumped into her at the theatre last week. She and Harry Stone are living together in Cardiff and, apparently, she's a regular visitor to the Theatre Bar. Oh Rhi, it was obvious to me that she hadn't missed me one bit. I wanted to show her how well we were doing without her. You should have seen the way her eyes lit up when I mentioned that we were staying at the Angel Hotel."

"Mmm — I bet. But why didn't you tell me that you'd seen her?"

"I'm sorry, Rhi. I just didn't want to admit how little I meant to my *so-called* mother."

Rhiannon could well understand Mair's secrecy. It must be very difficult — having to admit that your own mother does not care for you. But knowing the truth only made the mystery deepen as to the reason behind Nellie's visit.

Outside the Angel Hotel Nellie stopped and stared at Mair.

"What now?" Mair asked.

"You may well ask! I'm in a fine pickle, I can tell you."

"And I suppose it's my fault?" Mair quipped.

"Well, in a way, yes. If only that damn woman hadn't been so . . . so unreasonable."

"Aunt Florrie, you mean?"

"She's no aunt of yours," Nellie scoffed. "She, with all the airs and graces, has certainly shown her true colours. How right you were when you said she never wanted you."

"Just like you then, eh?" Mair snapped. "Why couldn't you have let me be? I was all right with Rhiannon — at least she wanted me with her."

Mair felt her mother's gloved hand strike her face.

"Ouch, that hurt."

"So where's Rhiannon now? I didn't see her run after you. No! From now on you're stuck with me, so, if I were you, I'd keep a civil tongue in my head. Now, come on. Harry will be wondering where I've got to."

"Is he expecting me?" Mair asked still rubbing her face.

"No, he bloody well isn't. And what's more, my Harry don't like surprises. If I were you I'd be on my best behaviour — no backchat! Harry's got a right temper on him. You'd do well to remember that. If you upset him, you're on your own."

No change there, then, Mair thought.

It was with great trepidation that Nellie, with Mair and her suitcase following behind, entered the flat that she shared with Harry. How was she going to explain Mair and the fact that she had been outdone by Florrie Grayson? Her only saving grace was the fifty pounds in her pocket — at least she had that.

Harry Stone stood larger than life in the bay window. Mair's first impression was of a man not long from his bed. He looked unshaven and dishevelled; the braces of his trousers were hanging at his side and his vest was not yet properly tucked in.

"Where the hell have you been, dressed up like a dog's dinner?" he growled.

Mair sensed her mother's uneasiness.

"Harry, I've —"

Harry spotted Mair. "And who might this be, then?"

Mair didn't like the way Harry was eyeing her up and down.

Nellie turned to Mair and, taking her by the shoulders, presented her to Harry. Mair felt Nellie's hands shake. Why was she so nervous?

"Harry . . . love. This is Mair." Nellie swallowed hard.

Harry eyes lit up. "Well hello, Mair," he gushed as he crossed the room to her.

He turned to Nellie. "She's perfect. She looks so sweet and innocent. She could earn us a fortune. How old is she?"

"If you must know, I was thirteen in January," Mair snapped, annoyed by the way he was talking about her as if she wasn't there.

"The perfect age, I'd say. Nellie you are such a clever girl."

Nellie looked puzzled.

"Don't you remember our little conversation the other night, about you taking on a new apprentice? He turned and stared at Mair, his mouth curved in a lecherous smile. "Well, I say we need look no further. Mair here will do very nicely, thank you."

Nellie cast Mair a worried glance. She watched in horror as Harry ran the back of his hand slowly down the contours of Mair's face and neck and then down to her breast . . .

"Harry. Stop!"

"Why?"

"Harry! Mair is my daughter!

CHAPTER
TWELVE

The next morning, as Rhiannon readied herself for work, she felt weighed down by an overwhelming sense of guilt. She had spent a restless night tossing and turning, convinced that she should have done more to stop Nellie from taking Mair. There could be no denying that she had let her sister down and she could only imagine how disappointed her dear father would have been with her.

One thing was certain: she had to find Nellie, and the sooner the better. If Nellie was a frequent visitor to the Theatre Bar, then that was where Rhiannon would begin her search. Nellie knew the truth. Nellie knew where Mair was now. Rhiannon vowed to visit the bar behind the gods at every opportunity until Nellie showed up, maybe then she would get the answers she needed if she was ever going to find Mair.

She was thankful that Walter, ever the diplomat, had arranged for Rhiannon's breakfast to be sent to her room with a note saying that he would be waiting in the foyer at ten to escort her to theatre in time for rehearsals. Aunt Florrie always followed later in the day, usually arriving an hour before curtain-up. Rhiannon and Walter travelled to the theatre in silence, he obviously sensing her mood. As soon as Rhiannon was safely delivered to the theatre Walter, before bidding her goodbye, handed her an envelope "This letter arrived for you this morning."

"A letter for me?"

"Yeah. Well go on, take it."

Taking the letter Rhiannon instantly recognized Frank's uneven scrawl and her heart missed a beat. At last, some news from home.

"I'll be off then. Catch you later," Walter said.

Rhiannon gave him a token nod then turned and pushed open the stage door, eager to get inside and find a quiet place to read Frank's letter.

"Good morning, Miss Hughes," Fred the doorman called as she entered.

"Morning, Fred," she replied.

"Miss Hughes, Adam Fletcher's been asking for you. He told me to tell you to get yourself to the front stalls."

Rhiannon slipped the Frank's letter into her skirt pocket. Much as she wanted to read it, if Adam Fletcher was asking for her then something must be wrong, As Rhiannon quickly made her way to the auditorium, she complimented herself on how quickly she had learned to find her way around the dimly lit maze that was backstage, expertly weaving her way through the narrow corridors lined with obstacles: ladders, guy ropes, angle rods and various flats and backdrops for numerous scenes. She found herself squeezing past groups of artists, everyone nervously chatting, eagerly awaiting their call on to the stage.

From the wings Rhiannon heard the orchestra tuning up and immediately felt butterflies in her stomach. She loved everything about the theatre, from the excitement of anticipation that was backstage to the glamorous splendour of front of house.

Adam Fletcher stood in front of the orchestra pit reading his notes. As she took the few steps from the wings to the door that led to the auditorium he looked up.

"At long last; there you are, Rhiannon."

"Is something wrong?"

"How do you feel about understudying Sally Webber's street-urchin performance today?"

"What! Are you serious?" Rhiannon couldn't believe what he'd asked.

"Yes, very! It's an emergency. Last night the stupid bitch . . . excuse language . . . only went to a party with, wait for it . . . her understudy and, unbelievably, both ate the shellfish. As I speak the two of them are in hospital with food poisoning and puking for Wales!"

"But what will the other girls think? Shouldn't you consider one of the chorus girls before me?"

"In theory maybe. But, in practice, I don't think it would work. The girls of the chorus would be the first to admit that they're all far too tall and, if the truth be known, far too old, to carry off the part of a young street urchin. They'll understand that, with you being, more or less, the same size as Sally, you'd be my obvious choice. So . . . what do you say?"

Rhiannon hesitated. Part of her, flattered by this vote of confidence from Adam, wanted to jump at the chance; another part was scared stiff, terrified at the thought of letting him down.

"Come on, you know you can do it. I've seen you singing along at rehearsals and you're word perfect," Adam encouraged.

"I may be able to sing the song, but what about the dance steps?"

"Well, we've got hours before tonight's first show, so what are you waiting for? Get yourself off to the dressing-room and change into her costume. If you need it altered in any way, the wardrobe mistress will be standing by."

Sally Webber shared a dressing-room with the Empire Belles. As Rhiannon entered the dressing-room she took a deep breath and inhaled the familiar scent of attar of roses, inexpensive rose-water cologne that the girls generously splashed over their bodies. As she ventured forward she was still apprehensive about how they would react when they found out that she, a complete novice, was going to stand in for Sally.

One thing was for sure: they had to be told, and sooner rather than later. In less than half an hour Adam expected her to appear on stage dressed in Sally's costume. So, taking another deep breath, she took the plunge.

"Girls, I've something to tell you . . . you're not going to believe this but . . . Adam has asked me to stand in for Sally. What do you think?" She hoped she hadn't sounded as nervous as she felt. She really wanted them to be pleased for her.

140

To her great relief she found that she needn't have worried. They all welcomed her with open arms.

"Have you told Mair? I bet she'll be green with envy," Clara Boxall asked.

"Mair — no she's . . ." Rhiannon couldn't believe that, faced with the prospect of appearing on stage, she had so quickly dismissed Mair's predicament from her mind.

"She's what?" Clara asked.

"She's gone. Last night Mair's mother came to the hotel and took her away. I've been so wrapped up in my own good fortune that I haven't spared a single thought for her. How shallow does that make me?"

"Welcome to the world of theatrical performance! That's what I say," Clara scoffed. "Now listen to me, my girl. Today you've been given a chance of a lifetime and you can't afford to let anyone, not even Mair, stand in your way. Trust me, this is a cut-throat old world, you'll not get far if you waste your time with guilt," Clara offered.

It was true. Rhiannon did feel guilty but somehow she managed to convince herself that her stepsister would understand. So what if it took Rhiannon a few days to find her? It wasn't as if Mair was alone. She was with her mother, for goodness' sake. Now where could the hardship be in that?

"Clara, will you help me? I need to get into Sally's costume and be on stage to rehearse Sally's dance routine."

"Of course I will. Come on, follow me."

Clara led the way to Sally's chair and dressing area, situated at the far end of the room. She took Sally's costume from its hanger and handed it to Rhiannon. "If I were you I'd get changed quickly into this; it wouldn't do to keep Adam waiting. You never know, he might change his mind," Clara teased.

As Rhiannon accepted the small costume she smiled and quipped, "He'd better not." Then, not used to undressing in front of strangers, she hesitated.

"Come on, don't be shy, I doubt if you've got anything us girls haven't seen before," Clara encouraged.

As Rhiannon slowly slipped out of her clothes she glanced down the room and was relieved to find that the other girls were too busy titivating themselves to pay any heed to her state of undress.

Clara proceeded to help Rhiannon into the street urchin costume. "I must say Adam got it dead right when he picked you to cover for Sally," she said. "It fits you perfect. Well, what do you think?" Clara turned Rhiannon round to face the mirror.

Rhiannon stared at her reflection; dressed in the coarse serge shirt and trousers, and with her hair forced under a cloth cap slouched over her dirt-grimed face, she had been totally transformed into a young lad. "I look so different."

"Well, you certainly look the part, I'll give you that. Now get yourself on stage and, if I were you, I'd work my arse off until I got the performance as good as the look!"

★ ★ ★

Two hours later, due in the main to Adam's professional expertise and patience, and her dogged determination, Rhiannon had the song and, more important, the dance routine mastered.

"Well done. Now go and rest. You've over an hour before your five-minute call. When you hear that, be sure to get yourself into position in the wings and wait for Gus to announce you, then — go break a leg," Adam Fletcher encouraged.

"Thank you, Adam; I'll try not to let you down." She reached up and gave him a peck on the cheek.

If her action surprised him, he didn't show it. He simply smiled and said, "I've every confidence in you."

Florrie Desmond and Walter Cahill were almost out of the door of the Angel Hotel, on their way to the theatre, when the hotel manager called them back.

"Mr Cahill, a cable has just arrived from America for you. It's at the reception desk."

"America you say? Thank you," Walter said. Turning to Florrie, he flashed a smile. "Take a seat, my dear. I'll not keep you waiting long."

Florrie watched as Walter headed back to the reception area. She hoped the delay wouldn't make her late for the theatre — that just wouldn't do.

A few minutes later an excited Walter, with a noticeable spring in his step, returned waving the cable above his head. "Florrie, after all this time, why, I'd almost given up hope . . ."

"Walter, what is it?"

"It's such wonderful news. The Americans want you."

Florrie stood up. "They do?"

"Yes. They want you to replace . . . wait for it . . . Alice Lloyd — the great Marie Lloyd's talented sister, at the Colonial Theatre, New York. Alice Lloyd, one of the highest paid music hall stars in America has decided to make a ten-week return visit to Britain. The Colonial Theatre need someone to replace her short time. You were their first choice."

"How soon do they want me?"

"Alice Lloyd is booked on the White Star line out of New York on the sixteenth April. If we want to be there by then we shall have to move quickly in order to make the necessary arrangements."

"But how can I leave? I'm contracted to the Empire Theatre for almost another three months. Oh Walter, please say that there's a way out? You know how long I've waited for a chance to make an American début."

"You leave it to me. I've an idea that might just work."

The girls' dressing-room was buzzing with excitement in anticipation of Rhiannon's stage début.

"Whatever you do, don't rush on stage. Take your time. It gives the audience a chance to give you the 'once over', and you, time to steady your nerves. A confident smile can help too," Clara advised.

There was a knock on the door and without waiting to be answered Gus Davenport entered.

"Well, what's this I hear, Princess Rhi? You're to appear in Sally's place for tonight's shows. I do hope that you're up to the job. For while I admit to you making as good-looking a young lad as Sally, the question is, have you got her talent?" he asked, nonchalantly leaning against the dressing-room door.

Rhiannon thought how handsome he looked in his stage apparel.

"Adam Fletcher has confidence in me," she quipped, determined to show him that she could give as good as she got.

"Ah, yes. But it's the Empire's audience you need to convince. They're a canny lot. You'll have to be good to get them on your side. Sally's a favourite."

"I . . . I . . ." Rhiannon stammered, her confidence starting to wane.

Gus gave a loud laugh.

"Gus Davenport, leave the poor girl alone. She's nervous enough without your attempted black humour. Anyway, why are you here?" Clara asked.

"As I've only just been told about the performance change, it would help me to know what this little song-bird wanted to be called." Gus raised his eyebrows and looked to Rhiannon for an answer.

"I don't understand. You know my name." She scowled at him. Her confidence was now restored as she found out that he'd only been trying to goad her.

"I do. I just thought that you might want to use a glamorous stage name — you wouldn't be the first." He beamed a smile.

"No thank you, Mr Davenport. Rhiannon Hughes will do just fine."

"I've told you before, the name's Gus."

Dressed in her stage costume Rhiannon stood nervously in the wings. On stage the Empire Belles were coming to the end of their dance routine. It was almost time for her big moment and Rhiannon struggled to quell the butterflies in her stomach. As the dancers linked arms and, in unison, high kicked their way off stage to great applause, Rhiannon stood aside to make room for them.

"Break a leg, kid," she heard Walter whisper from behind. She turned, and to her surprise saw Aunt Florrie standing alongside him. Her aunt flashed a smile and mouthed, "Good luck." Rhiannon felt a lump in her throat, touched to think her aunt and Walter had come to give her their support. Then, as the audience quietened, she heard Gus Davenport's commanding voice.

"My lords, ladies and gentlemen, today I'm afraid I have to be the bearer of sad news. Miss Sally Webber, your beloved little street urchin, is indisposed and sadly cannot be with us for tonight's show."

Rhiannon watched him raise his hand to his ear to encourage a loud "Aahh" from the audience. It worked.

"Yes, I know. It's very sad. But . . . cheer up. I also bring good news. Tonight, standing in for Miss Webber's cockney urchin, we have a new Welsh song-bird! She's young . . . she's beautiful . . . she's also very talented. So please, put your hands together and give a big Empire Theatre welcome to . . . Rhiannon!"

In the wings Rhiannon hesitated as she waited to hear her surname. Then, realizing it wasn't coming, and prompted by a nudge from Clara, she ventured on stage. As rehearsed, and remembering what Clara had told her, she slowly made her way to centre stage and, facing the auditorium, smiled a confident smile, hoping it masked her inner turmoil.

Although she was aware of its being a packed house she was thankful to find that all she could see was the glow of the footlights at the end of the stage and, beyond that, a smoke-filled darkness.

Rhiannon heard the orchestra begin the opening bars of her song. She took a deep breath . . . this was it. The cockney song began with a slow tempo. Luckily, on cue, Rhiannon found her voice . . .

Now, all me life I wanted to be a barrow boy
A barrow boy is all I've wanted to be.
I own the title I sticks to it with pride.
I'm a coster, a coster
From over the other side.

As the music became louder and stronger so did Rhiannon's voice.

I turned me back on all the ol' society.
I mingle where the big bananas grow.
I buys 'em twenty shilling
That's how I makes me living.

147

I ought to have been a barrow boy long ago.
Get off me barrow!
I ought to have been a barrow boy long ago.

Then, as the orchestra played the melody, Rhiannon broke into a jaunty dance, dancing from one end of the stage to the other before returning to centre stage.

It was a slightly breathless Rhiannon who encouraged the audience, with a gesture of her hands, to sing along with her for a final chorus of:

I buys 'em twenty shilling
That's how I makes me living.
I ought to have been a barrow boy long ago.
Get off me barrow!
I ought to have been a barrow boy long ago.

At the end of the song, an overwhelmed Rhiannon listened as the audience showed their appreciation with loud applause, whistles and by stamping feet. As she removed her cloth cap, revealing her long unruly chestnut hair, she gave an elaborate bow. She couldn't believe that with just one song, she'd won over the whole house. She soaked up the applause. It was then that she knew — this was what she wanted.

As she left the stage her eyes glanced across at Gus. He smiled and showed his approval by joining in the audience applause.

Off stage Adam Fletcher caught around her. "Well done. You're a natural. I told you you could do it."

"Thank you, Adam. I can't wait to do it again."

"Well, it seems you'll not have to wait long; the next show starts at ten past eight and, with no news as yet from Sally Webber, it looks as if you'll be going on again."

Back in the dressing-room, while Clara helped her out of the costume the other girls were full of praise.

"What's this? It's addressed to you." Clara picked Frank's letter off the floor.

"Oh, it must have fallen from my skirt pocket." Rhiannon quickly retrieved it. "It's a letter from home. It came this morning. With all that been going on I haven't had time to open it. I think I'll save it until I'm back at the hotel."

"A love letter from an old boyfriend, is it?"

"No, don't be daft. It's from my neighbour's son; we're just friends."

"If that's the case, how come you're blushing, then? Fancy him, did you?"

Rhiannon poked her tongue out. "Now wouldn't you like to know?"

After returning the letter safely to her skirt pocket, she made her way to her aunt's dressing-room.

"Well done, child. I'm really proud of you," Florrie gushed.

"I'll second that," Walter piped in.

"Oh, Aunt Florrie, Walter, I loved doing it. Do you think the audience liked me?"

"Yes, child, I do believe they did."

There was a tap on the dressing-room door.

"Come in," Florrie called.

"Miss Grayson, Walter. I came to congratulate your niece on her performance."

"Thank you, Gus. We were just doing the same."

Gus turned to Rhiannon, and as he did, reached out to take her hand. "Congratulations, Rhi. You did really well. The audience loved you." He gently brushed the back of her hand with his lips.

The touch of his warm lips on her flesh aroused her. She blushed. The way he looked at her told her that he was fully aware of the effect he was having on her. His piercing eyes stared into hers. "I thought that, with your aunt's permission, and of course if you were agreeable, I might take you out for refreshments during the interval between shows."

Rhiannon's heart skipped a beat. She was just about to accept his invitation when Florrie interjected.

"What a kind thought, Gus. And, once again, we are of the same mind. I was just about to send out for a tray of tea and sandwiches. With Rhiannon having another show in less than an hour, I think it best that she stays put, don't you?"

"Of course — I understand," he answered. "Another time, maybe?" With that he headed for the door.

Rhiannon's disappointment was obvious.

"Come, come, child. I assure you it's for the best."

Aunt Florrie had spoken and Rhiannon knew there would be no further discussion.

At seven o'clock, just over an hour before the second show performance, Rhiannon, with Clara's help, was just about to get into the street urchin costume when she heard, "I'll take that, if you don't mind?"

Rhiannon turned and, much to her surprise, saw Sally Webber marching the length of the dressing-room.

"As you can see, I'm fully recovered. I've spoken to Adam Fletcher and he agrees that I should take over for the next show."

"Are you sure? I really don't mind doing it," Rhiannon almost pleaded.

"No, I bet you don't. But forget it. The spot is mine. By the way, Adam wants to see you."

Rhiannon left the girls' dressing-room feeling totally dejected. Clara followed her out. "Don't feel too bad, eh? You did really well this afternoon. If the truth be known, Sally got to hear how good you were too. I'm sure there'll be other chances. Adam Fletcher can recognize talent a mile away."

Rhiannon made her way to the front of the auditorium, where she knew she'd find Adam.

"Hi, Rhi, you've obviously seen Sally," Adam said.

Rhiannon nodded.

"Disappointed, eh?"

Again she nodded.

"I'm afraid there was nothing I could do. After all, it is her slot."

"I know, but Adam I loved it so much, and now . . ."

"So, why not give the kid a slot of her own?" Gus called from his table at the side of the stage.

Rhiannon hadn't even noticed he was there.

"If only it were that easy, Gus. You know the show is timed out. Where would I find an extra slot?" Adam asked.

"One song, a four-minute slot. One less joke from Tom or one less illusion from Jack. An even simpler solution would be to merely shorten the interval by four minutes and your problem is solved."

Adam rubbed his chin. "I suppose I could —"

"Oh please, Adam. One song . . . my own song? You know I can do it."

"I'll tell you what I'll do. In three days' time I'm prepared to give you a proper audition. If you pass that, we'll take it from there."

"Thank you, Adam. You'll not regret it," she said as she planted a kiss on his cheek.

Then, turning to Gus, she called. "Thank you. I owe you one."

He smiled and said, "I'm sure there'll be something you can do for me one day."

"Now I wonder what that might be," Adam scoffed.

Adam's sarcasm was lost on Rhiannon. She had already left the auditorium, heading for her Aunt Florrie's dressing-room. If she were to find a suitable song for the all-important audition, who better to advise her?

Rhiannon gave a light tap on the dressing-room door.

"Come in," Florrie Grayson called.

Rhiannon entered.

As usual Florrie's dressing-room was a blaze of colour and filled with the heady perfume from the dozens of baskets of flowers, regularly sent from her adoring followers. The scent of the beautiful lilies closest to the door caught in Rhiannon's throat and made her cough. Florrie sat at her dressing table, the bright lights surrounding the mirror highlighting her still youthful-looking face.

Walter, relaxed on the *chaise-longue* in front of Florrie's ornately decorated changing screen, peered over *The Stage* newspaper and welcome her with a "Hello there, young Rhi."

Rhiannon, unable to control her excitement for a moment longer, blurted out, "Aunt Florrie, Walter, I've such exciting news."

"Have you dear, now there's a coincidence — so have we. But you first."

"Well it's all down to Gus — Gus Davenport."

With a raised gloved hand Florrie interrupted her. "Rhiannon, must you be so familiar? Surely, at your age, it would be more appropriate to address him as Mr Davenport?"

"Sorry, Aunt, but both Gus Davenport and Adam Fletcher insist I use their Christian names."

Florrie gave a loud "Tut-tut, it would never have happened in my day." Then, "Very well, carry on."

"Anyway," Rhiannon continued, "Gus suggested to Adam that I might be given my very own spot in the show and . . . wait for it . . . Adam is prepared to give me a 'proper' audition and, if I pass that, then . . . I'm on my way!"

"Now that is good news. How very exciting for you, and how very kind of Gus to interject on your behalf. Don't you agree Walter?"

Rhiannon didn't pick up on the sarcasm in Florrie's voice or the look of disapproval she flashed at Walter.

Walter muffled a cough, "Quite. But I think your good fortune has more to do with the great performance you gave as stand-in for Sally Webber this afternoon. Adam Fletcher is no fool. He, like the rest of us, couldn't have helped but spot your obvious potential."

"Oh Walter, thank you. I do hope so. It's all happening so fast, I have to pinch myself to make sure that it's not a dream. Adam has given me the chance to prove my worth. All I need now is the right song . . . Aunt Florrie? I thought, with your expertise, that you might be able to suggest one."

"Of course, I'd love to. If this is truly what you want, then Walter and I, at least while we're still here, will do everything we can to steer you in the right direction. But be warned. This career you have chosen can often be a hard road to travel. And you'll do well to remember that only a lucky few ever reach the top of their profession. I've seen many a talented performer fail to achieve their true potential. Success has a lot to do with luck; getting the right breaks and being in the right place at the right time. That said, I can't deny that your good news has helped to ease my conscience."

"Why? I don't understand. What do you mean "while you're still here?"

"I can't say too much, because it's not settled yet. But Walter and I may soon be leaving for New York."

Back at the Angel Hotel an exhausted Rhiannon lay on the bed. What a day it had been: her magical appearance on stage, the disappointment when Sally returned in time for the second show, Gus speaking up for her, Adam agreeing to give her an audition. To think that in just a few days she might actually be given her own spot in the show. And what about the bombshell when her Aunt Florrie announced that she and Walter might be leaving for America? Could this really be? And then there was the letter . . .

Rhiannon stared at Frank's letter, glad that she'd resisted the temptation to open it sooner; reading it now would make a fitting end to an almost perfect day.

> 8, The Terrace, Ponty,
> Near Bridgend,
> Glamorgan
> S. Wales.
> 26th March 1909

Dear Rhiannon,
It was so good to hear from you. Fancy you two girls living it up with the toffs at the Angel Hotel. You won't want anything to do with us valley folk soon.

My mother sends her love, she hopes your aunt Florrie is looking after you and keeping you away from "the rougher element of theatre life" whatever that means.

Is Mair still behaving herself? I know how difficult she can be. But then, if your mother had walked out on you? She's lucky to have a sister like you looking out for her. Although, having said that, you've been dealt a raw deal too. I often think of your dad and what he did for me and I want you to know that I will always be here for the two of you.

I'm doing my best to arrange a trip to Cardiff but, with my shifts down the pit, it's proving difficult. I'll try and wangle it somehow. It would be so good to see you.

Regards,
Frank

Rhiannon slowly folded the letter, wondering what Frank would say if he knew the truth about Mair. She'd thought the letter would be a great end to a great day. Instead it had made her realize how selfish and full of her own success she had been. She vowed to make things right with Mair. So that when Frank eventually made it to Cardiff the three of them would be together again.

CHAPTER
THIRTEEN

May 1909

Mair Parsons, alone in the Westgate Street apartment she shared with Harry and Nellie, lay on their crumpled double bed in the main room. Her own bedroom, although it had a double bed, was smaller, darker and much colder. She hated being here with Harry and Nellie and longed to be back at the theatre with Rhiannon and her friends. Since her arrival she hadn't even been out through the door.

Most mornings Harry left the digs early for work, leaving Nellie and Mair in their beds. Mair had taken an instant dislike to Harry. She didn't like the way he looked at her, the way his eyes almost undressed her, or the liberties he took, throwing his arms around her at every opportunity. The way his hands always managed to brush her chest area made her skin crawl.

Every morning, and only when she was sure that Harry had left for work, Mair would get herself out of bed and, before seeing to her own toilet and mindful not to wake Nellie, would proceed to light the small coal fire in the main room.

At around half past ten Nellie, usually suffering a hangover, surfaced and made a pot of tea while Mair toasted bread on a fork in front of the small open fire.

By twelve o'clock Nellie would be all dolled up and ready to go out, leaving Mair to spend another day cooped up in the apartment.

"Where are you going?" Mair had asked her earlier that day.

"It's Saturday. There's a matinée at the theatre today, so I'm off to meet some friends in the Theatre Bar. Your being here has made it very awkward for me to bring anyone back. Thank goodness Harry thought to rent me a room at the King's Head," Nellie mumbled under her breath.

Mair didn't understand what her mother was going on about.

"Can I come to the theatre with you?" Mair asked, eager to see Rhiannon.

"No, you certainly can't! I'll be back around six before Harry gets home from work. I'll bring us some hot pies for tea."

Most nights, depending on how much money Nellie handed him, Harry and Nellie went to the King's Head. Tonight was no exception.

"How'd you do today?" Harry had asked, as he tucked into a huge plate of meat pie and mash.

"I did really well," Nellie replied, handing him a wad of white five-pound notes.

"That's my girl. We're in the money and on the way up. There's a lot more where this came from."

"Harry, how much longer do I have to . . .?"

Harry didn't let her finish, "I've been thinking, now that Mair has joined us, we might look for a bigger

158

place. A place with maybe three or four rooms for . . . more privacy, eh?"

"Can we afford it?" Nellie asked.

"Yes, if all goes to plan." He chuckled.

"What plan? Harry Stone, what are you up to?"

"I'll tell you when we get home."

On Saturday, a week later, Mair, with just the small flickering flame of the dwindling coal fire for comfort, covered herself with the coarse blankets.

Alone in the near darkness she felt so vulnerable and . . . unloved. With Harry and Nellie even later than usual getting back from the pub, Mair's mind began to play tricks. Where were they? What if they never came back? Every day, to no avail, she had waited and hoped that Rhiannon would come to look for her.

"That little madam's just like her Aunt Florrie — with all her airs and graces, she thinks she's too good for the likes of us," Nellie had scoffed. "They begged me to take you away from them. And I, out of the kindness of my heart, did just that. They didn't want you — you'd do well to remember that."

Was this true? Had Rhiannon really been glad to be rid of her? If so, then maybe Harry and Nellie had just upped and left her too.

At that moment the door burst open and Harry, obviously the worse for drink, almost fell into the room.

Unusually, there was no sign of Nellie.

"There she is. There's my little hidden treasure . . . my own little pot of gold," Harry slurred. Then, holding the door open, he called out, "Come on in, Jake, don't be shy. Come take a look at your prize."

In the three days since she'd been there, no one had visited their digs. Who was this man Jake? Through the darkness Mair heard the shuffle of feet coming towards the bed and a terrible feeling of foreboding engulfed her. She lay perfectly still with her eyes closed tight. Maybe if they thought she was asleep they would both leave.

Mair heard a match strike alongside her. She opened her eyes slightly and watched as Harry lit the candle on the small table alongside the bed. As her eyes became accustomed to the light, she caught sight of a large ginger-haired man standing behind Harry.

"Mair, are you awake?" Harry gave a loud belch and a strong smell of stale beer wafted over her. "Mair, this is Jake . . . he's my friend." He gave a low, sinister chuckle, "And if he likes what he sees, soon to be your friend, eh Jake? Come on, girl. Look lively, get yourself out of bed, and let Jake see what a real prize you are."

"No — I don't want to," Mair moaned.

Harry marched over to the bed and, making a grab for her wrist, roughly pulled her towards the edge of the bed. "You'd better start heeding my every word, my girl, or else."

Mair, freeing her wrist from his grip, threw him a look of defiance.

This caused the man called Jake to laugh aloud. "She's a spirited little thing, isn't she?"

"Nothing I can't sort out," Harry assured him.

160

"No — no, it was not a complaint, I like it." He sniggered, his eyes practically undressing her.

Mair, aware of how her winceyette nightdress hugged her naked frame, reached for her woollen shawl, quickly draping it across her shoulder and breast.

"So, what do you think?" Harry urged.

Jake continued to eye her from top to toe. "She's lovely . . . a virgin you say?"

"If you find out otherwise, feel free to belt her one . . . and me too for that matter," Harry said. "So, what do you think?"

"I'd say I'm interested — very interested. How's the bidding going?"

"It's creeping up nicely. But I'm sure a man of your standing, if he was so inclined, would find it easy to outbid the rest of them," Harry assured him.

Jake moved closer to Mair and, reaching up, made to stroke the side of her face. Mair responded, frantically snapping her teeth at his hand, only Jake's quick reaction saving a serious nip to his fingers. "What a little minx! She's certainly got spirit. I'll give you that." Jake gave a loud belly-laugh. "Harry, my man, my interest has suddenly increased. Come let's head back to the pub to discuss the finer details."

Before leaving, Jake leant towards Mair, "Goodnight, you sweet child, until the next time, eh?" He gave a sinister chuckle.

Mair felt sickened. Having overheard Harry and Nellie's many whispered discussions when they thought she was sleeping, concerning their "little nest egg", "forthcoming auction" and "young virgin", usually

161

fuelled by drink, she was now only too aware of the seriousness of her predicament. As she was locked in from morning to night, she could see no way to escape her fate. If only Rhiannon . . . She stopped herself. Who was she fooling? Nellie was right, her stepsister probably never gave her a second thought.

CHAPTER
FOURTEEN

Rhiannon awoke in a cold sweat. She'd had another bad dream about Mair. This wouldn't do. For days now she'd had this terrible feeling of foreboding regarding Mair's safety. She so wanted — no — needed to find her.

A few days ago she'd broached the subject with her Aunt Florrie and was left in no doubt of her aunt's true feeling on the matter.

"Aunt Florrie, I thought I might visit the Theatre Bar during the interval this evening."

"Why on earth would you want to do that? I'm well informed that all sorts of unscrupulous folk mingle up there. It's no place for a young, impressionable girl like you."

"I believe it's where I'll find Nellie; you know, Mair's mother. When Mair bumped into her in the foyer, Nellie told her that she and her friends were frequent visitors the Theatre Bar. I thought . . . the thing is, Nellie's the only one who can tell me where to find Mair."

"No. I forbid it! When are you going to get it into your head that Mair is no longer our concern?"

"But Aunt Florrie, I promised her," Rhiannon pleaded.

"A promise which, while well-intentioned, you made on the spur of the moment, with no thought of the consequences. Now that Nellie and Mair are reunited, they have a wonderful opportunity to make a fresh start — to begin a new life. The last thing they need is for you to be raking over old ground. You'd do best to leave well alone."

"But —"

"Rhiannon, I'll not hear another word."

While common sense told Rhiannon to let the matter rest, her conscience said otherwise. She had made a promise to Mair . . . and finding her was the only way to prove to Rhiannon that all was well between them. If, as Aunt Florrie assured her, Mair wanted to be with Nellie then Rhiannon would have to accept it. With this in mind, a determined Rhiannon made the brave decision to go against her Aunt Florrie's wishes.

It was Friday night and, as usual, the show was playing to a packed theatre. Rhiannon was convinced that tonight, the start of the weekend, there would be a good chance of seeing Nellie and her friends in the Theatre Bar.

With the sound of the band's rendition of the National Anthem signalling the end of the first show, Rhiannon, with much trepidation, quickly weaved her way through the maze of backstage, heading for the stage door. From there she intended to enter the front door of the theatre into the foyer and then go up the sweeping staircase past the Lounge Bar and then on up to the Theatre Bar. Rhiannon believed there was less chance of her Aunt Florrie or Walter catching her if she went that way than if she used the stairway in the main auditorium.

She was thankful to find that she had made it to the stage door without arousing suspicion. She breathed a sigh of relief. So far so good.

"Well now, what's this? Now where might you be going in such a God almighty hurry?"

Gus Davenport's loud voice startled her. He stood just outside the stage door, smoking a cigarette.

"Shhh! Please Gus, I'm on my way to the Theatre Bar. It's a secret."

"I bet. I dread to think what your aunt would say. A secret, you say . . . sneaking off to meet some young fellow, eh? If that's truly the case, may I say how green with envy he's made me."

He moved to stand in front of her, blocking her way.

Rhiannon felt her colour rise. "Well, you're wrong! It's nothing like that."

"I'm intrigued." Gus waited for her to elaborate.

"Look, if I'm to be back in prompt corner in time for the second performance, I have to go now. I need to find my stepmother and there's a good chance she'll be up there. Please Gus — let me pass."

"Have you been up there before?" Gus asked.

Rhiannon shook her head.

"Then, if that's the case, there's no way I can let you go up there on your own."

Her eyes pleaded with him.

He smiled and offered her his hand. "Come on, there's only one thing for it — I'm going to have to escort you."

★ ★ ★

165

Nellie and Mair entered the smoke-filled Theatre Bar.

"Now you be on your best behaviour, mind. Or this will be the first time and last time I bring you," Nellie warned.

"Why are we here?" Mair asked.

"We're here to meet one of Harry's friends and you know what you have to do? Just parade yourself in front of them and try to look interested."

Mair stopped in her tracks, she felt physically sick. "Please, mam, I don't want to. I hate the way they look at me."

Nellie grabbed her arm and squeezed hard.

Mair grimaced with pain.

"Listen to me, you ungrateful little bitch. You'll do what me and Harry tell you to do, or else! And how many times do you need reminding? My name is Nellie. What's my name?"

"Nellie," Mair whispered.

"Sorry, I can't hear you." Nellie placed a hand to her ear.

"Nellie," Mair repeated in a louder voice.

"That's better. My Harry says that if the punters . . . sorry, his friends, knew our true relationship, it wouldn't be good for business."

Mair looked past the bar area and quickly scanned the packed auditorium. There was no sign of Rhiannon.

"If you've a mind to seek out your precious Rhiannon, forget it. It'll do you no good to go whimpering to the likes of her. From now on, your life is with me and Harry."

"But it's been ages. I'm sure she'd want —"

166

"What?" Nellie interrupted her. "Want to see you?" She sniggered. "From what I hear, that young madam is far too busy buttering up to men with influence to bother about likes of you."

"Rhi isn't like that! She wouldn't —"

"Wouldn't what? Offer a favour for a favour? Grow up. How else do you think she got the chance to appear on stage? And I say good for her. You get nothing for nothing in this world."

Mair didn't for one moment believe her.

Mair had overheard Nellie's friends at the King's Head talking about Rhiannon, the girl who'd made such an impression on the Empire's audience. How Mair wished she could have been there to see it.

Somehow Mair just had to get in touch with Rhi. If Rhi knew what Harry and Nellie were going to make her do she'd — Mair stopped herself. Who was she fooling? Rhiannon couldn't help her. And, more to the point, she probably wouldn't want to. Up to now Rhiannon hadn't even attempted to find her. *I promise to always be there for you*, Rhiannon had assured her. So where was she now?

Rhiannon willingly let Gus lead her from the stage door and down the dark, narrow alley, that led to the brightly lit front entrance of the theatre. The touch of his firm hand in hers felt good. She tried to imagine what it might be like to have his strong arms around her, then she scolded herself for having such sinful thoughts about a man she hardly knew. Yet there could be no denying the effect this handsome, charming, masterful

167

man had on her; arousing new and exciting feelings, that screamed to be set free.

Gus led her through the entrance, deftly manoeuvring his way through the crowds of theatregoers in the foyer, all awaiting the second show.

"We'll have to be quick. Adam will have our guts for garters if we're late back for curtain up . . . I must be mad." Gus quickened his pace taking the stairs leading to the bar, two at a time. It was as much as Rhiannon could do to keep in step.

A somewhat breathless Rhiannon entered the Theatre Bar alongside Gus. Through the haze of cigarette smoke she couldn't believe her eyes. The room was a maelstrom of men, women, girls and young boys, drinking, laughing and chatting, each competing to be heard above a cacophony of noise. Rhiannon was shocked to see the way well-dressed, and obviously well-to-do gentlemen were behaving; openly fondling coarse-looking women, who wore low-cut bodices, while other women sat atop tables, their skirts hitched up showing far too much ankle, laughing and drinking. And what were those young boys doing in the company of those lecherous looking old men? Was this what Frank's mother had meant by the "rougher element of the theatre" and the reason her aunt had been so against her coming here?

Among the noisy crowd, Rhiannon was surprised to see some of the older chorus girls and a few of the cast from the show.

"Any sign of your stepmother?" Gus asked.

"No. I can't tell if she's here. It's far too busy."

"And what do we have here? Now there's a turn up for the books. Gus Davenport, you sly old thing." Sally Webber sniggered. She stood no more than a few feet away from them, still wearing her street urchin costume from the first show.

Gus immediately let go of Rhiannon's hand.

"Too late, me laddo. I saw you holding hands with little miss innocent, there."

Rhiannon felt her colour rise. "It's not what you think. Gus —"

"Oh you can't tell me anything about our Gus. Most of us girls backstage have fallen for his charms at some time or other. He can be a right charmer and that's for sure." Sally turned to Gus. "I'm a bit surprised at you bringing her to a place like this. Mind you, after the speed with which she jumped into my shoes on stage, there's no doubt that she's a fast learner."

"Sally, if I were you I'd not judge everyone by your standards. Just go about your business and leave us alone."

"Sorry, I'm sure. I'll not stay where I'm not wanted," she scoffed and, with an elaborate turn, moved away.

Gus turned his attention to Rhiannon. "Look, Rhi, I can see you're not comfortable being here. So, why don't you make your way back to the auditorium? I'll make some enquiries regarding your stepmother. What did you say her name was?"

"Her name's Nellie Parsons."

"Will you be all right heading back on your own?"

Rhiannon nodded, "Thank you, I'll be fine."

★　★　★

169

Nellie Parsons was quick to spot Rhiannon and Gus Davenport entering the bar. He wasn't half a bit of all right. Rhiannon, the lucky bitch, had landed herself a good catch there. But what the hell were they doing up here? The last thing she needed was that little madam quizzing Mair.

"Mair, follow me, I need the privy."

Nellie knew that as the show chairman, Rhiannon's escort would need to be on stage for the start of the second show. She thought it prudent that she and Mair should lie low in the ladies' cloakroom until then.

Rhiannon was waiting in the prompt corner when Gus returned from the Theatre Bar.

"Well? Did you find out anything?"

"Yes. Apparently, we must have just missed her. She was there with another girl."

"I knew it. I knew I should have gone there earlier. Goodness knows when she'll be there again."

"Listen, all's not lost. I found out that she and her friends regularly meet at the King's Head on Westgate Street."

"How far is that?"

"It's not far. About a ten-minute walk, but don't you go having any ideas about wandering the streets on your own. Promise me that you'll speak to me first."

Rhiannon nodded. At last she felt that with Gus's help she would find Mair. Gus was turning out to be her knight in shining armour.

★ ★ ★

It was early Sunday morning and Rhiannon readied herself for her planned trip. She was dressed in a long navy skirt, white high-necked blouse trimmed with lace and a dark-blue velvet jacket, just one of the outfits purchased on a recent shopping expedition with her Aunt Florrie.

"Aunt Florrie, giving of your time and money like this is so very kind of you," Rhiannon had said, and meant it.

"You're so welcome my dear. It's about time you had a new wardrobe. Just you remember that the way you look and carry yourself throughout life is as important as the success you now crave. In the few weeks since you arrived in Cardiff I've watch you blossom into a confident young lady. And, as a young lady, I trust you'll always conduct yourself in a proper manner, whether I'm here to look out for you or not."

"Thank you, Aunt, I'll not let you down."

Rhiannon was just about to reach for her elegant new hat when there was a tap on the door. She quickly removed her velvet jacket, casually placed it on the bed and opened the door.

"Good morning, Rhi. So glad to see you up and about so early," Walter gushed.

"Good morning, Walter," she replied.

"The thing is, this morning your aunt has arranged for us to have breakfast in her room.

"Why? Is anything wrong?" Rhiannon was only too aware of how her aunt usually preferred to breakfast alone.

"No, not at all, she just felt it would be nice if we all had a little chat. You know? About your forthcoming stage début and our trip to America." He gave a nervous cough. "Come along now, she's waiting."

Rhiannon reluctantly followed Walter, annoyed in the knowledge that her planned secret trip would now have to wait until after breakfast.

"There you are."

Her aunt, dressed in a long, pink, silk housecoat sat at the table near the large French window overlooking Cardiff Castle.

"I took the liberty of ordering some champagne and strawberries by way of a little celebration. Come on, Walter, pop the cork."

Walter, first removing the gold foil and twisted wire from the champagne bottle, expertly teased out the cork, which exploded noisily across the room.

"What are we celebrating?" Rhiannon asked, as Walter filled three elegant, bowl-shaped, champagne glasses.

Florrie picked up her glass and held it aloft. "To my forthcoming trip to America!"

"What? You mean it's settled? You're actually leaving? When?"

"We leave at the beginning of next week. Isn't that exciting?"

"What about your contract at the Empire?" Rhiannon asked.

"Walter, the clever love, has managed to wangle my early release from the contract."

172

Rhiannon was completely taken aback. "B-but who will replace you?"

"Again, thanks to Walter, it's all worked out perfectly. With me taking over from Alice Lloyd in New York, Walter thought it worth getting in touch with her agent and . . . well, to cut a long story . . . Walter has managed to get her signed up to do a show a night with top billing here at the Empire."

"And Adam agreed?"

"Agreed? He jumped at the chance at having Alice Lloyd fresh from her American success, appear in his show. What a draw she'll be, even if it is for one show a night," Walter enthused. Then, noticing the frown on Florrie's brow he added, "The only act good enough to replace you, my dear."

"Quite." Florrie smiled. "Adam has already expressed how sad he'll be to lose me."

"I still don't understand. So who will top the bill for the matinée shows?" Rhiannon asked.

"Adam has given it to Sally Webber."

The disappointment on Rhiannon's face was obvious. If Sally hadn't made such a quick recovery, it might have been herself.

"Don't look so glum," Walter said. "What this means is that when Sally Webber is topping the bill there'll be a whole six-minute spot going begging for . . .?"

"Me!" Rhiannon screamed.

"Exactly," her Aunt Florrie enthused. "The good news is that Adam is all for it and has extended the second show so that you can appear in that too. He was very pleased with your aunt's choice of song. And instead of attending an audition, he wants you to begin rehearsals on Monday."

Pleased as Rhiannon was with this news, it was all happening too fast — and it all seemed a bit too contrived. She noticed a look pass between Walter and her aunt and knew she was right.

"What is it? There's something else, isn't there?"

"Well yes, there is. The thing is my dear, on the day of our departure we all need to book out of the hotel."

"You mean — me too? Where will I go?"

"We've already arranged for you to move into theatrical digs. A respectable boarding house just around the corner from the Empire, owned by Mrs Gordon, the theatre's housekeeper, and Mavis, her spinster sister. It already accommodates many of the cast, so you'll not be on your own."

Rhiannon noticed how her aunt avoided eye contact.

"But how am I to manage? How much will it cost?"

"Now don't you go fretting yourself, young 'un. Your aunt has already paid three months in advance and tomorrow she has arranged a visit to her bank to secure an account in your name with a modest allowance to get you started."

Rhiannon looked to her aunt. "Thank you, Aunt Florrie, that's very generous of you."

"It's just a little to help you get started. Walter also took it upon himself to speak to Adam on your behalf. He managed to secure you a fifteen guineas a week wage at the theatre. I'm all for you standing on your own feet. I suggest the need to be frugal, at least until you establish your career in the theatre."

174

Rhiannon was speechless. Between them they had thought of everything. But, acceptable as the arrangement was to her, she couldn't help feeling that their efforts on her behalf were partly made to ease their own consciences.

For a while no one spoke.

Walter was quick to break the awkward silence. "Come on, you gals! We all know what a wrench this will be, but look on it as a new start for us all. I think it's time for us to raise our glasses and toast. To the future!"

Rhiannon went through the motions of raising her glass to her lips, all the while fighting back the tears. In less than a week they'd be gone and, no matter what her Aunt Florrie said, she would be on her own.

Back in her room Rhiannon, more determined than ever to seek out Mair, reached for her hat and jacket. Once fully dressed she left the room heading for Westgate Street and the King's Head public house. Although Gus had advised her not to venture out alone, what harm could possibly come to her in broad daylight?

CHAPTER
FIFTEEN

"Good morning, miss," the doorman said, as Rhiannon left the Angel Hotel.

"Good morning," Rhiannon answered. "I wonder would you mind pointing me in the direction of Westgate Street?"

"Of course, miss. He stepped down onto the pavement. Then raising his arm pointed down the street. "Just you head to your left. That's the beginning of Westgate Street. Mind you it's a long street. Where exactly do you want to go?"

Rhiannon hesitated. "Oh, nowhere really. I just felt like a stroll," she lied, not wanting to divulge her true destination.

"Well, you certainly picked a nice day for it." He smiled, and doffed his top hat.

Rhiannon returned his smile before hastily heading in the direction of Westgate Street.

The doorman had been right. It was a beautiful day, with a clear blue sky and only a few fluffy white clouds. A hint that summer was well on its way.

It being Sunday and the shops all closed, Castle Street was eerily quiet. There were no trams, street hawkers or motor cars. A lone cyclist, a single horse-drawn carriage and a couple of pedestrians were the only signs of life in the normally bustling city street. Following the doorman's instructions, Rhiannon took the first turning into Westgate Street.

Halfway down the street a couple of young lads, both dressed in cloth caps and grey serge suits, stood on the pavement. Rhiannon didn't want any trouble from them, so she paused for moment and pretended to adjust the buttons on her shoe. Looking up she spotted the "King's Head" sign hanging above their heads. She stood up and, taking a deep breath, ventured forward.

"All right love, out for a bit of a stroll, then?" the taller of the two lads asked.

Rhiannon didn't answer. Instead, she gingerly made her way towards the pub entrance.

The other lad stepped in front of her, blocking her path. "Where are you off to then? Fancy a bit of company, do you?"

"Excuse me. I need to enter the public house."

"Oh, you do, do you?" The young man raised his nose in the air as if mimicking her.

"Come on, Albert. Don't you know a young lady when you see one?"

"A young lady in need of a stiff drink, I'd say. Now if it's something stiff you're after . . ." Albert sniggered.

Rhiannon felt her colour rise. "If you don't let me pass, I shall call for help." She took a deep breath, prepared to carry out her threat.

"All right, keep your hair on." He stood aside, "But it'll do you no good. It's Sunday. The pub's *officially* closed."

"Well, if it's closed, where's all that noise coming from?" Rhiannon snapped.

"I said *officially* closed. Every Sunday the landlord holds a private party — just for the regulars. There's no law against holding a private party, and it keeps everyone happy. No complaints from Bible-punchers or the local constabulary."

"Mind you, private party or not, we still have to pay for our ale," the other lad piped up.

"We were just about to knock on the door. If you want you can come in with us," Albert offered.

Rhiannon shook her head. "I don't think . . ."

"Look, I'm sorry about earlier. It's not often that me and Tommy get to see the likes of you down at the King's Head. We didn't mean anything by it, honest."

The door of the pub opened. Albert and Tommy quickly entered. "Well are you coming in, or what?" Albert urged.

Against her better judgement she followed them in. Once inside the door they entered a dark dingy taproom, dimly lit by pale gas lights, reeking of stale beer and cigarettes, sparsely furnished with a few well-worn tables and chairs. The bar was full of men. Through a hatch she spied another room behind. A room filled with heavily made-up women, wearing far too much lipstick and rouge, knocking back tankards of ale.

Rhiannon felt the urge to turn and run but, for some reason her legs wouldn't move.

"What's your pleasure?" the buxom barmaid asked.

"Two glasses of your best ale please, Dolly," Albert answered.

178

While the barmaid expertly served the two foaming ales, her eyes stayed firmly fixed on Rhiannon. "And what'll she be having, then?"

There was a moment's awkward silence, then Rhiannon, realizing that Dolly was waiting for her, answered. "Oh, thank you, but I don't want a drink."

The barmaid stood with her hands on her hips, her heavy bust straining the ribbons of her grubby bodice. "Well, pray tell me what the hell you're doing here if you don't want a drink?" she demanded.

Rhiannon imagined that all eyes were on her. "I'm looking for someone?"

"What, your old fella up and left you?" The barmaid sniggered.

"I-I'm looking for Nellie Parsons . . . I was told that she often frequented this establishment."

Around the room she heard muffled laughter.

"Nellie!" the barmaid shouted through the hatch. "There's a snooty cow out here asking for you. I'm sending her through."

The thought of entering a room full of larger-than-life women terrified Rhiannon — akin to sending a lamb to slaughter. She knew she was out of her depth but felt she had come too far to stop now.

"Nellie's in the snug out back, and enter at your peril, I say . . . Well, go on then, what you waiting for?" the barmaid taunted her.

Rhiannon began to weave her way slowly pass the men in the tap room. She wished she hadn't dressed so smartly. She looked and felt so out of place.

The snug door flew open and there, surrounded by rough-looking women, stood Nellie. She looked different. Although quite tidily dressed, her heavy make-up made her look harder and coarser.

"Well, if it isn't daddy's little girl. What the hell do you want?" Nellie snapped.

Rhiannon would have wished for a better reception. "I'd like to see Mair," she replied.

"Oh, you would, would you?" Nellie spat.

"Yes — yes, I would." Rhiannon failed to mask the tremble in her voice.

Nellie moved closer, Rhiannon could smell her beery-breath. "Well she don't want to see you, so why don't you just bugger off?"

Then from behind she felt a man's hand move around her waist. "What say you and me go out back for a bit of fun then?" he said as he began kissing the nape of her neck.

Rhiannon pulled away. As she did so, Nellie grabbed her shoulders. "What a good idea, Harry. Little miss perfect here could do with being pulled down a peg or two. Come on girls, let's take her out back and watch Harry and anyone else have their fun with her."

As the women began to jostle her towards the back door, Rhiannon became filled with dread. "You can't do this, it isn't right. Let me go," she insisted.

Harry and Nellie just laughed.

"You heard the girl, let her go!" a man commanded.

Rhiannon instantly recognized Gus's strong voice. She almost collapsed with relief.

180

"And what's it got to do with you? We're not greedy. You can have a piece of the action too, if you like," Harry scoffed.

"If you don't let her go, this instant, the only action you're likely to see is my fist on your chin."

"That's brave talk, mister. Especially, when there be only one of you and at least six of us."

"He's not on his own, Harry. Me and Tommy are on his side," the lad called Albert piped up. "So why don't you leave the young lady alone?"

While the men considered their options, Rhiannon attempted to struggle free, but Nellie and the women were having none of it.

"Break it up, lads. If you don't leave off with this bloody nonsense, I'll be forced to stop Dolly serving and throw you all out," a larger than life bearded man bellowed.

"I'm sure there's no need for that, landlord," the man next to Harry called. Then, turning to Harry, he urged, "Come on, mate. You've had your fun, now let them be."

A nod from Harry was all it took for the women to release their grip on Rhiannon. She instantly ran towards Gus. He caught an arm around her. At last she felt safe. Taking her hand Gus led her out of the pub. As they passed Albert and Tommy, Rhiannon mouthed "Thank you."

"You're welcome, miss," they said, and, as a show of respect, both removed their caps.

Once outside the pub Gus pulled her into a doorway.

"Whatever possessed you to do such a stupid thing? Didn't I tell you not to venture down here on your own?"

"I'm sorry, Gus. I just thought —"

"I dread to think what might have happened if I hadn't found you."

"I'm so glad you did. How did you know I was here?"

"I called at the hotel. I thought, with it being such a nice day, I'd call and ask your aunt's permission to take you for lunch. When the doorman told me you'd left, heading for Westgate Street, I guessed you'd gone to look for your stepmother. The King's Head was the obvious choice.

"Nellie *was* there," Rhiannon meekly offered.

"So I gathered. And what a right charmer she turned out to be."

"She told me that Mair didn't want to see me."

"And do you believe her?"

"I'm not sure. If it were true, I wouldn't blame Mair. She probably thinks I've deserted her." Rhiannon dropped her head.

Gus put his arms around her and pulled her to him. She felt his lips brush her forehead. She had never been this close to a man before. Part of her felt she should pull away. After all, it was broad daylight and she could almost hear her Aunt Florrie's disapproval. But it felt so good that, for a while, time stood still.

Then, taking her chin in his gloved hand Gus slowly raised her head and kissed her gently on the lips. She felt an awakening of strange new feelings and her whole

182

being longed for more, when she responded his kiss deepened. She was totally entranced.

From the pavement someone coughed. Gus released her. And her magic moment was no more.

In front of them stood the two lads from the pub. "I thought this might be of help to you, miss," Albert said, holding out a piece of paper. "It's Harry and Nellie's address."

"Thank you," Rhiannon said, as she reached out to take it, but Gus's hand beat her to it. For a few moments he studied the piece of paper in silence.

The suspense was too much for Rhiannon. "Gus, tell me. Do they live very far away?"

"No. Going by this address, they live a five-minute walk away."

"You mean Mair may be that close? Come on then, what are we waiting for?" Rhiannon urged.

"If I was you, I'd leave it for today," Albert interjected. "Harry, Nellie and her cronies will all be heading for home soon. I don't think . . . after what happened in the pub . . ."

"Thanks. That's probably good advice. I think there's been more than enough excitement for one day," Gus said.

"All right then, we'll be off. Good luck," the lads called as they turned and headed down Westgate Street.

Rhiannon's disappointment was obvious. "A case of so near and yet so far, eh?" she said.

"Come on, Rhi. You know it makes sense." Gus took her hand in his. "I suggest we head back to the Angel Hotel in time for a late lunch. If your aunt or Walter

183

asks, you went for a walk to Sophia Gardens and we met by accident."

It was almost 3.30 in the afternoon when Harry and Nellie returned from the pub.

Mair, having had a week of so-called freedom, allowed to visit the Theatre Bar and the King's Head pub, to be paraded in front of lecherous men, as if she were a prize cow at a farmers' market, was now strictly confined to her digs: locked in. "Now that everyone has had a chance to see her, all we have to do is sit back and wait for the highest bidder," she'd heard Harry boast to Nellie. Mair had strict instructions to prepare a meal for their return. With limited cooking facilities, a few pots and pans and an open coal fire, a stew was by far the easiest option.

Mair heard the key turn in the lock and her stomach churned, wondering whether this would be the night when they handed her to the highest bidder.

"I still can't fathom out how that brazen bitch knew where to find you. Unless you've been speaking out of turn," Harry spat, as he roughly grabbed Nellie's arm.

"Please Harry, you're hurting me. I swear it wasn't my fault. I was as surprised as you to see Dai's daughter in the pub today," Nellie pleaded.

"Well, she'd better watch her step. I'm not going to let anyone spoil my plan," Harry warned.

"Rhiannon — you've actually seen Rhiannon?" Mair asked, fighting to control her excitement. "Is she coming here to see me?"

"No, she bloody well isn't," Harry snapped.

184

"But she did come looking for *me*, didn't she? Please Mam — Nellie, I really want to see her."

Releasing Nellie's arm, Harry's hand whipped across Mair's buttocks.

"Ouch!" Mair cried.

"Think yourself lucky. If I didn't need you looking your innocent best, you'd have felt my hand across that pretty face of yours. Now, where's my food?"

CHAPTER
SIXTEEN

On Monday morning a nervous Rhiannon entered the stage door on her way to rehearsals.

"Rhi, wait for me," Clara Boxall called from behind. Rhiannon turned and smiled.

Clara put an arm around her. "I hear via the grapevine of theatre gossip that you're to have your very own spot in the show. Well done, you," she gushed.

"Thanks. I really can't believe my luck. I just hope I'm up to the job."

"Of course you are. Having seen how well you did as Sally Webber's street urchin, I can't wait to see you perform your own song."

"You're very kind."

"Don't mention it. I think it's lovely to see a newcomer get on. Mind you, some of the other girls might give you a bit of a hard time. A few think that your Aunt Florrie had more than a little to do with it."

"Well, I do admit that my aunt helped with my choice of song and that Walter did have a hand in securing my fee. But Adam Fletcher had already agreed to give me an audition, even before he knew about Florrie's planned trip to America, honest."

186

"I believe you. But be warned, jealousy can be a terrible thing. Come on, we'd better get a move on. It wouldn't do to be late for your first band call."

As both girls headed through the maze of backstage Clara carried on talking. "Anyways, another little bird told me that you're moving into our digs."

"Blimey, news certainly travels fast. But yes, I'm moving in on Friday, the same day as my aunt and Walter leave for America."

"Don't feel glum. I've spoken to Mrs Gordon's sister Mavis, and she's agreed to give you the bedroom next to mine — that'll be good, eh?"

Rhiannon didn't answer. The sound of the musicians tuning up and the cast's noisy chatter told them they had arrived at the prompt corner. As the girls stepped on stage a few heads turned, but most simply carried on chatting.

"So tell me, what's the boarding house like," Rhiannon asked, in an effort to take her mind off the sick, nervous feeling that welled in her stomach.

"Oh, it's comfortable enough and the food is exceptionally good. Mind you, you'll probably find it a bit of a come-down from the Angel Hotel. Ten of us girls stay there. No men, unfortunately. Both landladies are very strict. They'll not stand for any hanky-panky. Woe betide anyone found entertaining a male visitor."

"So where do the men stay?" Rhiannon asked.

"There are several other boarding houses down our road, where the stage hands stay, and a few more expensive guest houses, run more like hotels than theatrical digs, that house some of the main acts."

"What about the likes of Adam and . . . Gus?"

"Adam owns a house near Sophia Gardens and Gus, being his nephew and all, lives with him."

"Gus is Adam's nephew?"

"Yeah, although you'd never guess, would you? Adam doesn't want to be seen showing any favouritism. Truth be known he's stricter with Gus than with the rest of the cast. Interested in our Gus then, are you?" Clara teased.

"N-no I only —" Rhiannon felt her colour rise.

"Don't be embarrassed. You'll not be the first. We've all fancied Gus Davenport — Davenport being his stage name, sometime or another."

The musicians tuning-up became louder.

"All right, everyone. Quiet please. Clear the stage," Adam ordered.

The band and cast became quiet and within seconds everyone had taken their places in the wings. You could have heard a pin drop.

"I trust you all know the order of play?" Adam called. "Belles, get ready, you're first. Then the acrobats and jugglers, followed by the comedy spot, and then Rhiannon. After Rhiannon we'll take a fifteen-minute lunch break. By which time I expect the main artistes to grace us with their presence." The conductor raised his baton indicating on the count of three . . . one — two — three." Right on cue the band struck up the overture to the show and the Empire Belles began their high-kicking dance routine from wings to centre stage.

Rhiannon's heart missed a beat. While part of her loved the rush of blood she felt as the show began,

188

another part struggled to control the butterflies turning cartwheels in her stomach. As she watched each act perform, she felt a strange detachment, light-headed even. Then came a muffled voice and the sound of distant, yet familiar music . . .

A huge nudge in her back sent her flying on stage. "Rhi, it's your cue. Move it!" Clara urged.

"Stop there!" Adam called. "Rhiannon, you're supposed to glide on stage like a demure young lady. Not a clumsy oaf. Go back and try again. And on cue this time, please."

As Rhiannon gingerly headed back to the wings she mouthed a "Sorry" in Adam's direction.

"All right, let's go again." Adam nodded to the conductor "One — two — three —"

This time, after taking a deep breath, Rhiannon left the wings and, as the band played the introduction to her song, with head held high she sauntered to her centre stage. Then, looking up, her eyes fixed high up to the gods began . . .

I'm a young girl, and have just come over
Over from the country where they do things big
And amongst the boys I've got a lover
And since I've got a lover, why I don't care a fig.

The boy I love is up in the Gallery,
The boy I love is looking down at me.
There he is, can't you see, waving his handkerchief,
As merry as a robin that sings on a tree . . .

Rhiannon felt in good voice. She sailed through the next two verses with ease. Her aunt had been right, this song really suited her. As she reached the final note Rhiannon, again on the advice of her aunt, positioned the back of her hands under her chin and coyly dropped her head. She held this pose until the music stopped. Only then did she look up and take her bow.

A slight ripple of applause from the cast gave it their seal of approval.

"That was great," Adam called. "I loved the touch of melodrama at the end of the song. You and your aunt must have worked hard — and it shows. I think, by the end of the week, you'll be more than ready to début on Saturday."

"Oh, thank you." Rhiannon smiled.

"Don't be too quick to thank me. There's still a lot of work to do. After the break get yourself off to wardrobe. Mrs Gordon needs to fit you with an appropriate costume. Dress rehearsal's tomorrow. Don't be late."

Rhainnon felt relieved. Her first rehearsal had gone better than she could have wished. She couldn't explain the high she'd felt when she performed. It was like nothing on earth — like all your birthdays rolled into one. She instinctively knew that this was what she was meant to do.

Much to her surprise she suddenly felt hungry. She'd skipped breakfast this morning, too excited — nervous — apprehensive about the rehearsals. As she joined the queue for the refreshments — tea and sandwiches laid on in the auditorium for all the cast — she heard —

"Well, how did it go?" a voice behind her asked.

She turned to find Gus's handsome face smiling down on her.

"Fine — I think. Adam seems to think that I'll be ready for Saturday's matinée show."

"That's great," he said, leaning forward, his mouth almost touching her ear. She felt his warm, sweet breath on the nape of her neck and, remembering their first kiss, she visibly trembled. His lips brushed her ear. "Were there any awkward questions on Sunday?" he whispered.

Rhiannon pulled away. Having Gus Davenport this close to her she struggled to compose herself. "N-no. I-I kept to the story. I'm not sure my aunt believed that we'd met accidentally, though," she said, in a quiet voice.

"She's a wily old bird. No doubt she's seen it all before, eh? Still, I've had no questions my end."

"Gus, I really need to find Mair. You have the address, so . . ."

"I think we should let the dust settle for a few days. Look, what say we meet on Sunday morning, go to the address and wait for your stepmother and Mr Stone to leave. Then, when the coast is clear, pay your Mair a visit?"

"But that's almost another week away."

"I know, but I think it best to wait until your aunt and Walter are well on their way to America. Anyway, do you really need this distraction? I think you'd be better off concentrating on perfecting your act."

"I suppose you're right. But I'll not be fobbed off again. On Sunday I intend to find Mair, with or without your help."

"Agreed," Gus said.

"Come on, you two. Get a move on, you're holding up the queue. What's the matter, Gus? This one playing hard to get? Losing your touch, or what?" one of the backstage crew called from behind them.

Gus didn't reply, he just turned and glared at the young man. Rhiannon, picking up her tea and sandwiches, quickly moved away.

"All right Gus — what's the deal with you and young Rhiannon, then?" Adam asked later that night.

"I'm helping her to find her stepsister, that's all."

"Well, I never had you down as a good Samaritan," Adam said, with more than a hint of sarcasm in his voice.

"I like her."

"Fancy her, more like," Adam quipped.

"Yes, that too."

"She's far too innocent for you. Trust me, you'll not get anywhere with her."

"You want to bet? She already thinks of me as her knight in shining armour," Gus boasted.

"Be advised. Valley girls are notoriously strait-laced," Adam offered.

"That's what makes it such a challenge." Gus flashed a wicked smile.

"You're a real swine. Why don't you leave her be? Remember what happened to your last *young* protégée?"

Gus glared at Adam. "Trust you to throw that in my face. That was over four years ago and you still can't leave it be, can you?"

"Four years, three months and five days to be exact. And there's not a day goes by that I don't ask myself why I didn't stop you seducing Helena Biggins."

"You talk about her as if she were an innocent young thing. She was a streetwise chorus girl, for goodness' sake. She knew the score. How was I to know that she'd go top herself?"

Rhiannon glanced at the clock. It was 6.30 and time to get up. She hadn't slept well, she'd known she wouldn't. Ever since her aunt had told her the "good news" about the American contract she'd been dreading this day.

Last night her aunt had given a farewell speech:

"Dear friends, what can I say? America wants me! I've been dreaming of this for years. If they like me, and I'll make sure they do, then the sky's the limit."

Her aunt had never believed in false modesty. Rhiannon had long since realized how driven by success her aunt was. Florrie had never made a secret of her ambition, nothing and no one stood in the way of her career. But with Rhiannon about to make her own stage début and, as far as her aunt was concerned, there still being no news about Mair, how could she just up and leave? Rhiannon, finding it harder by the hour to be happy for her, left the party early.

Walter tapped his silver-topped walking-stick impatiently. "Come on, you gals, get a move on. The tide won't wait, not even for the Great Florrie Grayson!"

193

Walter had arranged for a carriage to take them to Cardiff docks where they were to sail on the *Celtic 2* — the pride of the White Star Line. She was an Atlantic liner bound for Southampton from Cardiff and then on to New York, with a turn-around time of only seven days.

"Are you sure you want to come to the dock? Maybe it would be best if we said our goodbyes here." Aunt Florrie didn't look Rhiannon in the eye; instead she nervously fumbled with the buttons of her glove.

Rhiannon knew it made sense, but it was as if, all of a sudden, having Rhiannon around made her aunt feel uncomfortable. Why else would Florrie be so eager to take a speedy departure? Rhiannon felt hurt. Well, she had no intention of letting Florrie off the hook that easily.

"Your going seems so final. I really need to come and see you both off," she insisted.

"Very well, but we'll have to get a move on," Florrie agreed.

"You're ready — at long last." Walter sighed, his frustration obvious, as he proceeded to help Florrie and then Rhiannon into the carriage.

With Walter's arm gently supporting her, Rhiannon caught a whiff of his musk cologne. It smelled of pine trees and brought back memories of walks across the pine-covered mountain of her beloved Nantgarw Valley. For the first time for a long while she felt homesick, and vowed to take a trip back to the valley soon. After all, it was only a train ticket away.

The streets of Cardiff were almost deserted. The only sign of life was a couple of barrow boys pushing their carts, on their way to market no doubt. Florrie, Rhiannon and Walter rode in silence, even Walter, normally not at a loss for words, remained quiet. The eerie silence, only broken by the clip-clop of their horse-drawn carriage and the rattle of its wheels on the cobbled stones, made the ride seem endless.

When they eventually arrived at the dock gate visibility was low, the sea mist sweeping in from the south causing a grey blanket of low clouds. Through the mist they heard a vendor call out, "Read all about it . . . Welsh song-bird leaving for New York!"

Walter stopped the carriage and, leaning out of the window, handed the man on the corner of the street a shiny penny in exchange for a newspaper.

The carriage entered the quayside and pulled up alongside the loading bay. Walter, Florrie and Rhiannon stepped onto the quay while, amid the hustle and bustle, porters eagerly off-loaded their luggage. The quay area was packed with people all saying their goodbyes. It brought home to Rhiannon the full significance of her situation. With Florrie and Walter gone she would be completely alone.

"Come on, Rhi, don't look so down. Be happy for me." Florrie's voice was unable to hide the excitement she felt for the trip ahead.

Rhiannon forced a smile, "I wish you could stay, at least until we find Mair."

"Rhi, Mair is with her mother. She's no longer your responsibility and certainly no concern of *mine*."

Rhiannon, realizing she'd touched a nerve, decided to try a different tack. "I can understand you not being interested in what happens to Mair, she's not related to you, but what about me? I can't believe you don't want to be here for my first night!"

"Rhiannon, you're acting like a spoilt child. I know it's a hard lesson to learn, but in show business you have to look out for number one. That's what I intend to do. I suggest you do the same. It's time to grow up!"

Florrie's outburst left Rhiannon speechless. She was on her own and from now on she had to learn to live with it.

Florrie's hands went to the gold locket around her neck. She unclipped it and handed it to Rhiannon. "This is for you. It was your grandmother's. She gave it to me when I first left for France. I know she'd want you to have it."

"It's beautiful. Thank you."

"Whenever I touched it I could almost feel my mother willing me to succeed. I hope it brings you as much luck as it did me."

"Will I ever see you again?"

"Who knows? I certainly hope so. In the meantime I expect you to write frequently. I shall watch your career with interest — do well! Remember, success breeds success and with it the freedom to choose your own destiny. A word of warning. Stay away from Gus Davenport. I'm not at all sure I approve of the sudden and, to my mind, unhealthy interest he's been showing you of late."

Rhiannon felt her colour rise.

"Florrie, old gal, it's time we boarded. Rhiannon, I'm afraid this is it." Walter's arms reached out to her. "It's been a joy having you with us these past months. I'm gonna miss you." He squeezed her to him, then quickly stood back and, raising his handkerchief, lightly blew his nose.

There was no such show of emotion from Florrie. She simply brushed Rhiannon's cheek with a small kiss before turning and, taking Walter's arm, headed for the gangplank.

CHAPTER
SEVENTEEN

Armed with her new fashionable valise, a parting gift from Walter, Rhiannon entered the boarding house.

"Miss Hughes — Rhiannon, welcome." Mrs Gordon smiled warmly. "If you'd care to follow me, I'll show you to your room." She didn't wait for an answer; she simply turned and headed down the hall.

Rhiannon followed Mrs Gordon, a smart, if somewhat primly dressed, middle-aged woman, down the hall and up a flight of stairs, taking in the strange surroundings that, for the time being at least, were to be her home . . . home? — Perhaps not. Home would always be the colliery house in Ponty where she'd lived with her dear father.

"I trust your aunt and Mr Cahill got away safely?"

"Yes, thank you." Rhiannon swallowed hard, determined not to give way to tears. What good would her crying do? No amount of crying would change the fact that her aunt had left and, with still no sign of Mair's return, she was on her own.

"Here we are. We've put you in the room next to Clara Boxall. She's a good girl, that one. She'll set you straight on the rules of the house," Mrs Gordon said, as she unlocked the bedroom door.

Rhiannon entered the light, airy and surprisingly spacious room. The furnishings consisted of a large double bed, wardrobe, dressing table, sofa and writing-desk. While not being as sumptuous as her bedroom at the Angel Hotel, it felt somehow more inviting, and not as . . . impersonal.

"I'll leave you to settle in. You'll find your own set of keys on the dressing-table. Later, I shall introduce you to my sister, Mavis. Since I have my wardrobe duties at the theatre, Mavis usually deals with the day-to-day running of this place. So if there's anything you need, she's the one to ask. I'm sure you'll find her amiable."

It was Saturday afternoon and Rhiannon stared into the long dressing-room mirror. The reflection of the girl staring back at her was almost unrecognizable. Mrs Gordon had surpassed herself — Rhiannon's costume with its high choker neckline, tight figure-hugging bodice, long straight skirt, an elaborate ruffled bustle and train was a dream of white organza. Rhiannon's hair was tied back in a fashionable chignon and, with a wide-brimmed matching hat and gloves, Mrs Gordon had created a look of such innocent beauty that it quite took your breath away.

"Five minutes to curtain-up," Percy called.

Rhiannon felt a buzz of nervous excitement. During the week rehearsals had gone extremely well. Now all she had to do was focus on her performance. She heard her aunt's advice repeated over and over in her mind's ear:

"The audience has to believe in you. When you sing, imagine your first love sitting up in the gallery waving at you. You have to pull the audience closer to you, let them feel your innocence and vulnerability, make them . . . *believe*," her aunt had advised. "Play it right and you'll have the audience eating out of the palm of your hand. Trust me; it's a feeling like no other."

As Rhiannon made her way to the wings she heard Percy's whispered call, "Break a leg, Rhi."

From the wings Rhiannon watched the comedian, Tom O'Reilly. He had the audience shrieking with laughter. She knew from what she had heard during rehearsals that he was nearing the end of his act. Her time was almost here . . . she watched the comedian make an elaborate bow, then, waving to the audience, he left the stage to spontaneous applause.

"Great crowd today!" Tom O'Reilly announced to everyone in earshot.

As the applause subsided Rhiannon had a crisis of confidence. Tom O'Reilly had gone down so well. The butterflies in Rhiannon stomach started doing somersaults. How could she, a complete novice, be expected to follow that?

She watched Gus at the table on the side of the stage and, as he raised his gavel, she knew it was too late to back out now.

"My lords, ladies and gentlemen! Just as the comedy genius of Tom O'Reilly had you in shrieks of laughter, the next act, I'm sure, will bring you to the brink of tears. Please believe me when I say that this young lady is destined for greater things. Now put your hands together for a star in the making . . . Rhiannon!"

Encouraged by Gus, the audience's applause was so loud that Rhiannon struggled to hear the overture to her song.

"You're on," the prompter whispered.

As Rhiannon walked on stage the audience, as if totally spellbound by her appearance, fell silent. This slightly unnerved her, but with the overture to her song nearly at an end, she, as rehearsed, made her way to the mark at centre stage and, turning to face the audience, beamed a smile. Then, lifting her face towards the gallery audience, the highest point of the auditorium, and, with a sea of faces staring down on her in anticipation, she began her song.

I'm a young girl, and have just come over
Over from the country where they do things big

As soon as she started to sing, her confidence began to grow and all her doubts and fears disappeared. She sang with such heart-felt emotion that within seconds she had the audience hanging on her every word. With the first verse completed Rhiannon beckoned with her hand, and the audience, singing very quietly, joined in the chorus — *the boy I love is up in the gallery* — and when the song reached the part — *there he is, can't you see, waving of his handkerchief* — everyone in the auditorium took out a handkerchief and waved it furiously at her. She smiled. She had them! Her aunt had been right; there was no other feeling like it!

201

Once again she focused on the gallery, it was then she thought she spotted a familiar face. She did a double take: it was Frank — Frank Lewis. Rhiannon's heart missed a beat. At long last Frank was here!

With her eyes fixed firmly on Frank who, like all the rest, was smiling and frantically waving his handkerchief, she began the second verse.

When Rhiannon ended the song with the well-rehearsed touch of melodrama, the audience erupted; their applause, whistles and stamping feet seemed to last for ages. Rhiannon glanced towards the orchestra pit, awaiting Adam's signal. He smiled then, a slight nod of his head told her it was time to make her exit. Raising herself up from her curtsy Rhiannon blew a kiss to the audience and sauntered off stage.

As usual most of the girls in the dressing room congratulated her on a job well done. Rhiannon's spirits were high, feeling good about her performance, made even better to think that Frank had been there to see it.

As Rhiannon changed into her street clothes Sally Webber came up to her.

"I don't know whose idea it was to choose that particular song but, if I were you, I'd be prepared for a backlash from Marie Lloyd." Sally Webber sniggered.

"I don't understand. Why would Marie Lloyd concern herself with me?"

"She's the one who made 'The boy I love' famous. I'd not wish to be in your shoes when she gets to hear about it. Her sister's due to appear here tonight, she's sure to tell her."

202

"It's just a song. I'm sure that neither my aunt nor, for that matter, Adam, would have let me sing it if they thought I'd upset anyone."

"We'll see." Sally sneered. Glancing into the mirror, she made a final adjustment to the street-urchin cap on her head and headed for the door.

"Don't let her get to you, I think Nellie Powers sang it long before Marie Lloyd and I'm sure Adam would have asked permission before he let you sing it," Clara offered. "Sally Webber's just out to steal your thunder. You were great and she knows it."

At that moment Percy poked his head around the door. "Rhi, there's a lad asking for you at the stage door, he says he's a friend."

"Yes, thanks Percy. Could you please ask him to wait? I'll be there in five minutes."

"What's this then, Rhi? Have you been hiding a secret admirer?" Clara teased.

"No, don't be daft. His name's Frank. His family lived next door to us up the valley. He's just a friend."

"Yeah, we believe you," one of the chorus girls called, causing titters from all the others.

As Rhiannon made her way to the stage door she could hardly contain her excitement. After all this time Frank was actually here.

"Good afternoon, miss," the doorman said.

"Afternoon," Rhiannon politely answered.

Outside the stage door a small crowd had gathered.

"Well done, Rhiannon," one lad called out.

"Any chance of a private showing, Rhiannon?" another quipped.

"Leave her be," said a stern female voice. Rhiannon looked across to see Mrs Gordon. "Let her pass," the wardrobe mistress commanded. And, as if by magic, the crowd parted.

"Thank you," Rhiannon called.

"That's all right. Wherever you're off to, just don't be late back," Mrs Gordon said.

"I won't be."

Rhiannon spotted Frank leaning up against the wall across from the stage door. He was smoking a cigarette; he looked taller, older and more handsome than she remembered.

His eyes lit up when he saw her.

"Frank! Oh Frank, it's so good to see you."

"You, too," he gushed.

For a moment there was an awkward silence.

"Look, there's a teashop about four doors away, I can't go far, I have to be back for the next show," Rhiannon said.

"That'll be just great. But where's Mair? I thought she'd be with you."

"It's a long story. I'll tell you over a cup of tea."

Rhiannon dreaded having to tell him about Mair. What if he blamed her?

As was usual after a busy show at the theatre, the tearooms were extremely busy; the only unoccupied table, luckily for two, was tucked away in a dark corner. It suited Rhiannon perfectly, providing the privacy she needed to tell Frank about Mair.

Once seated, Frank immediately took charge, ordering a pot of tea for two and an assortment of dainty cakes.

204

"Fancy you on the stage. I thought you were great, a real star, eh?"

"I don't know about that. All I can tell you is that, when I'm performing on stage I'm transported to another world, a world of . . . make believe."

"Is this world so bad, then?"

"Yes-no — oh, I don't know. I thought that coming to Cardiff to be with Aunt Florrie would be the answer to my prayers. Now Florrie has left for America and Mair —"

At that precise moment the waitress arrived to serve their tea. They waited in silence until she'd gone.

"What about Mair? Where is she?" Frank asked.

Taking a deep breath and lowering her voice to almost a whisper, not wanting others to hear the sordid story, she relayed the events leading to Mair's leaving with Nellie and the subsequent disappearance of both of them.

At the end Frank's face looked ashen.

"You're right. There has to be more to it. Nellie must have had an ulterior motive. She is too selfish by far to want to care for Mair."

"Oh Frank. I can't explain why but I have this awful feeling that something terrible might happen to Mair unless I find her soon."

"Look, I've got to go home tonight, my mother's expecting me. But I'll come back next week, book into a boarding house and then I'll be here to help you find Mair."

"But what about your job down the pit?"

"Well, that's just it. That's why I'm here. I came to tell you that my mother and John Jenkins the butcher are to be wed. My mam wants you and Mair to attend the wedding breakfast."

"Aunt Ethel and John Jenkins are to be wed? Well I never."

"I know. Apparently, not long after my dad died, the butcher started calling to the house with a sob story of being let down and having to make his own deliveries. Mam fell for it and not long after they started courting."

"Well, I think it's great news and I wouldn't miss it for the world. I'm so pleased for your mother: such a caring, lovely lady. But what about you? I know how close you were to your dad. So how do you feel about your mam being with someone else?"

"John Jenkins is a good man. As long as he does right by her and the kids, I'm happy for them. They plan to move the family into the house next to the butcher's shop."

"And you?"

"The army. That's the other reason for my being here, I came to enlist. Now that Mam no longer needs the colliery house I'm free to do as I please."

"But the army? Are you sure?"

"Rhi, the day your dad gave his life to save mine, I swore I'd make something of it — to prove that his death —"

"Frank, I never blamed you."

"I know. Anyways, in four weeks' time I'll be Private Frank Lewis and proudly wearing the uniform of the

Volunteer Brigade of the Welsh Regiment. This next week will be my last down the pit. After Friday I'll be free to come to Cardiff. I hate to think of you having to look for Mair on your own."

"Well, actually . . . Gus is helping me."

"Gus? Who's he?"

"Gus Davenport. You saw him on stage tonight. He's the show's master of ceremonies — he's helping me."

"Oh yeah?"

"Yes. And I'll thank you not to suggest there's anything improper. He's been very kind to me. In fact, we've already discovered Nellie's new address. I've arranged to meet Gus tomorrow morning. And, if everything goes to plan, there's every hope that we'll find Mair then."

"Just you be careful. Promise?"

Rhiannon nodded.

They stood outside the tearoom.

"Well this is it, then."

"Oh Frank, I wish you didn't have to go."

"Me too . . ." he hesitated then pulled her to him. "Come here, *cariad*," he said, hugging her.

Rhiannon instinctively snuggled up to him. It felt good to be held in Frank's strong arms, it reminded her of how her dad used to hold her and call her "my lovely girl". Rhiannon gave a deep sigh.

"Come on, Rhi, I'm sure everything will work itself out. I'll be back to see you, and I hope Mair, next Saturday."

"Let's hope so."

★ ★ ★

207

Rhiannon returned to the theatre, passing as she did so the long queue of people outside the theatre who were patiently waiting for the doors to open so that they could take their seats in the auditorium. She felt such a mixture of emotions: sadness at having to say goodbye to Frank after such a brief and, for her, heart-wrenching visit, while at the same time, she was fearful of the outcome of her planned meeting with Gus in the morning and what she'd do if, once again, they failed to find Mair? What confused her most was how, with all this going on, could she manage to feel such excitement at the prospect of once again performing her act for the second show? But as Adam had, as Gus had once suggested, shortened the interval to accommodate her song, the thought of appearing in the same show as Alice Lloyd made everything else pale into insignificance.

As Rhiannon made her way to the dressing-room she accidentally bumped into Adam who was heading the other way.

"Hey, watch where you're going, young lady."

"I'm sorry. My mind's all over the place."

"That'll be with excitement, then, eh?"

"Yes, something like that."

"There's a packed house tonight. Ever since the advertisement appeared in the *South Wales Echo*, announcing the opening night for Alice Lloyd, the box office has been rushed off its feet."

Rhiannon grimaced. "I can't believe that I'm actually appearing on the same bill as Miss Alice Lloyd. And, if I'm honest, I find it all a bit scary."

"Well you shouldn't. If you perform as well as you did for the matinée, you'll set the standard and might even give Miss Alice Lloyd food for thought."

"I doubt that, but I can't wait to see her. Gus has already told me what a class act she is."

"Listen, Rhi, you can tell me to mind my own business, but what's the deal between you and Gus? You seem very . . . close, of late."

"We're friends, that's all. What are you implying?"

"Nothing, it's just . . . well, as Gus and I are related I feel I know him than better most. I know what a charmer he can be, so you just watch your step, eh?"

"If you know something —"

"No-no. Look, I must go. Have a great show."

The evening show at the Empire was a complete sell-out; the stalls and circle were packed with an older, more sophisticated audience than usual, all dressed in their finery: ladies in elaborate hats and elegant gowns, accompanied by gentlemen dressed in tail-coats and top hats. Of course the gallery was still full of ordinary folk, but even they had taken the trouble to don their Sunday best. It made the whole theatre experience somehow . . . more special.

Rhiannon, spurred on by Adam's words of encouragement earlier, walked on stage determined to give the performance of her life. It worked. Her performance had the audience calling out for more . . . she left the stage . . . their applause still ringing in her ears.

After Rhi's performance Sally Webber's street urchin went down well with the audience. Only when the applause had subsided did Gus take to the stage. It was time for Miss Alice Lloyd.

"My lords, ladies and gentleman, be prepared to be transported to another world . . . a world of beauty . . . a world of sublime enchantment . . ." he paused, determined to keep this audience and the rest of the cast, all watching from the wings, in suspense for as long as he could . . . "It's with great pleasure that I present to you the fabulously talented, international star . . . I give you —" he turned his back on the audience. As the heavy gold-and-red brocade stage curtain slowly rose up to give everyone their first glimpse of her, Gus announced with great gusto, "Miss Alice Lloyd!" The audience erupted into great applause in anticipation of a memorable performance.

In the end, no one was disappointed. Like Florrie Grayson before her, Alice Lloyd had real star quality. She commanded the audience's attention, and they loved every minute of it.

At the end of the show, Alice Lloyd led all the cast into the grand finale. As the orchestra loudly played a medley of songs from the show, Alice Lloyd turned and, reaching for Rhiannon's hand, pulled her to stand next to her at the front of the stage.

Alice Lloyd moved closer. "Congratulations, my dear. I would never have believed that anyone, especially someone as young as you, could do justice to that song. But you did. Well done. I know my sister will be as touched as I am."

"Thank you. You're . . . too . . . kind." Rhiannon's voice cracked with emotion.

When Alice Lloyd leaned over and kissed Rhiannon's cheek the audience went wild, aware that tonight they'd witnessed not one, but two "star" performances. With all the excitement Rhiannon was entirely unaware of the venomous looks Sally Webber was giving her.

"We're all going to the Lounge Bar after the show. Do you fancy joining us for a celebratory drink?" Gus asked. Beaming a smile, he added, "It's not every day that 'a star is born'."

Rhiannon blushed.

"Save the blushes. You must know how good you are," he teased.

Rhiannon didn't know what to say, she really was embarrassed, ill at ease with receiving compliments.

"If you like I'll walk you back to Mrs Gordon's boarding house later?"

"How did you know I'd moved?" she asked.

"It's hard to keep a secret from us theatre folk. Mind you, I did call in the girls' dressing-room to congratulate you after the matinée and Clara was acting very mysterious. When I asked her where you were, all she said was, 'wouldn't you like to know?'"

"There's no mystery. I had a visitor. An old friend from up the valley — he took me out for tea."

"He? And how old exactly is this 'old' friend?"

"Frank? I'm not sure, eighteen or nineteen, I think. He worked alongside my dad. My dad —" Rhiannon was about to tell him the story of how her dad had saved Frank's life, but Gus cut her short.

"Look, forget tonight. I'll call for you around eleven in the morning." With that he was gone.

For a while Rhiannon didn't move, puzzled at Gus's sudden mood change. What could she have said to upset him?

CHAPTER
EIGHTEEN

June 1909

It was a beautiful sunny day when, just after eleven on Sunday morning, Gus and Rhiannon patiently hid in a side alley across the road from what they believed to be Harry and Nellie's address. They waited for what seemed like an age. Suddenly there they were, all dressed up in their Sunday best, leaving their digs and heading in the direction of the King's Head.

"That's them. Stand back. Wait until they're out of sight," Gus instructed.

Rhiannon did as he bid. She shut her eyes as if, somehow, not being able to see somehow decreased the chance of being seen.

Gus took her arm. "Come on. They've turned the corner. The coast is clear, let's go."

They entered the apartment building and climbed the stairs.

"This is it, 21A," Gus said.

Rhiannon banged on the door. "Mair! Mair! It's me. Open the door!"

"Rhi? Oh Rhi . . . is it really you?" Mair's voice sounded desperate.

"Yes-yes, love, I'm here, and I've brought a friend. We've come to help you. Open the door!"

"Rhi, I can't. It's locked."

"What do you mean, locked? Just get the key and open it!"

"You don't understand. Harry and Nellie have the only keys. They keep me locked up. Please, Rhi, you've got to get me away from them." Mair was sobbing.

"Gus, what can we do?" Rhiannon pleaded.

"I'm afraid I'm totally stumped. The door's too solid to kick down. I can't believe those evil bastards. Fancy locking her in like this."

"Gus, we've got to do something?" Rhiannon pleaded.

"Rhi," Mair called, "I must get away before next Saturday night! Rhi — you don't know what they've got planned for me."

"Tell me." Rhi urged.

"I-I can't. It-it's too awful."

"Listen, Mair. You don't know me but my name is Gus and I'm a friend of Rhiannon's. Mair, if we're to help you, you've got to tell us."

Mair stayed silent.

"Mair please . . . I beg you," Rhiannon coaxed.

"They plan to s-sell me t-to the highest b-bidder," Mair's frightened voice stammered.

"Sell you? What do you mean, sell you?" Rhiannon demanded.

This time there was no answer from Mair, just the sound of her muffled sobs.

Taking Rhiannon's arm Gus pulled her to him, his warm lips pressed against her ear. "Rhi, she's a young virgin, I think it may be their intention to sell her to the highest bidder," he whispered.

214

Rhiannon caught her breath. "No! Not that? I can't believe that even they would —"

"Believe it," Gus said.

Rhiannon's eyes filled with tears. "Mair, my love, don't worry. We'll think of something. And whatever happens, I promise to have you out of there before next Saturday!"

"Rhi, I've an idea that I think could work," Gus whispered.

"What is it? Tell me?" Rhiannon urged.

"We need to find Adam. Then, if he agrees, and if we're quick, I'll still have time to get to the King's Head before Harry and Nellie leave for home."

"Adam? What's Adam's part in this? I don't understand."

"It will soon become clear. Now, come on. We really must get a move on." Rhiannon hesitated, loath to leave Mair, but she trusted Gus; if he had a plan that would free Mair from Harry and Nellie's clutches, she needed to go with him.

"Mair, love," Rhiannon called softly through the door. "We've got to go now. But take heart. We'll be back before Saturday, I promise."

"We'll head for Adam's house. Just keep your fingers crossed that he'll be in; it's our only chance."

Rhiannon sensed the urgency in his voice and asked, "Is it far?"

"No. Only a ten-minute walk."

Adam's house was a large, detached Victorian, city-centre property overlooking the beautiful Sophia Gardens.

If Adam was surprised to see Rhiannon with Gus he didn't show it.

"What a pleasant surprise. Please come in."

They entered the spacious hallway behind Adam and followed him into the parlour. "This is something of an occasion. I think it may call for a glass of sherry. Gus would you do the honours?"

"I'm afraid that, as pleasant as that would be, there's no time," Gus urged.

"I'm intrigued. What's the big rush?"

"Adam? We need a big favour," Gus said.

"What sort of a favour? Gus, if you've . . ." he threw Gus a challenging look, then turned to Rhiannon, "Rhiannon, are you in some sort of trouble?"

"No. It's my stepsister, Mair," Rhiannon assured him.

Adam shook his head. "I don't understand."

"If you'll be quiet and stop that overactive mind of yours jumping to the wrong conclusion, I'll explain," Gus said.

"All right, but this had better be good," Adam warned.

Gus, keeping it short, relayed Mair's story.

"I see. I'm sorry Gus, I thought —"

"I know what you thought."

"So what can I do to help?"

"Well, I've this idea. I'm sure that if we could raise enough money between us, I might be able to persuade the unscrupulous pair to release Mair."

"How much money are we talking about here?" Adam asked.

"Well, I can get my hands on one hundred pounds. I thought that, if you could match it, then two hundred pounds should do the trick," Gus replied.

Adam nodded. "It may take me a few days but I'm sure I can do that."

"Gus. Adam. No! I couldn't possibly let you do this. It's such a lot of money. It would take me ages to pay you back," Rhiannon argued.

"Rhiannon, be sensible. Don't let your silly pride stop you accepting our help. After all, what's money compared with saving an innocent child from some degenerate?" Adam urged.

"Put like that, I suppose —"

"That's settled then. Now, Rhi, you stay here with Adam while I get myself down to the King's Head. With a bit of luck Harry and Nellie will still be there and I can get this matter sorted out, once and for all."

"I'm coming with you: safety in numbers and all that. Rhi, you just make yourself at home. We'll not be gone long." Adam smiled.

"Thank you both. Good luck," Rhi called, as she watched them leave the house.

The two men entered the King's Head pub and, with Gus leading the way, pushed their way through the lively crowds in the bar area. There was no sign of Harry and Nellie, so Gus headed towards the snug and, opening the door, heard Nellie jibe, "Well, if it isn't our Rhiannon's fancy man."

She and Harry were seated, with beer tankards in hand, surrounded by their cronies in the corner of the snug.

Gus, closely followed by Adam, edged his way to their table.

"I need a word in private," Gus announced.

"In private, you say? Now what would that be about, then, eh?"

"Do you really want me to discuss your plans for Rhiannon's stepsister right here, right now?" Gus said warningly.

"Go on, Harry, take them outside to the back yard; they're fair turning my beer sour."

Harry stood up. "I suppose out back to the privy wouldn't hurt." He gave a loud belch. "As it happens, I could do with a piss."

Harry led the way and, on reaching the dilapidated outbuildings that served as toilets, turned to face Gus and Adam.

"Well? What's this you've heard about Nellie's daughter, then?"

"I've heard there's to be an auction." Gus said.

"If what you've heard is true, what's it to do with you?"

"I-we are here to make you an offer. And if you've got any sense you'll take it." Gus tried to stay calm.

"An offer, is it? Now there's a thing. What's the matter? Rhiannon getting too old for you, eh?"

Gus made to lunge at Harry, but Adam pulled him back. "Don't, Gus, he's not worth it."

"Look, we haven't met before, but my friend and I have a proposition I think you might find interesting," Adam offered.

"All right, I'm listening. What's the proposition?"

"We're here to offer you, and Mair's mother, the princely sum of two hundred pounds, we —" Adam was cut off in mid-sentence.

218

"What's the catch?" a woman's loud voice called from behind.

Adam and Gus both swung round and saw Nellie standing in the doorway with hands on hips.

Gus struggled to hold his temper. He so wanted to give this woman a piece of his mind, yet instinctively he was aware that now was not the right time. "No catch," he said through gritted teeth. "All you have to do is hand over Mair, together with a signed statement giving Rhiannon sole responsibility for her future care and upbringing."

Nellie sniggered. "Two hundred pounds, you say?"

"Yes, I'm sure it's more than you could possibly get if you were to proceed with this immoral auction."

Gus's gaze followed Nellie as she sidled over to Harry. "What you say to this then, Harry love?"

"I say it all depends." He looked over at the two men. "If, and only *if*, I were to agree, when would we see the colour of your money?"

"All we need is a few days to secure the funds. How does five o'clock Friday evening sound?"

"Where would we meet?"

"We'd pick Mair up from your digs."

Harry looked surprised. "Know where I live then, do you?"

"Oh yes, we know where you've been keeping Mair, locked up like a caged animal."

"How do I know you won't bring the rozzers?" Harry asked.

"Believe me, if I thought calling the police would help, I might consider it," Gus snapped.

219

Harry laughed aloud. "Why, the police would be more likely to cop the pair of you for wasting their time. You see, we've not done anything against the law. Mair's Nellie's daughter, so it's our word against yours."

"Of course, you're right. Who'd believe that a mother could stoop this low?"

"You think you're so high and mighty, don't you?" Nellie spat.

"That's enough," Harry ordered. "All right, you're on. Two hundred pounds, five o'clock Friday, it is. Don't be late." Harry began urgently unbuttoning his flies. "Now will you all bugger off? As I said — I need a piss."

CHAPTER
NINETEEN

Harry and Nellie, having treated themselves to a few extra drinks on the strength of their promised two-hundred-pound windfall, left the King's Head feeling even more tipsy than usual.

"Harry, love, why didn't you make it known in the pub that the — you know — the auction thing — was off?" Nellie slurred her words as she hung on to Harry's arm for support,

"Off? Who says it's off?"

"But I thought . . ."

"Well, you thought wrong. It's not off. It's just a simple case of bringing it forward a day, that's all."

"B-but Harry, now that we're to have two hundred pounds, we don't need to —"

Harry's hand whipped across Nellie's face. "Since when do you tell me what we do and do not need, eh? I say we bring it forward. That way we'll get double money, do you hear?"

"Sorry, Harry," Nellie whimpered, her hand holding her burning cheek.

"That's better. As I see it, the deal is to hand Mair over to them on Friday evening. This I intend to do, just slightly damaged." Harry laughed. "If those jumped-up toffs think to get the better of Harry Stone they've another think coming. Now, get a move on. I hope the young 'un has cooked us something good, I'm starving."

Mair's spirits had lifted. How could she have ever doubted Rhiannon? When Nellie boasted about the fifty-pound pay-off for Florrie Grayson to be rid of her, and, fuelled by Nellie's constant jibes about her stepsister being selfish and only thinking of number one, Mair assumed that Rhiannon must have been party to it. But, on reflection, how, with no forwarding address, could Rhiannon have possibly found her? Mair had surely done her stepsister an injustice.

For weeks Mair had been dreading the moment when Harry and Nellie would leave her at the mercy of some stranger, willing to pay to have his way with her.

When Mair pleaded for Nellie's help, her reply had been, "I don't know what all the fuss is about. I lost my virginity at the back of Carne Terrace to a lecherous old bugger, a supposed friend of my father, who promised to look after me. Of course he'd lied. I didn't get a penny. Then there was your Jack-the-lad father; promised me the world he did, only to join the army and turn his back on us. In hindsight, I should have listened to my parents and got rid of you. Don't look at me like that! You should try bringing up a young 'un on your own! At least this way there'll be money in the bank."

That was the day Mair ceased even to think of Nellie as her mother. What mother would agree to set her daughter up for this? No, from now on Mair would only ever think of her as Nellie Parsons.

222

Now, against all odds, Rhiannon had not only found her, but had promised to get her away before Saturday.

Mair heard the door being unlocked. Harry and Nellie were home. Judging by the way they practically fell in the door, they were obviously the worse for drink.

"Well hello, you conniving little bitch, you. Got something to tell us then, eh? Had any visitors?" Harry lunged towards her.

"No — no," Mair said, stepping out of his way.

Harry continued to lunge forward. Almost losing his footing, he made a grab for the chair to steady himself. "Don't lie to me girl! Tell her Nellie. Tell her how we came to be talking to Rhiannon's two sugar-daddies back at the King's Head."

"It's true, Mair. You'd best come clean," Nellie urged.

"I . . . I —" Mair hesitated.

"The truth now, or as sure as my name's Harry Stone, I'll give you the hiding of a lifetime," he growled.

"Please, Mair. Tell him the truth," Nellie pleaded.

"Yes, all right. Just after you both left for the pub Rhiannon and a man did come to the door."

"And you — you couldn't wait to tell them 'bout our little arrangement, could you?"

"No . . . yes! I told them everything and Rhiannon has promised to have me away from here before — before Saturday — so there!" Mair blurted out.

Harry slumped in the chair. "At last the truth. Well done."

Mair was confused. Why was he taking it so calmly?

"Well, the good news is that your precious Rhiannon was also speaking the truth," Harry mocked.

"She was?"

"Oh yes. Your mother and I have agreed to let you go. We think it's for the best. Don't we, Nell?" He looked towards Nellie and smirked. "Anyway, truth be known, you're cramping our style."

"Mam — Nellie. Is this right? Am I really going back to stay with Rhiannon?"

"Y-yes, it's all arranged. They're coming for you at five o'clock on Friday evening." Nellie avoided meeting Mair's eyes.

Mair looked skyward, "Oh thank you, Lord, thank you!"

"Now, what is it the Bible says? Oh yes, the Lord giveth and the Lord taketh way." Harry smirked. "Now, enough of that. Let's eat."

Gus and Adam returned to the house.

Rhiannon greeted them at the door. "Well?" she asked, in eager anticipation.

"Good news. It's all settled, we've arranged to pay them the money," Gus said.

"They agreed?" Rhiannon shook her head in disbelief, "When? Where?"

"It's true. The two hundred pounds definitely did the trick. They've agreed and we've arranged to pick up Mair, together with a written statement giving you full parental control for your stepsister's well-being, from their digs at five o'clock Friday evening," Adam assured her.

"Oh Gus — Adam . . . thank you so much. It may take me a while but I promise to repay you every penny."

"Not necessary, glad to be of assistance," Adam insisted. Then, walking towards the spacious kitchen area, he said, "Hey, something smells good."

"I hope you don't mind. Waiting here on my own, I needed a distraction. I took the liberty of raiding your larder and managed to cook a corned-beef pie."

"Great. I do believe I've just the bottle of wine to wash it down with. Come on let's eat and raise a glass to celebrate a successful result of our day's endeavour," Adam said.

They ate their meal sitting around the large kitchen table. When they had finished Gus and Adam enjoyed a cigar and a glass of port, while Rhiannon busied herself clearing away.

"There's really no need for you to do that," Adam said, "Gus and I are quite capable, you know."

"No, please. I want to," Rhiannon insisted. Spending the day in Adam's house had made a welcome change from life in a hotel and boarding house. It felt real; she'd missed being able to prepare and cook home-made food.

"I for one won't stop you spoiling us; being greeted with such a warm welcome, home-cooked food and clearing away to boot. We could get used to this, hey Adam?" Gus teased.

"Yes, but sadly, I don't think we stand a chance. I'm sure this budding star is destined for greater things." Adam raised his glass of port. "To Rhiannon!"

Gus followed suit.

Rhiannon felt her colour rise.

The clock struck six o'clock.

"It's getting late. I'd better be off, before Mrs Gordon and her sister send a search party."

The men stood up from the table.

"I'll walk you back," Gus offered.

"There's no need, really," Rhiannon said.

"There's every need," Adam insisted. "Can't have you wandering the streets of Cardiff on your own. Gus, you make sure to deliver her safely home, do you hear?"

"Trust me. She'll be safe with me."

Did Rhiannon imagine a stern look pass between the two men?

"Goodnight, Rhi. See you at tomorrow morning's band call. Half past ten sharp. Don't be late!"

"I'll be there. And Adam, thanks again." Rhiannon reached up and kissed his cheek.

Adam took her hand and gently brushed his lips across her palm. "My pleasure," he whispered.

"All right, where's mine?" Gus teased.

Adam, taking Gus's hand, immediately kissed the back of it.

Rhiannon laughed. "You two are quite mad!"

As Gus led the way down the hall she noticed him hesitate, then, almost as if it were some sort of secret, deftly remove a set of keys from a hook near the front door and place them in his waistcoat pocket.

"Catch you later," Gus called to Adam.

★　★　★

226

The first two weeks in June brought the hottest weather of the year, and the early-evening sky, aglow with red tinges, promised yet another fine day tomorrow.

"Oh Gus, I feel so happy. I can't explain the turmoil my mind's been in over the last few weeks. Pleased as I've been with the way my career has progressed, the nagging guilt about Mair has left this gaping hole — my Aunt Florrie and Walter's sudden departure didn't help. It just brought home to me how utterly alone I am."

Gus stopped and caught her around the waist, pulling her to him. "My dear, dear Rhi. Please believe me when I tell you that you're not alone. I'm here for you. Rhiannon, you must know how I feel about you?"

"I-I wasn't sure."

Gus leant down and kissed her. Rhiannon eagerly returned his kiss. It felt so good to be in his arms once again. He responded tenderly, brushing his lips across her face, her cheeks, her ears and then her neck, before returning to kiss her lips again and again, each time with heightened passion.

Rhiannon felt light-headed, she swayed gently. Maybe the two glasses of wine she'd had with the meal had not been such a good idea after all.

Gus supported her, holding her, kissing her. How many nights while lying in her bed had she dreamt of this moment?

"Oh Rhi — listen. I'd like to take you somewhere special. What do you say?"

While Rhiannon's heart yearned to say yes, her head said otherwise. She so wanted to be with him. Yet in the end she heard herself say, "Gus, it's getting late. I really should be heading back to my digs."

"Is that what you really want?" He kissed her again. This time it was a long, lingering and passionate kiss.

Rhiannon trembled.

"Are you cold?" Gus whispered.

"Not really. It's just — with all that's happened today."

"And it's not over yet. Rhiannon, do you trust me?"

"Yes, of course I do."

"Then what's the matter?" He didn't wait for an answer. He simply took her hand.

"Where are we going?"

"A slight detour, it's a surprise."

She hesitated.

"Come on, it'll not take long. Where's your sense of adventure?" He led her swiftly, weaving his way through the city's back streets, most of which she hadn't known existed.

Rhiannon felt so happy to be with this dream man; if the truth be known, she would have followed him anywhere. How much better could the day get?

Much to her surprise, they arrived at the stage door.

"Gus, what are we doing at the theatre? It's Sunday night. The theatre's closed."

Gus smiled, before removing a set of keys from his waistcoat pocket. He dangled them in front of her for a second, then unlocked the stage door.

"The theatre might be closed but," he pushed the stage door open, "hey presto — we're in!"

"Gus. We shouldn't," Rhi whispered.

"Oh yes, we should. Follow me." Gus led her through the stage door.

As expected, it was very dark inside. "If we follow the wall around, I know where the junction box is for the new emergency lights.

Rhiannon followed him gingerly. Aware of his hand reaching above her, she heard him pull a lever and, as if by magic, the dim lights came on.

"Gus, what are we doing here?"

"Be patient, it'll soon become crystal clear," he whispered.

As he expertly negotiated the maze that was backstage, they eventually ended up standing in the wings. She couldn't fail to be impressed.

Gus slowly led her on stage. Stepping away, he left her.

For a few moments she stood, overcome with emotion, in awe of her surroundings. She was looking out to the vast, dimly lit auditorium; it was silent, yet eerie. She breathed in the mixed aromas of greasepaint, heady perfume, cigar smoke and stale beer that filled the air.

"Gus? Where are you?" she nervously whispered.

"I'm up here," she heard him call.

Glancing up at the gallery, she saw his faint outline.

"Well, go on. What are you waiting for? I want you to sing to me." Gus called.

Rhiannon giggled. "You're quite mad."

"Go on. Consider it a 'private performance' just for me."

She smiled. After all he'd done for her, why not?

Taking a deep breath she began, her voice echoing around the empty auditorium, and when she came to the chorus, "The boy I love is up in the gallery," as if on cue, Gus frantically waved his handkerchief.

At the end of the song Rhiannon made an elaborate curtsy and waited for his applause. There was none. She looked up at the gallery only to find him gone. She felt a sinking feeling in her stomach. Where was he? What would she do if he'd left her? "Gus!" she frantically called out. The silence seemed endless.

"Yes-yes, my love, I'm here," he said, walking out from the shadow of the wings. As he reached her, his arm encircled her waist, pulling her to him.

She fell against him. Their kissing was more passionate than ever before. Lifting her into his arms, as if she were but a feather, he carried her off stage towards the dressing-rooms.

With her arms wrapped firmly around his neck, wherever he was taking her at that precise moment was all right with her. She never wanted this feeling . . . this longing . . . to end.

With one hand Gus opened the door of the "star" dressing-room, and carried her in.

It was so dark she couldn't see a hand in front of her. But, remembering the days spent in this very room when Aunt Florrie had held "star" spot, she, like Gus, knew only too well where the *chaise-longue* was situated. So, when he laid her down, the softness of the familiar plush velvet material seemed to embrace her.

230

Gus lay next to her. She felt his hands sensuously explore her back, her neck, her arms . . . her breast. She didn't make any attempt to stop him. It felt too good.

"If you'd like me to light the gas lamps, just say," Gus whispered.

Rhiannon knew she should have insisted that he did. Insist that he must stop fondling her . . . insist that he took her home . . . but instead she quietly whispered, "No-no."

"My darling Rhi." His mouth found hers and Rhiannon knew that their passion could no longer be denied. He loved her and she loved him. Surely that was all that mattered? As they urgently fumbled to undress one another, they both seemed reluctant to release each other from their passionate kisses. Then, as their bodies connected, he whispered, "My love. I promise to be gentle." And then they became as one.

True to his word and aware it was her first time, Gus was a gentle, considerate and, she sensed, an experienced lover. Any nerves or inhibition she might previously have felt were soon replaced by the urgent longing for his closeness — his touch — his all.

When it was over, Gus continued to hold her. For a while they just lay there, neither wishing to spoil the moment.

It was Rhiannon who eventually broke the silence. "Gus, I really should be getting back. I dread to think what trouble I'm in."

Gus quickly rose to his feet.

"Yes, of course, what must I have been thinking of? Come on, I'll walk you back to your digs."

"Thanks. But don't you think we should get dressed first?" Rhiannon giggled.

They both laughed, each aware of a new intimacy.

Rhiannon, sensing his naked body standing next to her, felt her colour rise, though she felt no embarrassment at what had gone between them and had no regrets.

When they were dressed, Gus took Rhiannon's hand, led her from the dressing-room and back to the stage door. Once outside Gus carefully locked up and replaced the keys in his waistcoat pocket.

Before moving off Gus pulled her to him. "Any regrets?"

Rhiannon vigorously shook her head. "Have you?" she asked.

"Me? How could I possibly regret making love to such an adorable, gorgeous, loving creature?"

"Gus, you know I love you. Don't you?"

"I'm sure you *think* you do. I just wish I'd met you . . . Rhi . . .?"

"Yes?" Rhiannon sensed he wanted to tell her something important . . . a secret maybe?

His eyes looked desperate.

"What is it, Gus?" she urged.

He shook his head. "It's nothing. I agree, we really should get a move on. I dread to think what sort of reception we'll get from your landladies when we get back."

Rhiannon wished that instead of fobbing her off he'd said what was really on his mind. Could what he had failed to say have been so bad? Maybe he was trying to tell her that he didn't love her and their intimacy had, for him, been just another encounter. Was that it? And if so, would she ever know?

Although they walked hand in hand, Rhiannon felt a rift between them. Their earlier closeness had been severed by . . . what? She didn't know.

They were nearly at her digs.

"Here goes, it's time to face the music. I think we should keep it brief. All we need to say is that Adam and I talked you into staying for dinner and we simply lost track of the time. I don't think we should mention stopping off at the theatre. That'll be our little secret, don't you agree?" Gus fidgeted, as if embarrassed.

Rhiannon sensed he wanted to be rid of her. "Y-yes, I'm sure that would be for the best. Look, on second thoughts, there's no need for you to walk me to the door. I'd rather face them alone. Of course I'll make sure they know you walked me home, but I think it best if we part here."

He didn't argue, he just said, "All right, if you're sure?" He bent over and placed a friendly kiss on her cheek. "I'll see you tomorrow. Let me know how you get on. And Rhi, sleep well. Mair's going to be fine."

As he turned to leave Rhi bit her lip. "Thank you," she whispered.

She felt confused, had she imagined him cooling towards her?

CHAPTER
TWENTY

Rhiannon reached the front door of her digs and, taking a deep breath, was just about to knock and face the music when she heard a voice.

"Rhi, I'm up here!"

Rhiannon looked up to see Clara hanging out of the second-storey window.

"Rhi, I've been waiting ages. Where the hell have you been? Whatever you do don't knock on the door. Mrs Gordon's on the warpath — she sent her sister to bed hours ago. Stay where you are and, I'll sneak down to let you in."

Minutes later Clara opened the door and, holding a flickering candle in one hand, beckoned Rhiannon in with the other. "Shhhh, the old dragon's lying in wait in the dining-room. Take your boots off, we need to tiptoe across the hall and up the stairs," Clara whispered.

As she bent down to untie her boots, Rhiannon's heart was in her mouth. What if they were caught? Kind as Clara was, it just wouldn't be fair to get her into trouble, and maybe thrown out of the digs for something Rhiannon had done.

"Well now, what's going on here?" a stern voice demanded.

Rhiannon immediately stood up to see Mrs Gordon, also with a burning candle in hand, standing in the hallway.

Quick as a flash, Clara piped up, "I came down to answer the door and, lo and behold, there was Rhiannon."

"Is that so? Well maybe you can explain how I didn't hear this 'phantom' knock?"

Clara scrunched up her shoulders. "I really don't know. But —"

"All right, that will do. It's late — much too late for mysteries. I think it best if you two get yourselves off to bed." Mrs Gordon walked over to Rhiannon, "And, as for you, young lady, I shall deal with you in the morning. At this moment I can't tell you what a disappointment you are to me. I dread to think what your Aunt Florrie would make of you coming in at this ungodly hour."

"Sorry, Mrs Gordon."

"As I said, we shall talk in the morning. Now follow me." With that, she turned on her heel and led the way across the hall and up the stairs.

Mrs Gordon left them on the landing outside their respective bedroom doors. "I'll thank you to take to your beds, do you hear?"

"Yes, Mrs Gordon," the girls answered in unison.

When Mrs Gordon was safely out of the way Rhiannon unlocked her bedroom door and entered her room, closely followed by Clara who proceeded to light the gas lamp on the writing-desk.

"That went well. At least we managed to postpone Mrs Gordon's wrath until the morning. Enough time for you to think up a feasible story, eh? That said, having stuck my neck out for you, I'll take no less than the truth. So, where the hell did you get to tonight?"

"Oh Clara, what a day I've had. I didn't tell you before, in case it all went terribly wrong but, we've found Mair and, if all goes well, we should have her back by Friday." Rhiannon's excitement was obvious.

"That's great news. And would Gus Davenport be the other half of the 'we' you refer to, by any chance?" Clara asked.

"Well, yes." Rhiannon, puzzled by Clara's look of disapproval quickly added, "Gus and Adam have both helped me so much. That's why I'm late back. Adam invited me to stay for a meal at his house."

"Doesn't Gus live there too?"

"Yes. The three of us had a meal and a drink to celebrate Mair's impending return."

"And . . . after the meal? I don't have to guess who put that look in your eyes?"

"Look? What look?"

"The look that tells me you've come of age. Got something to tell me, eh?"

Rhiannon felt her colour rise as she cast her gaze to the floor.

"No. Well let me guess. I bet Gus Davenport, ever the gentleman, offered to walk you home and on the way, made a pass. I can see it now. It's common knowledge how persuasive our Gus can be. And you,

236

obviously flattered by having such an attractive man fawn over you, fell for his charms."

"It wasn't like that! Yes we did . . . but I love him and he —"

"He what? Oh Rhi, I should have seen this coming and warned you. I've known Gus Davenport for a long while. Please believe me when I say you're not the first to succumb to his charms and you probably won't be the last. I just hope that what you two did tonight doesn't result in your ending up in the family way, because one thing's for sure, Gus Davenport is not the marrying kind."

"How can you say such a nasty thing? I thought you were my friend."

"I am. That's why —"

Rhiannon raised her hand. "No! I think you've said more than enough. I'd like you to go now. I need to be alone."

Gus entered Adam's house. He walked across the hall and deftly replaced the theatre keys on the hook before entering the parlour.

Adam, relaxing in armchair by the fireplace, looked up from *The Times* newspaper. "So you're back, then? Good night, was it?" Adam snapped.

"Yes. Rhi is safely delivered to her digs. I shouldn't think she'll be in too much trouble. We both know that Mrs Gordon's a softie at heart. I told Rhiannon to blame us, to say that we insisted she stayed for a meal and the time just —" He was about to elaborate when Adam interrupted.

"Stop off anywhere on the way, did you?"

"No-no, why do you ask?"

Adam leapt from his chair. "You're a lying swine! Did you really think I wouldn't notice the theatre keys missing from the hook?"

"Look, Uncle Adam, you don't understand —"

"Oh yes, I do. And don't Uncle Adam me! What was I thinking? Trusting you, who's never been known to miss an opportunity for a dalliance with a pretty young girl? I stupidly believed that your feelings towards Rhi were different, that you truly cared for her, but all the while you were nursing your usual schemes."

"It wasn't like that," Gus protested.

"No? I don't believe you. We both know how indebted she felt concerning the money we put up for Mair's safe return. Well, it didn't take you long to find a way for her to repay you, eh?"

"I can see how it might look. I'm only too aware of what an uncaring bastard I've been in the past. But Rhiannon — you're right — Rhiannon is different."

"Who are you trying to fool? It might work on a vulnerable young girl, but I for one am having none of it! First thing in the morning I intend to do what I should have done weeks ago: tell her about what happened to Helena Biggins and how, like now, all you were interested in was having your fun and to hell with the consequences. I did try to warn you that, like most girls, Helena wanted more — but would you listen? And when you'd done with her and moved on to your next conquest —"

"I never, not for one moment, thought she'd take her own life."

"That's your trouble. You never bloody well think! You just let your dick rule your brain. When that young girl took her own life I felt partly to blame for not warning her off you. Well, it'll not happen again —"

"Adam. Please. I beg you. Please don't spoil my chances with Rhiannon. I want —"

"I don't particularly care what you want. I want you out of my house, out of the theatre and out of my life!"

"I can see there's no reasoning with you. If that's what you want, I'll leave in the morning."

"No. Not in the morning. I want you out of here tonight! And I'll thank you to leave your keys to the front door."

Gus awoke with a headache; he'd had too much whisky the night before. Having just managed to throw some clothes and toiletries into a suitcase, he'd left Adam's house and booked into the Angel Hotel for the night. For as long as he had known him, he had never seen his uncle so upset. When Gus had been ten, after the tragedy of losing both parents in a house fire, Adam had taken him in. Since then Adam had been his rock; so dependable and non-judgemental; a perfect friend as well as uncle.

Gus knew only too well how his casual, uncaring use of the many women he'd encountered over the years had left him with something of a reputation. A reputation that, up until now, he'd enjoyed, believing as he did that most of the women who succumbed to his charms all knew where they stood. What they saw was what they got. Which was why he'd been so shocked by what had happened to Helena Biggins. Gus had thought she understood the rules: to have fun with no commitment and no strings. When Adam had tried to warn him off Gus hadn't listened. Now Adam was going to tell Rhiannon about all of Gus's past misdemeanours and of the callous way he'd treated Helena Biggins . . . and its dire consequence. Gus was in no doubt that when she found out what type of man he was, she would turn against him.

The irony of the situation was not lost on Gus, for his feelings for Rhiannon were so very different from those he'd had for any other woman. For a long time he'd tried to deny the way he felt about her, telling himself that it was just another of his dalliances, but tonight after their shared intimacy he knew what he felt for her was different: he truly loved her. She was like a breath of fresh air and he loved everything about her: from the way her unruly chestnut hair fell on her small shoulders, her slim yet well-formed tight little figure, to her shapely legs, right down to her tiny feet; she was a perfect package of innocent beauty. Oh yes, he was well and truly smitten.

Gus had thought of going back to Adam's, to plead his case one more time but, remembering the grim determination on his uncle's face he knew how futile it would be. No, there was only one thing he could do. The time had come for him to move away. The thought of Rhiannon not seeing him in a good light, maybe even hating him, would be too much to bear.

240

"Mrs Gordon, forgive me for calling at such an early hour," Adam apologized, "but I really need to clarify what really happened — to explain the reason for Rhiannon's late return."

"Well, I must say, I expected better from you."

"It really was my fault. I'm afraid I got carried away, discussing new shows and the possibility of Rhiannon joining our next tour. I should have realized the time. I'm sure you of all people are aware of what an exciting new talent she really is?"

"More reason to keep her feet firmly on the ground, I say. It wouldn't do to put too many high ideas into such a young head. I'm all for nurturing new talent, but not at the cost of one's sense of decency and decorum."

"Quite. Have you spoken to Rhiannon yet?"

"No, not yet. I've asked her to meet me here in the parlour after she's had her breakfast."

"I wonder . . . would you mind if I joined you? There are a few changes to the scheduled performance that I think you both should know about before the band-call."

Rhiannon gave a light tap on the parlour door; it was time to face Mrs Gordon.

"Come in," Mrs Gordon called.

Rhiannon entered and was surprised to see Adam Fletcher seated alongside Mrs Gordon. On seeing her he rose to his feet. "Good morning Rhiannon," he said.

"Adam — Mr Fletcher, I didn't expect to see you here."

"Mr Fletcher came to explain how your late return last night was entirely his fault. I have accepted his apology on the understanding that it will not happen again."

Rhiannon's eyes met Adam's; she hoped he would see in hers her heartfelt thanks for taking the blame. Turning to Mrs Gordon, she said, "Thank you for being so understanding, I promise it'll not happen again."

"Good. Now let that be the end of it. Mr Fletcher, you mentioned a change in schedule?"

"Yes, Mrs Gordon. Rhiannon, it'll soon become common knowledge but I wanted you to be the first to know that Gus Davenport has left the company. I —"

"Gus has left? When? Where? Why?"

"Miss Hughes. I'll thank you to watch your manners. Sudden as it may seem, the reason for Mr Davenport's departure is surely no concern of yours." Mrs Gordon's voice was stern. "Now, please leave the room. It's almost time for you girls to leave for the theatre, you'd better go chase up Clara. Band call is at ten-thirty this morning, remember."

Rhiannon reluctantly did as Mrs Gordon ordered and left the room.

"Mr Fletcher, I do hope you'll excuse the child's outburst, although I must say the news about Mr Davenport was a shock. I can see what a disruption to the show his leaving might cause."

"Yes, the suddenness of his departure has caused me quite a headache, I can tell you. I've been up half the night, thinking of who could fill the MC spot. I've come up with this idea: I thought to dismiss the whole idea of the MC and use a member of the cast to

242

announce the acts instead. Tom O'Reilly seems favourite. I'm sure his comic banter between acts would go down well. What do you think, Mrs Gordon?"

"I'm flattered you think me worthy of an opinion."

"You've been part and parcel of the Empire since even before I took over the company, and that's nearly ten years ago, so who better to ask?"

"Well, put like that, I think your idea to change the format a good one. I, like you, think it would be hard to find an MC as capable as Mr Davenport at such short notice. I'm sure Tom O'Reilly as compère would work well."

Rhiannon was in shock. Surely Adam was mistaken. Gus wouldn't just up and leave her like this. Not after what had gone on between them last night. If it were true, she needed to speak privately to Adam. He would put her straight.

"What's up with you? Still pouting over what I said last night?" Clara asked. "Rhi, I'm sorry if I upset you. I only wanted to set you straight regarding the likes of Gus Davenport, honest."

"I know. And there's been a development but I really don't want to talk about it. All I'll say is that you'll find out at band-call. Now, come on, get a move on, I don't want to be late."

"Development, what sort of a word is that? At band-call you say? I'm intrigued."

At 10.30, with the cast assembled for band-call, Adam told them the news regarding Gus's sudden departure.

He gave no reasons, although no doubt there'd be much speculation; all he said was that Gus had moved on. "I'm sure we all wish him well. Without an MC I intend to change the set-up."

Adam's changes were greeted with mixed feelings, especially regarding Tom O'Reilly's new role, but they all admired Adam Fletcher's work and decided, at least for the time being, to trust his judgement.

Band-call seemed to go on for ever, restructuring the timing, the set; the removal of Gus's table and gavel seemed particularly final. Rhiannon was desperate to speak to Adam and, if necessary, would wait all day.

Eventually she heard Adam call, "That's it for today, folks. Thanks for all your hard work. Good luck for tonight — fingers crossed that the audience likes the changes made; we can but do our best. See you at curtain-up."

As everyone left, Rhiannon held back.

"Adam, I need to speak to you," she spoke quietly.

"That makes two of us," he snapped.

He sounded angry with her. Surely he didn't blame her for Gus's departure.

"Adam, I need to know why Gus left so abruptly."

"Rhiannon, I know what went on between you and Gus last night and I'm sorry."

"Why should you be sorry?"

"I blame myself. I knew only too well what Gus was like. I should have warned you."

"Adam, please don't reproach yourself, what we did was —"

244

"I should have insisted on walking you back to your digs myself last night, instead of letting him do it. The thing is, I truly believed that, where you were concerned, he could be trusted. What a fool I was in thinking he'd changed."

"Adam, please don't think too badly of him. What happened between us was with my consent. He loves me and I love him —"

"Oh Rhi . . . Rhi, I've heard that from his previous conquests so many times before."

"Please, Adam, I don't want to know. What's past is past."

"Well, you're damn well going to." Taking her hand he led her to sit in the stalls. He stood over her, visibly trembling. "I've stayed quiet for too long. Five long years to be exact. She was a young chorus girl — her name was Helena Biggins. And she, like you, fell for his overwhelming charms and, again like you, she believed he felt the same way about her. Of course he didn't. The upshot was that after he succeeded in seducing her he moved on to his next conquest without as much as a backward glance."

"That was then. The way he feels for me is . . . different."

"Rhiannon, stop fooling yourself. Face the truth. Gus is incapable of loving anyone but himself."

"Adam, why are you doing this? Surely as his uncle —"

"You mean blood is thicker than water? For years I've felt the same and have always given him the benefit of the doubt. He was my brother's son and close relatives don't stand in judgement . . . but I was wrong. What happened five years ago proved what a shallow human being he'd become."

"Was what he did five years ago so terrible?"

"Oh yes. Yes. You see, a few weeks after Gus walked away, the poor girl found herself in the family way and, with no family and no means of support, she took her own life and that of her unborn child."

"No!" Rhiannon gasped and placed a hand over her mouth to mask a pitiful scream.

"Yes! And I let it happen. Maybe, if I'd warned her . . .? And now look what he's done to you! When he returned to my house last night, I guessed what had happened between you. I told him I was going to tell you everything. I ordered him out of my house and out of my life, and, guess what? True to form, the coward ran away. The only good thing he did was leave this envelope for you."

"Is there a letter?" For a moment her hopes were raised.

"No letter, just his share of Mair's ransom money. At least he kept his word on that. Now he's gone and I say good riddance!"

"But Adam, I love him."

"I'm sure you do. But trust me — we're both well rid of him."

Rhiannon returned to her digs, still struggling to come to terms with what Adam had told her and the fact that in a matter of just a few hours she'd found and lost the man she loved. Had she been taken in? Had he used

246

her? She tried to recall Gus's actual words. Had he actually said he loved her? According to Adam he was incapable of loving anyone. Yet what they'd shared had felt so right. She didn't want to believe that it meant nothing to him. But if he truly loved her, why the sudden departure? No, Adam was right, he'd used her.

Rhiannon entered her room, threw herself onto her bed and burst into tears. But when the tears stopped, she went over and over in her mind every moment she had spent in the theatre with Gus the night before.

There was a tap on the door.

Clara entered. "Rhi, Mrs Gordon has called us for tea. Are you all right?"

Rhiannon rose from the bed, slowly making her way to the washbasin on a stand in the corner.

"Thanks, I'll be there in a minute."

"Oh Rhi, you've been crying. I'm so sorry. I can see how much Gus has hurt you. I'd give anything not to have said what I said about him last night. I hated falling out with you. Please say we're still friends?" Clara pleaded.

"Our falling out was my fault, not yours. I didn't want to believe he —" Rhiannon put her head in her hands.

"Come here," Clara crossed the room and threw her arms around Rhiannon. "Rhi, if ever you want to talk, I'm here for you. That bloody man has a lot to answer for."

That night, against all odds, the show went well. This was due in the main to the way Tom O'Reilly excelled himself in getting the audience rolling with laughter between the acts.

As usual, Rhiannon performed well. But her heart was not in it; every time the song called for her to look to the gallery she imagined Gus's handsome face smiling down on her. It was a cruel reminder of their first, and it would seem, their last night of passion. This couldn't continue. If she were ever to get over him, she needed to change her song. She vowed to speak to Adam after the show. Adam had made it perfectly clear that, from now on, he didn't want even to hear Gus's name. What Rhiannon needed to do now was to focus her mind on Mair's safe return; at least that was something to celebrate.

"Adam? What would you say about my having a change of song?"

"I'd say no. With only a few weeks to go until the end of this show's run, I wouldn't want to risk a further programme change. Up to now Gus's departure hasn't affected audience figures. Another change might be a change too far."

The disappointment on Rhiannon's face was obvious.

"Look, I'm not against you changing song. It's just that at the moment I think it is bad timing. Why not wait until we take the show on tour?"

Like the rest of the cast, Rhiannon was well aware of Adam's plan to take a smaller show on tour, something he did for three months every year, thus freeing the theatre for the pantomime season. Although he'd used discussions about it as an excuse for her late return to Mrs Gordon, this was the first time he'd mentioned it to her.

"Does that mean you want me on the tour?"

"Well yes; the plan is to visit selected small venues around Wales and the West Country. I thought you'd enjoy the challenge."

"Yes — yes! But . . . what about Mair?"

"I thought we could employ her as a dresser. What do you think?"

"Oh Adam! Thank you. That's a wonderful idea and what a great opportunity for a new start for Mair. You haven't forgotten the arrangement to pick her up on Friday, have you?"

"No, I hadn't forgotten."

"I thought, with him . . ." She still couldn't bring herself to say he'd gone, "I thought I'd come with you."

"I'm not sure that's such a good idea. The business transaction was strictly between us men. Your being there could spark trouble. No, you stay at Mrs Gordon's and wait. I promise to bring Mair straight there."

Rhiannon spent the next few days simply going through the motions: rehearsals, band calls, matinées and evening shows. Most nights she spent without sleep, tossing and turning, trying to understand why Gus had left her. She didn't doubt the truth of what Adam and Clara had told her, but it still couldn't stop her loving him. What if they were mistaken and Gus really had changed? Rhiannon had been so convinced of his

249

feelings towards her. He'd been so tender, caring and so . . . loving. But the question that nagged at her was, if he really loved her then why had he run away? Why hadn't he been man enough to stand and face the music? No, it was time to face the truth. Gus had gone and somehow she had to try to forget him.

CHAPTER
TWENTY-ONE

It was Thursday night and Mair couldn't help but notice how Harry appeared to be in unusually good spirits.

"I thought, as it's your last night with us, that I'd treat us to a special fish-and-chip supper, and maybe a few flagons of ale. How does that sound?" Harry gushed.

"I think that's a splendid idea, don't you, Mair?" Nellie urged.

Mair wanted to scream at the both of them. Did they really think a fish-and-chip supper would make up for the way they'd treated her for the last few months: keeping her locked up with the intention of selling her to the highest bidder? She so wanted to tell them how much she longed to be rid of them both. Instead she heard herself say, "Thank you. I'd like that. Fish and chips are my favourite." Common sense told her to go along with the charade. She didn't want to risk them backing out of their agreement with Rhiannon's friends — she'd bide her time; tomorrow she'd be free.

"Good, then that's settled. You girls set the table and I'll nip to the chip shop and the pub's taproom. Nellie, remember to set for four, eh?" he threw her a knowing look.

"Four? Why four?" Mair asked.

"A friend from down the King's Head is joining us. And I expect you to be on your best behaviour and to mind your manners — it's not too late for us to change our mind about you going tomorrow, so take heed. That said, I intend to make this a night to remember."

His chuckle aroused Mair's suspicions. What was he up to?

Almost an hour went by with still no sign of Harry, during which time Mair, not wanting to enter into conversation with Nellie, busied herself packing her few belongings into her old suitcase: the same suitcase she and Rhiannon had used when they first left the valley, it seemed now, a lifetime ago.

"I bet, instead of fetching our supper and a flagon of ale, the bastard's swigging back ale down the pub. If he's not back in the next ten minutes I'll be joining him."

At that moment the door opened and Harry entered, followed by a portly middle-aged man. Harry beamed a smile. "Well here she is, Jake, our Mair, ready and waiting as promised."

Mair recognized Harry's friend as the man who had come to the apartment a few days previously. She could never forget the way he had eyed her up and down, practically undressing her, salivating so much that the moisture dribbled from the corner of his mouth and down his chin. It had made her feel sick.

"What's the highest bid so far?" Jake asked Harry.

252

"Up to this morning, fifty guineas. Although with all the interest shown I expect that figure to more than double by the weekend."

"And still a virgin." He took a handkerchief from his pocket and wiped his chin.

"Yes, that's right. You have my word on that. Needless to say that, if you were to find otherwise, then you'd rightly be compensated."

"Harry, my man, your word's good enough for me. I'm prepared to top whatever offer you get between now and Saturday. I'll go to as much as one hundred and fifty pounds. Have we got a deal?"

Harry grabbed the man's hand. "Let's shake on it."

Mair watched in horror as the men shook hands and in doing so sealed her fate.

Mair heard the rustle of notes and the jingle of coins.

"There, that should do it," the man said.

"Right girl, it's time for you to start earning your keep. Nellie you get yourself off to the pub, I'll be along shortly."

A frightened Mair stared into Nellie's eyes. "Please, Mam . . . Nellie, please don't leave me here," she pleaded.

Nellie hesitated and looked across the room to Harry.

Harry walked over to her. "Come here woman," Harry said, then with both hands fondling her bosoms he pulled Nellie to him, placing a passionate kiss full on her mouth. "Don't you go fretting yourself about what's going on here. Remember what we agreed? This is just a means to an end. After tomorrow, there'll be no more working the streets for you, eh? Together with our little investments, we shall move away from these parts, and maybe I'll make an honest woman of you."

"You mean we really will get wed?"

"If everything all goes to plan tonight and tomorrow? Yes. Now get yourself down the pub and wait for me."

"Yes, Harry, anything you say, Harry." As she walked through the door, she didn't look back.

Mair felt suddenly light-headed. What was happening to her? She knew she wasn't tipsy; she hadn't taken but a sip of ale, although the taste of it still lingered on her tongue.

Mair was aware of Jake taking her hand and leading her towards the bed.

"Come on, what say we have a lie down." As he whispered in her ear, the smell of stale cigarettes and whisky invaded her nostrils. She struggled to pull away from him but it seemed all her strength had left her.

"What did you give her?" Jake asked.

"Only a little pill to quieten her down. She can be a feisty little bugger. Trust me, she'll not be giving you no trouble."

"I hope you haven't taken all the fight from her. I don't want it too easy."

"It won't be. I'm sure you'll not be disappointed. Have fun, we'll see you later." Then looking directly at Mair he said, "We'll not be gone long. Just long enough for you and Jake to get to know each other. Now you be nice to him, do you hear?" Harry threw her a look that said, "or else." Then turning to shake the man's hand he left the room.

As Jake moved closer to the bed Mair, sick with panic, made to get off it, but Jake's heavy hand stopped her. "Now where do you think you're going? I just paid one hundred and fifty for you, young 'un. That means I'm free to do with you as I please."

She knew only too well what he intended to do to her. Years of sharing a bedroom with Nellie, at the Tredegar Arms back in the valley, had meant that every time Nellie brought one of her men-friends to the room, Mair spent the night on a single mattress under her mother's bed. Oh yes, she knew what happened between men and women . . . but surely not to a girl of thirteen!

Mair attempted to scream, but Jake's large hand over her mouth muffled any sound, and with the other hand he deftly lifted her skirt and petticoat. Immediately she felt his heavy body crash down on her and his stale whisky-breath mouth smothering hers. She tried to fight Jake off but, even without whatever Harry had given her, he was such a big man she could never have moved him.

As his hands fumbled to remove the rest of her undergarments she felt sickened, helpless and unable to prevent the inevitable.

He entered her.

She screamed out.

He just laughed and carried on, grunting and gasping, while his hands cruelly mauled at her young breasts.

Mercifully her ordeal was soon ended. With one loud strangled gasp he slumped down upon her. At that moment, had she been able to put her hand on one, she could have willingly thrust a knife again and again into his flabby belly. She vowed that from now on she'd keep a weapon of some kind with her at all times.

It was early Friday afternoon and Rhiannon, together with the rest of the cast, left the theatre after band-call to find Frank Lewis waiting at the stage door. The sight of him made her eyes well up with tears. "Oh Frank, it's so good to see you."

"I said I'd be back. What's the news about Mair?"

"Harry and Nellie have agreed to release her at half past five this evening. Mind you, it took two hundred pounds of Adam and Gus's money to do it."

"Adam and Gus sound like good blokes. I can't wait to meet them, to thank them personally."

"I'm afraid Gus has left the company . . ." She gave a long sigh.

"Are you all right, Rhi?"

Rhiannon nodded and forced a smile. "Yes, I'm fine. In fact, I think it would be a good idea if you met Adam right now. Come on, he's still in the theatre." Taking Frank's hand Rhiannon turned and headed back into the theatre.

"Adam, this is Frank Lewis, the friend I told you about from the valley."

Adam offered his hand. "Pleased to meet you. Any friend of Rhi's, eh?"

Frank shook hands. "It's good to meet you, and thank you for your part in negotiating Mair's return."

"It was the least I could do. In fact . . . I don't know if Rhiannon has explained that Gus and I had arranged to collect her this evening but, now that Gus has up and left, how do you feel about taking his place? I don't expect any trouble but . . . ?"

"I'll be only too glad to accompany you. The sooner we get Mair away from that pair the better."

"Good man. Rhiannon, you stay put at Mrs Gordon's as arranged, yeah?"

"Yes, all right. No disrespect Adam, but Mair doesn't know you that well. I feel happier knowing Frank's going with you. Mair has always had a soft spot for him — a friendly face and all that. Truth be known, I still don't trust Nellie and her fancy man. What if they ask for more money . . .? What if they change their minds, or what if — ?"

"You mustn't go fretting yourself. I'm sure everything will go to plan and in a few hours you and Mair will be reunited. Now, cheer up."

Rhiannon forced a smile, but for some reason a strong sense of foreboding stayed with her.

Adam turned to Frank. "How long do mean to stay in Cardiff?"

"My time's my own. I was just on my way to find myself some digs."

"Forget the digs. You can stay at my house. In fact, if you'd like to hang around for ten minutes while I finish up here, I'll take you back to drop your suitcase off, and maybe have a little light refreshment before heading off to pick up Mair."

"That's very kind of you. If you're sure, it'll be fine with me. Will you be joining us, Rhi?"

"No, I really need to get back to my digs. Mrs Gordon will be expecting me. I wouldn't want to upset her." Rhi hadn't been back to Adam's house since the night with Gus.

"Your landlady sounds a bit of a tartar."

"Not really. She's really very caring. She's already agreed for Mair to come share my room at no extra cost and she's even making a special pre-show tea to celebrate Mair's return."

Adam smiled, "You tell her from me that I always knew she was an old softie at heart."

"I will, but I doubt she'll admit to it. I'd better be off. Good luck, you two. I can't wait to get Mair back."

"We'll not keep you waiting long. We should have her back with you well before six. Now off you go, and try to rest up. Remember you've another show this evening."

CHAPTER
TWENTY-TWO

Adam knocked on the door.

Harry opened it.

Adam couldn't fail to notice the smug look on Harry's face.

"We're here for Mair," Adam said.

"Where's the money?" Harry snapped.

Adam removed the envelope from the inside pocket of his overcoat and offered it to Harry.

Harry snatched it from him. "Don't mind if I check it, eh?"

"It's all there, all two hundred pounds," Adam assured him through gritted teeth.

Frank stood beside Adam. "All right, no more delays. You've got the money, now where's Mair?"

"All right, keep your hair on." Harry turned and called out, "Nellie, bring the girl!"

"Her name's Mair! And believe me, if you've harmed a hair on her head . . ." Frank was about to elaborate when Nellie came to the door, her arm wrapped around Mair's waist as if supporting her. "Mair, are you all right?" Frank asked.

Mair's glazed eyes stared back at Frank, as if she were struggling to recognize him.

"Mair, it's me Frank — Frank Lewis. Come on, love, you know me."

When Mair didn't respond, Frank stepped forward. He took her in his arms but soon realized that she could barely stand on her own two feet.

"What have you buggers done to her?" Frank demanded.

"We haven't done anything. The girl's caught a bit of a chill, that's all. Came on last night it did," Nellie offered.

Frank swept Mair up into his arms. "How many times do I have to say it? Her name's Mair, she's your daughter for Christ's sake, and this looks like more than a chill to me." Frank turned to Adam. "Adam, let's get her away from this evil bloody pair!"

As Adam and Frank made their way from the building to Adam's waiting car they heard Harry shout from an upstairs window, "And good riddance to you too, that's what I say!"

Once safely out on the street Frank stopped. "Adam, I really don't think we should take her to Mrs Gordon's looking like this."

"No. You're right. We'll take her to my house and call a doctor."

"No-no, I'm all right, honest. I just want to see Rhi." Mair's voice was but a whisper.

"And you shall. I promise you that Rhi will come to my house, but first we'd like a doctor to check on you."

"Mrs Gordon, where have they got to? What could have gone wrong?"

"I don't know, child. Try to be patient. I'm sure there's a perfectly good explanation."

There was a knock on the door. Rhiannon jumped up from her chair.

"You stay put, I'll go," Mrs Gordon ordered.

"Mrs Gordon, I'm sorry. May I come in?" Adam asked.

"Certainly, but whatever has happened? Where's the wee child?"

"Mair's not well. I didn't think it wise to bring her here. I thought it best to take her to my house and send for the doctor. The doctor said he'd be there in an hour. Frank's at the house waiting for him. Mrs Gordon, I fear the worst, I think the poor girl has been sexually assaulted."

Mrs Gordon, not wishing to alert Rhiannon, raised her hand to her mouth in an effort to muffle her cry of, "Oh my God!"

"I think it best if she stays at my house for a few days. I don't want this to become common knowledge, you know how given to tittle-tattle theatre folk can be?"

"Yes, quite. Mr Fletcher — Adam, would you like me to go and sit with her, and be there with her when the doctor arrives?"

Adam nodded. "I was hoping you'd suggest that."

"Then that's settled. I'll just get my coat. In fact, if it's all right with you I'll stay a few nights. I'm sure everyone at the theatre would relish a few days without my supervision."

"I think that's a grand idea. Although I'm sure wardrobe will miss you, you do such a great job. Now all I have to do is break the dreadful news to Rhiannon. And I can say, with all honesty, I'm not looking forward to it."

"Why don't you go, get yourself off to the theatre and leave it to me to break it to Rhiannon?"

Adam gave a notable sigh of relief. "Thank you. I really wasn't looking forward to it and perhaps . . . coming from a woman, it may help to soften the blow. Do you think I should get someone to fill in Rhiannon's spot for tonight's performance?"

"No, I do not! Rhiannon is a true professional and she'll not let you down. I'll let Mair know that Rhi will be at your house straight after the show."

Mair lay in the strange bedroom. She was confused as to why Adam and Frank had brought her to Adam's house instead of taking her to Rhiannon. When Mrs Gordon had arrived Mair asked her the very same question.

"The doctor's been called and well . . . if the doctor was to call at my boarding house, everyone at the theatre would know your business, you wouldn't want that, now would you? And as for Rhiannon, she'll be here straight after the show."

Mair was thankful that, when the doctor examined her, Mrs Gordon was there to hold her hand. The way his hands pushed and prodded her and the questions he asked made Mair feel both dirty and ashamed. Maybe that was how Rhiannon thought of her, too. If Mrs Gordon could be here for her then why wasn't Rhiannon? Surely she was more important than some stupid show?

Rhiannon's performance on stage that night, while totally professional, was not her best; her mind just wasn't on her job, she simply went through the motions. The audience didn't seem to notice, she did what was expected, enticing her audience to enter her world, to sing along, to clap and stamp their feet, to enjoy themselves. And they obviously did. But her heart just wasn't in it. Hearing the news from Mrs Gordon of Mair's terrible ordeal brought her stage performance into perspective; her performance on stage was a triviality, simply acting out a part — an illusion. While what happened to Mair was real life. The way Rhiannon had felt since Gus had left was nothing in comparison to what Mair had been made to suffer.

Rhiannon was consumed by guilt. Why hadn't she looked for Mair sooner? Why had she been too ready to believe her Aunt Florrie's version of why Mair had left in the first place? There could be no denying that she had let Mair down. So much so that if Mair chose not to forgive her who could blame her?

After the show Rhiannon hastily changed into her street clothes and headed for Adam's house. Adam had suggested she should wait for him to escort her, but Rhiannon knew that it would be at least another hour before he could leave and she couldn't wait a moment longer to see Mair.

At Adam's house Mrs Gordon was the first to greet Rhiannon.

"My dear girl, I know how eager you are to see Mair but I feel I should prepare you. The doctor confirmed our worst fears and he says that her condition is far from good. My dear, she's lost quite a lot of blood. I can't believe what that evil bastard . . . I'm sorry, I don't normally swear, but the child has been so hurt. The doctor assured me that, in time, she will heal. But the mental scars? They may take a lot longer."

"Where is she? I must go to her!"

"Follow me. She's upstairs."

Rhiannon entered the comfortable bedroom, well lit by gas lamps strategically placed at either side of the bed. Mair lay, apparently lifeless, in the large double bed, her small face peeping out from under the thick satin eiderdown.

"Mair love, it's me, Rhiannon."

Mair's eyes half-opened. "Rhi, is it really you?"

"Yes. It's me."

"Rhi, h-he really hurt m-me," Mair sobbed.

"I know, love. I'm so sorry. The agreement we made with Harry and Nellie was intended to save you from this. But they tricked us."

"Why, Rhi? Why did my own mother let this happen? Why does she hate me so?"

"I only wish I knew. I so wish I could make all the nasty memories go away. Honestly Mair — I'd do anything."

"Rhi . . . can you find me a knife?"

"Don't talk now. Just you rest."

"Rhi, I need a knife. Please get me a knife — in case he comes back."

"I promise you, he'll not find you here. No one is going to hurt you. While Adam and I are at the theatre, Mrs Gordon and Frank have agreed to stay with you. Mair love, you look so frail. You really must try to eat."

264

"How can I when I have no appetite?"

"Doctor Humphries says your body is still in shock."

There was a tap on the door.

"Come in," Rhi called.

A solemn Frank poked his head around the door.

"I'm sorry to disturb you both, but I just wanted to let you know that I'm going out for a bit of a walk. Rhi, if you like I can walk you back to your digs."

"You're both leaving me?" Mair whimpered.

"Now don't you go fretting yourself," Frank coaxed. "Mrs Gordon will be here with you and I'd dare anyone to get past her. The girls at the theatre have a nickname for her — they call her "the Dragon". And I for one wouldn't like to cross her."

"Frank's right, you know," Rhiannon assured her, "She's as good as any man. We all know that she's a member of the suffragist movement, the purple amethyst and green brooch she's taken to wearing is a dead give away." Rhiannon stood up and, bending over, placed a soft kiss on Mair's cheek. "But as it happens I've decided to stay with you tonight. I just need to have a few words with Frank and I'll be straight back."

"You promise," Mair pleaded.

"I promise. Now why don't you try to have a little sleep?"

Mair forced a smile, "All right, I'll try."

"Good girl. Mrs Gordon's down in the kitchen busy preparing supper. If you feel up to it, I could help you downstairs and then we could all enjoy a late supper around the kitchen table."

"I'd like that."

For a little while Frank and Rhiannon stood in silence outside Mair's bedroom door, both numbed by what had happened to Mair and both consumed with guilt for having failed her.

"I'll not be gone long, Rhi. There's just something I need to do," Frank whispered.

"Frank, where are you off to?"

"I told you. There's something I need to do."

"Frank, you're not thinking of paying Nellie and Harry a visit are you?" Rhiannon kept her voice low, not wanting to alarm Mair.

"Your father always said it was hard to get anything past you. If you must know, I want . . . no, I need, to give them a piece of my mind. What they did . . . allowing that animal to . . . to . . . Well, it was so bloody evil."

"You're right, they are evil. So what do you hope to achieve by going to see them?"

"It will make *me* feel better. Rhi, I need to do this."

"I can't stop you. If you must go, please be careful. Mair told me how quick-tempered and dangerous Harry can be."

"Maybe against defenceless women. But rest assured, he doesn't frighten me."

Rhiannon knew her warning had fallen on deaf ears. Frank's determination was obvious.

Frank banged his fist on Harry and Nellie's front door. There was no answer, so he banged again, this time much louder.

266

"What the hell are you playing at?" the tenant from the flat above called down.

"I'm looking for the occupants of 21A," Frank called back.

"You'll be lucky. They moved out late last night. That was yet another bloody racket I had to put up with."

"I'm sorry. I didn't mean to disturb you. Any idea where they've gone?"

"Yeah, I overheard down them down at the King's Head, bragging as to how they'd come into a windfall and were off to London. By all accounts, Harry seemed to think there were rich pickings to be had there."

"Thank you. I'll not be bothering you again," Frank said.

As he left the building Frank couldn't help but feel cheated. He so wanted to teach them a lesson. And if they knew what was good for them they'd do well to stay in London and out of his way. One thing was for sure: Rhiannon would welcome the news of their departure.

Four days later, with instructions from the doctor to continue to rest, Mair left Adam's house and moved into Mrs Gordon's boarding house to share a room with Rhiannon.

They were both thankful that Mrs Gordon had told everyone that Mair had sadly been let down by her mother and her boyfriend, who had left for London without a word. "What Mair needs now is our support. No awkward questions. No speculation or gossip, do you hear?" Mrs Gordon had ordered.

And for once everyone listened.

CHAPTER
TWENTY-THREE

August 1909

In the beginning progress was slow. Most of the time Mair was quiet and timid and not a bit like the Mair of old. But now, two months on, it pleased Rhiannon to see her begin to come out of her shell: an invisible wall put up, no doubt, to prevent her getting hurt. Although she still did not show any interest in returning to work in the theatre, Mair willingly helped Mavis, Mrs Gordon's sister, with some light duties in the day-to-day running of the boarding house and was even entering in to the friendly banter around the dining-table at night. However, much to Mrs Gordon's annoyance, Mair only ever managed to eat a small bowl of soup or a slice of bread and jam, before retiring early to her room.

With September nearly upon them, the show at the Empire was coming to a close. The show, having starred the likes of Miss Florrie Grayson and then Miss Alice Lloyd, with full supporting casts, had been an overwhelming success. And it was almost time for many of the cast to part company, move on to the next audition or the next booking. Those fortunate enough to be selected for Adam's new tour had had to endure a few weeks' hard work for, whilst still attending a daily band-call for the show at the Empire, they had to somehow find time to fit in extra rehearsals for Adam's touring show.

Rhiannon remembered her excitement on the night when Adam had announced the cast for the forthcoming tour:

"Head billing: Tom O'Reilly, comedian and compère. Second billing: Sally Webber, "The Street Urchin"; third billing: Rhiannon, "The Welsh Songbird"; Les Belles chorus girls to be led by Clara Boxall."

The next day he called them all together.

"The first thing you need to know is that as Mrs Gordon is committed to the job of fitting out the incoming pantomime company and, of course, running the boarding house with her sister, our touring show will be travelling without a wardrobe mistress."

Around the room this news was not greeted favourably. Straightaway Tom O'Reilly made his objection, "No wardrobe mistress? Well, I for one have never heard the like. Surely, within days the show will be in chaos and I'll be made a laughing stock . . ."

"I thought that was part of a comedian's job," Sally Webber quipped.

Everyone laughed, instantly easing the tension around the room.

Adam raised his hand and the room became silent. "I can understand your concern," Adam said, "but trust me when I tell you that I've done it many times before and, if we work together to ensure costumes are packed away after every performance, it can work like clockwork. With twenty venues in twelve weeks, we need to perform, pack up and move on quickly. Now if there are no more objections?" Adam's eyes went around the room.

No one said a word.

Rhiannon was pleased to be going on the tour under any circumstances, but wondered why Adam hadn't mentioned Mair travelling with them as dresser. But then why should he? After all, Mair hadn't even set foot in the theatre for weeks. To include her at this point would have shown favouritism. No, when the time came Rhiannon would simply tell everyone that Mair was travelling as her companion. If during the course of the tour Mair offered to help out, then all the better.

"Good." Adam smiled and nodded his appreciation before continuing. "What I can tell you is, that Clara Boxall has offered to oversee the packing process, but she can't be expected to do it alone. So let's pull together on this. Clara will also understudy, if the necessity arises, both Sally and Rhiannon. Are you sure you're ready for this?"

"Yes, Adam, I'm sure," Clara enthused, pleased to have the chance to prove herself.

"I'm glad. Now, before we leave I need to set some ground rules. For the duration of this tour I need — no — I *expect* your total commitment — commitment and professionalism. A happy troupe! This means — with living and working in such close proximity for the next three months, we all need to get on. There'll be no room for any artistic temperament or, to put it plainly, any bitching." Adam's eyes went straight to Sally

Webber, who was busily flicking through a magazine. "Sally, I hope you're paying attention. There are to be no snide remarks or bitching, do you hear?"

"I heard you the first time. And yes! But why pick on me?"

"Rhi?"

"Yes, Mair, love."

"I hope you don't mind but I've decided that I don't want to join you and the rest of the troupe on tour."

"Why ever not? What's brought this on? Are you unwell?" Rhiannon asked.

"No. I'm fine. I just don't think I'm ready to face all the travelling. We both know that Adam's only asked me to help out in wardrobe to make it easier for you to go."

"What's the alternative? The tour is scheduled to begin in two weeks, but I couldn't possibly leave you here on your own."

"Rhi, you know that Frank's mother's wedding is the week after next?"

"Yes, on Saturday the eleventh of September. Why? What's on your mind?"

"Well, I know that after the wedding, you'll be committed to return to Cardiff for the tour, but I'm sure Mrs Lewis wouldn't mind if I stayed on for a while. What do you think?"

Rhiannon was surprised. "I'm not sure. This has all come as a bit of a shock to me. But if that's what you really want, then I'll have a chat with Mrs Lewis when we're there."

"Oh, thank you, Rhi. You'll be much better off without me. I'd only be in the way. My mother never stopped telling me what a hindrance I was."

"Mair, love, you're not a hindrance to me. I promise. I love you. And, if Mrs Lewis can't see her way to letting you stay then I'm not going on tour either. I'm staying with you."

"You'd do that for me? What would Adam say?"

"Adam will understand. And as for me, I'm sure there will be other tours. Anyway, it may not come to that. Let's wait and see what Ethel Lewis has to say." Rhiannon crossed her fingers and prayed to God that Ethel Lewis would agree. Rhiannon would be devastated if she couldn't make the tour.

It was early Sunday evening. August was almost at an end and there was less than a week before the show at the Empire ended when Rhiannon left Mrs Gordon's boarding house on the pretence of taking a stroll.

Fifteen minutes later, with Adam's house in sight, Rhiannon was going over and over in her mind what she intended to say. She stepped up to the door, then, adjusting the lace shawl around her shoulders, lifted the brass knocker and lightly tapped the door.

"Rhi, how lovely to see you. Come in. Frank and I were just going to have a pre-dinner sherry. Please join us. There's more than enough for three."

"Thank you, I'd like that." Rhiannon followed Adam down the hall and into the spacious sitting-room. Although invited by Adam many times before to join him for dinner, she had always refused, not wishing to

272

be reminded of the fact that this house was where Gus Davenport had spent a large part of his life lodging with his uncle. That was . . . until she came into their lives. By doing so she had managed not only to make a complete fool of herself but, which was more serious, to break up Gus and Adam's long-standing family relationship.

"Hello, Rhi. To what do we owe this unexpected pleasure?" Frank asked, handing her a glass of sherry.

"I need to speak to Adam. I've something to tell him that can't wait."

"I'm intrigued," Adam said.

"Look, I've this letter to write to my mother," said Frank. "Rhi, you know how she frets if I don't keep in touch? I've been putting it off for days, what say I leave you two to have your chat, and I'll see you later for dinner."

"Good man. Dinner's in half an hour. See you then," Adam agreed.

"That's fine with me," Frank called, as he headed down the hall.

"Rhi, are you all right? Nothing wrong, is there?" Adam enquired.

"No . . . yes. Look, Adam. I'm sorry to drop this on you at such sort notice, but there's a slight possibility that I'll not be able to make the tour."

"What!"

Rhiannon shook her head. "It's true. I'm so sorry."

"Why? Whatever's happened?" Adam demanded, adding, "There had better be a damn good reason."

"It's Mair. She doesn't feel up to it and —"

Adam interrupted her, "That's it? You're going to give up an opportunity that many would kill for because Mair 'doesn't feel up to it'? Are you really happy with this?"

"Of course I'm not happy. I want nothing more than to come with you and the rest of the troupe but . . . Adam, you know the ordeal Mair's been through. And the truth is I feel partly to blame. If I hadn't been so selfish, putting my career before her, if I'd been there for her, if I'd —"

"Why must you always be so hard on yourself? How can I make you see that you were in no way responsible for what happened to Mair? Please believe me when I tell you that responsibility lay with the evil pair who set up the whole sordid thing."

Rhiannon dropped her head in her hands.

Adam took her hands in his and pulled her to him so that her head was resting on his chest. She gave a deep sigh.

"My dear, Rhiannon, I hate to see you like this. But this isn't just Mair, is it? I suspect my nephew might be playing a part in your distress — a case of gone but not forgotten, eh?"

Rhiannon raised her head from his chest and, freeing her hands, looked up at him. "I sometimes think you know me too well," she said, forcing a smile. "Oh Adam, I really have tried to forget him, to move on with my life. But every performance I give, every time I look to the gallery, I imagine him smiling down at me and . . . it hurts so much."

274

"I know, and I do understand. Despite everything I must admit that I miss him too. Maybe you were right and blood is thicker than water, after all. I only wish I could help."

"You did say that there was a chance I could change my song for the tour."

"I know what I said, but I now think that changing your song for the tour would be a grave mistake. This tour is intended to promote the success you've already had at the Empire. A success born from your singing that particular song. It's become your signature tune. Rhiannon, you have to come on this tour!"

"Well, I do have an idea. It involves Frank's mother, so please don't mention anything over dinner. But if all goes to plan . . . it'll mean I can make the tour."

"The tour starts in Chepstow on the eighteenth of September. The train tickets from Cardiff are all booked; Rhi, I'm depending on you not to let me down."

For Rhiannon the end-of-show party marked the end of her first season as a performer. Rhiannon realized how lucky she'd been to have made so many wonderful friends, each in their small way contributing to her coming of age. Her time in the theatre had brought many highs and many lows; the high of her theatrical success — the low of losing Mair. The high of falling head over heels in love with Gus Davenport — the low of losing him, the high of Mair's return and now . . . maybe the low of not making the tour. Oh yes, so much had happened. And, as her dear dad used to say, "Those that live the longest, will see the most."

"Rhiannon?" It was Mrs Gordon. "I just want to say how much I shall miss you and your sister. I wish I could have offered for Mair to stay with me but I need the room for the pantomime cast. But Mavis and I will always manage to squeeze you into our private quarters for a night or two, if need be."

"Thank you, Mrs Gordon. I may take you up on that. And please don't reproach yourself, both Mair and I understand your predicament. We have so much to thank you for."

"Fiddlesticks. It was my pleasure."

Rhiannon felt a warm glow engulf her. She had so much to look forward to; tomorrow, accompanied by Frank, she and Mair would be returning to the valley in time for Ethel Lewis and John Jenkins's wedding. She was going home.

CHAPTER
TWENTY-FOUR

September 1909

As they walked down Chapel Street, Rhiannon's eyes went straight to her old house. It looked the same yet different. It felt strange to think of another family living there.

"The couple living in your place have four small kids. They're a bit rough and ready, but my mother says their hearts are in the right place," Frank said, quickly adding, "Of course it's not the same as having you and Mair next door."

"Unfortunately, it wasn't to be. I'm glad for your mother though, it's so much easier when you can get on with the neighbours," Rhi said, mainly to make him feel better.

"Mam, we're here!" Frank called as they entered the familiar hallway of the Lewis's mid-terrace house.

Ethel Lewis opened the kitchen door. "Well now, there's a sight for sore eyes. Come here. Let me give you both a big hug." She wrapped her arms first around Mair and then Rhiannon. "You don't realize what a difference it'll make to have you both here for my wedding day. Having you live so close to me for all those years, I think of you as part of the family. My day wouldn't have been the same without you. It's so good to have you back home." Raising her wrap-around pinafore she dabbed her tear-filled eyes. "What a daft ha'peth I am, crying like a baby because I'm that happy to see you both."

"Mrs Lewis, it's so good to see you too. And as for your wedding day, we wouldn't miss it for the world," Rhiannon said, and truly meant it. She held fond memories of all the kind neighbourly things Ethel Lewis had done for them before and after her father's death.

"Well, there's posh you sound. Your Aunt Florrie's influence over the past months has definitely had an effect. You're quite the young lady now, aren't you?"

"I don't know about that. Although I will admit that I've changed; I feel a lot more grown up." Rhiannon almost added in more ways than you could imagine, but stopped herself.

"I suppose that living and working in Cardiff, surrounded by such well-travelled theatre folk, it was only to be expected."

"Anyway, we'll not impose on your hospitality for long. Tomorrow I'll start looking for somewhere to rent."

"And I've already told her that there's no hurry. Isn't that right, Mam?" Frank said.

"That's right, lad, no hurry at all. Our home is yours and you're both welcome to stay as long as you like. Now what must you think of me chatting away, when I should be offering you a nice cup of tea? Come on, you sit yourselves down and I'll put the kettle on the hob," Ethel offered.

278

"Mrs Lewis, if it's all right with you, I think I'd like a lie down." Mair's voice sounded weak.

"Why, of course, child. Travelling all the way from Cardiff in one day is no joke. I've sorted out the sleeping arrangements; you two can have Frank's bedroom."

"Oh no, we can't take your room, Frank," Rhiannon objected.

"Oh yes you can, Mam's made me a bed up on the settee in the parlour. I've slept there before, I'll be fine, I promise. Now come on, let's get young Mair settled." He picked up their suitcase and headed for the stairs.

"That's right, Frank, you show them the way. And Rhi, once Mair's settled, you come back down. I'll have the tea brewed by then, I can't wait to hear all your news."

"Here we are, then," Frank said, opening the door to his bedroom. "I'm afraid my mother insisted that I must clear out all of my personal bits and pieces, so the room looks a bit bare. Mam's changed the bedding this morning. The bed's really comfy, so I hope it suits you both."

"I'm sure it'll suit us fine. Thank you," Rhi said.

"Right, I'll leave you two on your own to settle in." He turned to leave.

"Frank?"

"Yes, Rhi?"

"Thanks again. It's feels good to be back."

"It's good to have you back." He flashed a warm smile before closing the door behind him.

When Frank had gone, Rhiannon turned to Mair. "Mair, love, are you all right?"

"Y-yes, I'm fine. I just need to lie down for a while." Mair slowly sank onto the bed. "Rhi, why do I always feel so weak and so tired?"

Rhiannon stared down at Mair's tiny frame. Since her ordeal she'd lost so much weight. And even with Rhiannon's and Mrs Gordon's daily efforts to tempt her with tasty snacks, she had refused to eat.

"I'm not surprised by your lack of energy. Look at you. There's nothing of you. Mair, you really need to build up your strength and the only way to do that is to find your appetite. I'm sure a few bowls of Ethel Lewis's famous lamb stew will soon make you feel better."

"I hope so, I really do." Mair closed her eyes and, almost immediately, she was fast asleep.

Lifting the patchwork eiderdown from the bottom of the bed, Rhiannon carefully covered her sister and placed a soft kiss on Mair's forehead. Quietly she left the room.

When she entered Ethel Lewis's homely kitchen; a huge coal fire burned in the grate, heating two black-lead ovens and hobs. On one hob stood a saucepan of simmering stew, while on the other sat a large black kettle of boiling water.

"There you are. Tea's made. Frank, pull up a chair near the fire for Rhi," Ethel instructed.

Frank did as his mother asked and gestured for Rhi to sit next to him.

"How's Mair?" Ethel asked, handing her a cup of tea.

"I'm sure she'll be fine after a little nap. I'm afraid she's not been very well of late," Rhiannon said.

"I can see that. I can't believe the change in her. Whatever happened to the feisty young girl who left the valley? Why, she looks a shadow of her former self."

Rhiannon shook her head. "It's a long story."

"Well, I've got all the time in the world," Ethel said.

"Rhi, I really think you should tell her," Frank urged.

"Tell her what?" Ethel looked puzzled.

Rhiannon looked towards Frank. She shook her head and turned her gaze to Sadie and Martha, who were sitting at the kitchen table playing a game of snakes and ladders.

Frank immediately understood. "Sadie, Martha, how'd you fancy a walk to the corner shop? I believe there's a jar of sherbet just waiting for you two, and I just happen to have a threepenny piece in my pocket to treat you."

"Oh yes! Come on Martha, I'll race you." The youngsters were soon on their feet heading for the door.

Frank looked at his mother. "It'll keep them out of earshot. What Rhi has to tell you is really not suitable for their ears."

When the girls had gone, Rhiannon took a deep breath and began to relay the whole sordid story of Mair's abuse and ultimate betrayal.

Ethel listened, most of the time shaking her head in disbelief. "Well, I always knew that Nellie Parsons was a bad 'un," Ethel eventually said when Rhi had finished.

"It makes you wonder what sort of a mother could stand by and let this happen to her own flesh and blood? It's not natural. When my Frank told me you were both returning to Ponty, I had a strong feeling that something was wrong. But I'd never in a million years have guessed at this . . . this is just unthinkable."

"I know. What that man did to her was so terrible, I can only imagine how she feels. But knowing her own mother was party to it . . .? Is it any wonder she seems to have lost the will to live?"

"Tell me, Rhiannon, what are your immediate plans? How long can you stay?" Ethel didn't wait for an answer, she just continued: "As you know, after the wedding I plan to move the family — except Frank that is, into Mr Jenkins's — John's house. Frank, rightly, needs to spread his wings and make a new life for himself, although I'm not so sure about his joining the army — something else for me to worry about, eh? Only don't tell him how I feel, will you?"

"I'll not say a word," Rhiannon promised.

"Anyway," Ethel continued, "John's house is one of the biggest in the valley. It has four large bedrooms — and you'll not believe it — an indoor bathroom and lavatory. I shan't know myself. I've had a word with John and he says that you're both welcome to stay with us for as long as you like."

"That's so very kind of you both. The thing is, Mrs Lewis —"

"You calling me Mrs Lewis all the time sounds very formal. I remember how, when you were little, you used to call me Auntie Ethel, I liked that."

282

Rhiannon smiled and nodded. "The thing is, Auntie Ethel, with the end of the show's run at the Empire, I have this dilemma."

"Which is?" Ethel urged.

Rhiannon took a deep breath. "Adam Fletcher, our musical director, has planned a twelve-week tour of Wales and the West Country for a small troupe of artists, and . . . well . . . I've been chosen to join them. It's such a great opportunity for me. Adam even offered Mair a job in wardrobe, so that we could be together, but she's adamant she doesn't want to go."

"Well, Rhiannon, if I may say so, having seen for myself the way Mair is, I really don't think that, in her present state, she's fit enough. So why not leave her here with me? You know I'll look after her as if she were one of my own." Ethel's voice was firm. "What that poor mite upstairs needs most of all is to feel part of a caring, loving family. It'll be the start needed to build up not only her strength, but her faith in human nature."

Rhiannon breathed a sigh of relief. Ethel Lewis had come up trumps and Rhiannon was free to go on tour, safe in the knowledge that Mair would be well looked after. Still, part of her wondered what she would have done if Mrs Lewis had refused to look after Mair. Would she have stayed at home and not gone on tour? She wanted to believe that that would have been so; thankfully this was a decision that now she wouldn't have to make, but that didn't stop her feeling a tinge of guilt for, once again, putting her career before Mair. She hoped Mair would understand how much this tour really meant to her. She truly loved Mair and she hoped that one day she would have a chance to prove it.

"Congratulations, Auntie Ethel. Or should I now call you Mrs Jenkins?" Rhiannon laughed.

"Auntie Ethel's fine."

"You look so happy," Rhiannon said.

"I am. John Jenkins is a good man. The truth is, I thought after my Jack died that I'd never feel this way again. But when I'm with John, it feels so — so right."

"I'm pleased for you. You're such a good generous person, you deserve to find happiness, whereas I'm . . ."

"You're what?"

"I'm selfish and . . . not at all good."

Ethel reached out and took Rhiannon's hand in hers. "Rhiannon, that's just not true. What you are is a young girl with ambition. And that's to be admired. Your dear father and mother would have been so proud of you. They both wanted so much for you. In my book, you've done them proud."

"I don't think they'd approve of the way I'm abandoning Mair."

"I take offence at you suggesting that leaving her with me constitutes abandonment! Why, your father often entrusted you, his special little girl, to my care . . . until Nellie Parsons came on the scene, that was."

"Oh Auntie Ethel, I didn't mean to imply that I don't trust you with her. Of course I do. You've always taken care of me from as far back as I can remember."

"Then you have to stop reproaching yourself. Mair will be fine, I promise. You go on the tour with a clear conscience . . . be successful . . . make us all proud. And when the tour ends I'll expect you back here to spend Christmas with us."

"Oh, thank you so much, Aunt Ethel."

Rhiannon went up to the bedroom.

"It's all settled. Aunt Ethel said that you're more than welcome to stay on with the family when they move into John Jenkins's house for as long as you want. My tour lasts for three months. As soon as it's ended I promise I'll be back in time for Christmas. We're to spend it with Aunt Ethel and the family. Now, you must be pleased with that."

"Oh Rhi, a real family Christmas — I can't wait. Although I will miss you; three months is such a long time. Mind you, I'll miss Frank too. This morning he told me how he's actually received his call-up papers."

Rhiannon looked surprised. "Funny. I wonder why he didn't come to tell me."

It pleased Mair to think that Frank had chosen to tell her before Rhiannon. But she knew better than to read anything into it. After all, she'd seen the way he looked at Rhi, the drooling sort of look that made her wonder if there wasn't something going on between them.

"Rhi, can I ask you something, personal, like?" Mair ventured.

"Ask away; what is it you want to know?"

"Rhi, you would tell me if you and Frank were . . .?"

"Were what?" Rhi asked.

Seeing the puzzled look on her sister's face, Mair decided just to come out with it. "Rhi, do you love Frank?"

"Of course I do, to me he's like the brother I never had."

"I don't mean as a brother. I mean . . . like . . . *in love* with him?" Mair persisted.

"You daft ha'peth, whatever's put that in your head? And no, I've never thought of Frank in that way. The only man I've ever felt that way about was . . . Gus."

"Well, if that's the case, then I really don't think you should lead Frank on so!" Mair snapped.

"I don't know what you mean?" Rhi looked genuinely puzzled.

"Come on, Rhi, are you trying to tell me that you haven't noticed the way his eyes light up every time you enter the room or the way he hangs on your every word? It's so obvious. He's besotted with you." Mair almost added *you lucky thing, you*, but stopped herself, confused as to how, after all that had happened to her, the thought of Frank loving Rhi hurt so much.

"Mair love, if what you say is true . . . then before I leave, I shall set him straight on the matter; make my feelings clear."

"There's no need." Frank's voice came abruptly from behind. "Mair has got it wrong." He entered the room. "I'm sorry, but I couldn't help but overhear." He turned firstly to Mair. "Mair, I can't imagine what's put such a silly idea into your head." Then, turning to face Rhiannon, "And Rhi, just to set the record straight, I'm pleased to hear that you think of me as a brother — an older brother, of course." He threw her a wicked smile, reached out and took Mair's and Rhiannon's hands in his. "That's how I truly think of myself regarding the two of you. And I want you both to know that I'll always look out for you."

Rhiannon forced a smile. "I really meant it when I said I'll miss you."

"Me too," an embarrassed Mair whispered.

Rhiannon and Frank made the journey to Cardiff together on Friday.

"When do you actually need to present yourself to the battalion?" Rhiannon asked, breaking what she thought to be an awkward silence between them. Since overhearing her and Mair's little chat he seemed to have distanced himself from her — or was she imagining it?

"Monday morning. I'm hoping Adam won't mind my lodging at his house until then."

"I'm sure he'll be only too pleased to have you stay. I'll be staying with Mrs Gordon and her sister. It's only for one night; we leave early in the morning to start the tour. Look, I know it's short notice but later tonight, maybe we could get together for a farewell meal?"

Frank smiled. "I'd like that."

"Do you know where you're heading?" Rhiannon asked.

"My initiation will be in Cardiff. After that, I'll be based at Maendy barracks. And after that — who knows?"

"We'll keep in touch, though?"

"I don't think that, with you on tour and me stationed God knows where, that it would be practical for us to write directly to each other. I shall of course be writing at regular intervals to my mother, so maybe you could do the same."

"Of course. I understand," she said, but in truth, she didn't understand at all.

CHAPTER
TWENTY-FIVE

The tour was going well. Every venue they visited was a complete sell-out. The tour was a real eye-opener for Rhiannon. It was much harder than she'd expected: living out of a suitcase, never staying in one town longer than a couple of days, frequently moving digs — some better than others. Even Sundays, usually their day off, were spent in rehearsals.

Rhiannon, keeping her promise, frequently wrote to Ethel and Mair, separate letters in one envelope. Unfortunately, while on tour, it turned out to be a logistic nightmare for, though she found it easy to send letters, receiving them — well that was another thing.

She sent Ethel and Mair the first letter from Chepstow the day she arrived. She had to wait nearly two weeks before getting a reply! Ethel's letter, together with a short note from Mair, had been forwarded from the venue in Chepstow, then on to Bristol before eventually finding her in Taunton.

Ethel's letter told her that, although Mair seemed happy enough and was now eating well, her health seemed slow to recover. Ethel said she was keeping a close eye on her and if things didn't improve she would seek the advice of the doctor. Although this was a worry to Rhiannon, it made her realize how right she'd been to leave Mair behind.

Ethel went on to say how proud she was of her Frank, who appeared to be getting on so well in the army. For years he'd not just been her son but the head of the family . . . the main breadwinner. Her marriage to John Jenkins had set him free to make a career in the army and maybe travel the world.

Mair's first note said that although missing Rhiannon, she was so happy to be staying with Ethel and the family, and how welcome they made her feel. Reading this went a long way towards easing Rhiannon's conscience.

Once again Rhiannon replied immediately. She thanked Ethel for looking after Mair and asked her to let her know straight away if another visit to the doctor became necessary. She asked to be remembered to Frank and hoped to see him soon. She answered Mair, telling her how much she was missing her and, as they were already three weeks into the tour, it wouldn't be long before they were together again.

Not for the first time, Rhiannon wondered what the future held for them. When the tour ended Adam Fletcher would return to the company's base at the Empire Theatre, Cardiff; a new season, a new show to run from March through to September. He had already placed an advertisement in *The Stage*, looking for artists and dancers; auditions were to start in February.

"There's a two-song slot for you in the show, if you're interested?" Adam offered.

Rhiannon's first reaction was to jump at the chance of joining another of Adam's shows, but she knew she had to discuss it with Mair first.

When no reply came to her letter, Rhiannon hoped all was well.

"Mair love, are you all right? You've been in that lavatory for ages," Ethel called.

"Yes, I'm fine, thank you," Mair answered, but she'd lied. She felt wretched. She'd been sick again, the fourth morning in as many days. With her monthly course almost nine weeks late, she knew it could only mean one thing. She was pregnant.

If being brought up by the promiscuous Nellie Parson had taught Mair anything, it was to keep track of when her monthlies were due. If Nellie was as much as a day late she'd reach for the tried and tested remedy of a good nip of gin and a hot bath — an "old wives' tale" maybe, but it seemed always to have worked for Nellie.

A week ago, in desperation, Mair had tried the hot bath but, with no access to gin, it hadn't worked. It had been more than ten weeks since . . . she couldn't even bring herself to give what happened to her a name; the fact was that, by her calculations, she was nearly three months gone. Soon her belly would start to get big and then everyone would know. Mair felt that, before it became common knowledge, Ethel Jenkins deserved to be told. She decided to confide in Ethel after supper tonight, preferably when all the others had gone to bed.

But that was later, right now it was time to face the family for breakfast.

Mair entered the kitchen and to her surprise found Ethel sitting alone at the breakfast table reading a letter.

Ethel looked up. "Good morning, Mair. Tea's brewed. Be a love and pour us both a cup."

"Where is everyone?" Mair asked.

"It's Saturday, so John — Mr Jenkins — invited the girls to accompany him to work in the shop next door. He offered them a sixpenny piece each if they'd help out. He rightly feels they should begin to get to know the workings of the butchery business. I do so hope they *are* a help, rather than a hindrance. You know what a pair of chatterboxes they can be? As soon as I've read this letter from Frank, I'll make you some breakfast."

"Thank you, but I'm not really hungry," Mair said. She lifted the large teapot from the hob in front of the coal fire and poured two mugs of hot steaming tea. She placed one on the table in front of Ethel.

Ethel reached over for the honey jar and proceeded to scoop a heaped teaspoonful into her tea. "I know I shouldn't, but I like my tea strong and sweet. Come sit next to me." Ethel tapped the multicoloured, hand-knitted cushion of the chair next to her and Mair did as she was bid.

"Good news. Frank's been given a weekend pass; he's on his way home. He sent this letter on Thursday, hoping it would get to us in time . . . he'll be home tonight," Ethel gushed.

Mair, although pleased to hear of Frank's return home, knew she would have to delay telling Ethel about the pregnancy. The thought of Frank finding out filled her with shame. Although he plainly only thought of her like a sister, to her there could be no denying that *she* idolized him. She had thought, after what that man had done to her, that she would hate all men, and at first she had. But Ethel had come to her bedroom one night and talked to her like a real mother, changing her way of thinking.

Mair, love, I don't want to delve too deeply into the dreadful experience you've had to endure at such a young age, but I keep thinking what I might say to help you. Since you've been here with us, I've come to think of you like one of my girls, and I've seen the way you, understandably, draw back when any man enters the house — even my John."

"I'm sorry, Auntie Ethel, I don't mean to. Mr Jenkins has been so kind to me. You must know that I don't for one moment think that he would . . .?"

"I know, child. And that's the thing, not all men are evil. What I'd like you to do for me before you go to sleep tonight is to close your eyes and think of every man you've had anything to do with since leaving the valley and assess each of them fairly — will you do that for me?"

"Yes, Auntie Ethel, I will."

Later that night Mair lay in bed and closed her eyes and tried to picture every man she'd met over the past months. As instructed by Ethel, she began to assess each in turn. The first man to come to mind was Walter

Cahill, the larger than life, kindly, American who insisted on pronouncing her name "Mayre". Mair smiled: he was one of the least evil men she knew. Next, Gus Davenport: although he seemed something of a thoughtless jack-the-lad, the way he left Rhi and all, he could never be thought of as evil. The fact that Rhiannon still loved him proved that. Next, there was Adam Fletcher: look how kind and generous he'd been, in putting up the money to set her free. Next came John Jenkins, a really good man who had welcomed her into his home without a second thought. Yes, Ethel had been right; the only evil men she'd met were Harry and Jake.

Her thoughts then went to Frank Lewis, the sweetest, kindest man she'd ever known. A man who had this way about him, to make her feel warm inside and safe in the knowledge that he would never hurt her.

But what did it matter how she felt? She was barely fourteen and pregnant . . . what man would want a shop-soiled girl like her anyway? No, the sooner she faced up to the fact that her life was totally ruined, the better.

Mair decided to hold back from speaking to Ethel until Frank had returned to barracks.

It was just getting dark. John Jenkins had lit the gas lamps and stoked up the fire with coal. Mair was sitting next to him with Ethel, Martha and Sadie at the kitchen table awaiting Frank's homecoming. An intricately embroidered white cotton tablecloth covered the table, which was heavily laden with plates of corned

294

beef, ham, home-made bread and a tin of freshly baked Welsh-cakes.

Ethel's eyes stared at the kitchen clock. "The next charabanc from Pontrhyl railway station should be arriving on Ponty Square any time now, with our Frank on it."

"Now, Ethel love, don't go building your hopes up. We can't know for sure that the lad even managed to make his connection from Cardiff, now can we?"

Ethel sighed. "No. But it seems such a long time since I've seen him."

"Well, I for one hope he's not too long. I'm starving," Martha groaned.

"I'm sure Frank won't be long. While we're waiting, why don't you tell your mother and Mair what a grand day you've both had?" John Jenkins suggested.

"Mam, it was great," Sadie said excitedly. "The customers were so kind to us. Mrs Williams the farm gave us both a sugared almond and Dai — the fruit man, an apple each."

"I hope you both remembered your manners and said thank you," Ethel said.

"Yes, you've no worries on that score. They were both a credit to you and it was a joy to have them in the shop." John Jenkins threw his wife a warm smile. "It felt good to show off my new family."

At that moment the back door opened and they all jumped to their feet. Frank entered and for a while time seemed to stand still. Dressed in his new khaki uniform, with his smart military cap — proudly sporting the plumed coronet of the Prince of Wales, held under his arm, he looked so . . . grand and so . . . grown up and somehow so . . . out of place.

"Good to have you home, son," a tearful Ethel said, throwing her arms around him.

John Jenkins reached out and shook Frank's hand. "Your mother's right," he said. "It's so good to have you back. I know it's early days but I hope in time you *can* think of this house as home."

"Rest assured, home to me will always be where my mam and the girls are." Frank reached over and affectionately ruffled both girls' hair. He flashed Mair a wicked smile and added, "and Mair of course."

Mair blushed. "It's good to see you Frank. And don't you look grand?"

"Well now, I could say the same about you. I must say, Mair, you look so much better than when I left. I do believe that, at last, you're starting to fill out," Frank enthused.

Mair quickly pulled her shawl over the small bump that was her belly. "Have I? I hadn't noticed," she lied.

"She has, hasn't she, Mam?" Frank persisted.

Ethel Jenkins eyed Mair up and down, her eyes stopping at Mair's hands shielding her belly. "Well, now that you mention it, yes son. Seeing her everyday, I must admit I hadn't noticed."

"Didn't I tell you, Mair, how hard it would be to resist my mother's home cooking? Teasing apart, it's so good to see you looking so well." Frank beamed a smile.

Mair felt her colour rise.

"Can we eat now?" Martha pleaded.

296

★ ★ ★

After tea, having spent the past hour trying to avoid catching Ethel's eye, Mair asked to be excused from the table and, on the pretence of needing a lie-down, went to her room. Less than an hour later came the knock on the door that she had been dreading.

"Come in," Mair reluctantly called.

A solemn-looking Ethel Jenkins entered.

For a while they just stared at each other; then, almost in unison:

"Mair . . ." Ethel said.

"Aunt Ethel . . ." Mair said.

Mair gave a nervous laugh. "Aunt Ethel, please let me speak first."

Ethel nodded.

Mair touched her belly. "You've guessed, haven't you?"

"Yes, child. And I feel daft for not having noticed before. Why didn't you tell me?"

"I planned to tell you this evening but . . . when you told me that Frank was on his way, well, I didn't want to spoil his homecoming."

"Mair love, Frank, like the rest of us, will understand that the condition you find yourself in is through no fault of your own."

"Pl-ease, you can't tell him! I just couldn't bear it!" Mair pleaded.

"But surely you must realize that sooner or later it'll become obvious to all?"

"I know. But does Frank really have to know today?" Mair begged.

"No, I suppose another few days wouldn't hurt. If it makes you feel better I'll delay telling him until he's due to leave. Will that suit you?"

Mair gave a sigh of relief. "Thank you." She felt that any delay, however short, would give her a few days' grace at least to enjoy Frank's visit.

"We'll need to let Rhiannon know," Ethel said.

"Couldn't it wait until the end of her tour? After all, there's nothing she, or anybody else for that matter, can do to change things."

"I think she'd feel hurt to be the last to know, don't you?"

"What harm could a couple of weeks do, eh?"

"Bloody hell, Mam — sorry, I know you don't like to hear me swearing but . . . a baby? It's so unfair. Hasn't that poor girl been through enough? If only I could get my hands on those responsible I'd —"

"You'd just get yourself in trouble. That's what you'd do! I'm afraid what's done is done and what we need to do now is what's best for Mair. Raking up old coals is the last thing she needs!" Ethel admonished.

"I know you're right. Has Rhiannon been told?" Frank asked.

"No. Not yet. Mair wants to delay telling her until nearer the end of the tour and part of me agrees with her. I thought . . . now say no if you don't want to, but I thought you'd maybe find out where the tour ends and pay Rhiannon a visit. I'd write to her, but it just doesn't seem right to give such news in a letter. What do you think?"

298

"Leave it to me, Mam. Now, if it's all right with you, before I leave I'd like to call and say so long to Mair."

"Tread softly, son. The lass obviously thinks a lot of you. Why, she almost begged me not to tell you about her condition."

"Truth be known, Mam, I think a lot of her, too."

"Well, all I ask is, be honest with her; don't go sending her mixed messages, she's far too vulnerable to deal with it," Ethel warned.

"I won't, Mam, I promise," Frank assured her.

Frank knocked on Mair's bedroom door several times, but there was no answer. "Mair — Mair, please open the door."

"She's told you, hasn't she?" Mair sobbed from behind the door.

"Yes, I know about the baby, if that's what you mean. And as far as I'm concerned, it doesn't change anything between us. Mair, love, I have to leave in a few minutes and I don't know when I'll be able to make it back. Please, don't let me go without seeing you."

The door slowly opened and a tearful Mair stood at the door. Seconds later Frank's open arms engulfed her and he was gently kissing her forehead. "Mair, trust me when I tell you that, while I've strength in my body, no one will ever hurt you again. You're not alone in this. Whatever it takes, we'll get through it — together."

With Frank's strong arms around her and, hearing his heartfelt words, Mair once again felt totally safe.

CHAPTER
TWENTY-SIX

December 1909

It was 4.30 and the afternoon was closing in. The cool
overcast day was replaced by a biting cold wind when
Rhiannon and Clara turned up to band-call for the
pre-show rehearsal at the Cwmbran memorial hall.
Both of them were dressed in long winter coats,
woollen hats and mufflers.

Clara was first to spot the young soldier, leaning
against the wall smoking a cigarette. "Well now, what
have we here? If you're a stage door Johnny you're a bit
too early. The show doesn't start until half past seven,
so you've a long wait," she mocked.

"Frank, is that you? My, don't you look grand in
your uniform?" Rhiannon cried, throwing her arms
around him." She felt his body tense and, feeling
somewhat embarrassed, she immediately stepped away.
"Clara, this is my good friend Frank Lewis. You've
heard me talk about him often enough."

Clara offered her hand. "I'm Clara Boxall, and
pleased to meet you, I'm sure." She deliberately kept
hold of his hand. Then turning to Rhiannon, she said,
"You never told me that your Frank was so
good-looking and a soldier to boot! You know what
a sucker I am for a man in uniform. If he wasn't such a

300

good friend of yours I'd make a pass at him here and now." She chuckled to herself. Frank visibly blushed.

"Clara. Will you stop embarrassing him and get yourself on into the hall. I'll be along shortly. Now, go away!"

"Sadly, I know that three's a crowd, so I'll leave you friends alone to catch up. Duty calls and all that. Maybe another time — another place, eh, soldier boy?"

As she turned to leave she threw him a wicked wink.

"Pleased to have met you," Frank muttered awkwardly.

"Sorry about that. She's got a heart of gold, really," Rhiannon apologized. After the way he'd reacted to her impulsive embrace Clara's innocent teasing, suggesting that Frank and Rhi were more than friends, was the last thing Rhiannon needed. She had to clear the air somehow.

Rhiannon sucked in a breath of cold air and shivered. "Frank, it's far too cold to talk out here. Let's go inside. We can use Adam's office. I'm sure he won't mind."

Frank smiled. "You're right, it's cold enough to freeze the whatnots off a brass monkey."

Rhiannon giggled. "Whatnots? There's polite you're being."

"Lady present, isn't there?"

Rhiannon bobbed a curtsy. "Why, thank you, kind sir."

They both laughed.

Once inside Adam's office, Rhiannon lit the gas heater and turned to Frank. "It really is so good to see you. And I'm so glad that, after your mother's wedding, we got things sorted out between us. Frank . . . we did get things sorted out, didn't we?"

Frank smiled and nodded. "Yes. But I wasn't entirely truthful with you."

"What do you mean?"

"Back home. The thing is that when Mair told you that I was besotted with you, she actually hit the nail right on the head."

"Fr-Frank, if I've in any way led you to believe . . ."

"Don't be embarrassed. I've known for ages that you didn't feel the same way about me."

"I'm so sorry."

"Please don't reproach yourself. I'm over it, I promise. In fact you did me a favour — but enough of that." Frank wanted to tell her of his growing feelings for Mair, but stopped himself — this was neither the time nor the place. "One thing's for sure; while I never had the pleasure of meeting Gus Davenport in person, in my mind he was a fool to leave you the way he did."

"I really don't want to talk about it. Maybe one day, eh? Anyway, it's so nice to see you. We're here in the Newport area for the next two days, before spending our final week in Swansea. How long can you stay?"

"Rhi, this isn't a social call. I'm afraid I can only stay for a few hours and then I have to catch the train straight back to barracks. A few of the lads have promised to cover for me. If the CO, that's the commanding officer, were to find out that I'm AWOL — absent without leave — I'd be up on a charge."

302

"I don't understand. What could be so important to make you risk getting into trouble? Is something wrong at home with the family or . . . Mair?" The look on his face said it all. "That's it! It's Mair, isn't it? When I'd been so long without a letter from them I had a feeling something was wrong!"

"My mother thought it best to give you the news face to face, like. She thought, with your tour coming to an end and you, no doubt, eager to get back to the valley to see Mair, she felt you should be warned . . ."

"Frank will you stop babbling on and tell me what's wrong?"

Taking a deep breath Frank said, "Mair — Mair's pregnant!"

"Oh, no, please, not that?"

"I'm afraid so — the result of that dreadful night at Harry and Nellie's apartment."

"That means she must be almost six months gone!"

Frank nodded.

"Did she know before we left Cardiff?"

"I'm not sure. She was nearly three months when my mother and I first found out. You had already left the valley by then."

"If you've both known for three months, why wasn't I told before now?"

"Mair made us promise to delay telling you."

"Why? Surely she didn't think I'd judge or turn away from her . . . did she?"

"No — nothing like that. She thought that if you heard the news earlier you'd want to be with her. She didn't want you to leave the tour and maybe endanger your career prospects on her account."

Rhiannon bit her lip. Mair hadn't wanted her to leave the tour on her account? Or was the real reason that Mair couldn't face the fact of Rhiannon, once again, choosing her career before her? Rhiannon remembered back to when she and Mair had first arrived in Cardiff; of how her Aunt Florrie, when faced with the question of letting them stay, had made it perfectly clear that "my career has to come first".

"I've become as selfish as my Aunt Florrie," Rhiannon said aloud.

"I'm sorry?" Frank said.

"Ignore me, I'm just thinking aloud."

"Rhi, I have to go. But look, there's no great hurry. No one's expecting you back in the valley until a week before Christmas, when the tour ends so —"

"So they're all in for a surprise then, aren't they? I'll need to clear it with Adam but, if all goes well, I should be at your mother's house in time for tea tomorrow evening."

Frank beamed a smile. "And a welcome sight you'll be too."

"Adam? There's no easy way to say this but . . . I'm going to have to leave the show."

"You're joking, yeah?"

"No, I'm afraid not. I need to get back to the valley. You know I wouldn't leave unless I felt it absolutely necessary. With only ten days to go before the end of

304

the tour — I'm sure that Clara is more than capable of filling in for me."

"The audiences are expecting you!"

"I'm sorry. I really am. But I have to go," Rhiannon persisted.

"At least tell me why?"

Although not wishing to announce Mair's predicament to the world she felt that Adam, having been instrumental in saving Mair from Harry and Nellie's clutches, had the right to know the truth. So feeling it best not to beat around the bush or babble on as Frank had done, she found herself blurting out, "Mair's pregnant!"

"What dreadful news, Rhi. I assume it's in consequence of that awful night."

"Yes. According to Frank she's nearly six months gone."

"Frank came to tell you? Where is he? I'd like to see him. He's such a nice, sensible lad. The night we picked up Mair, he was to be commended. I could never have managed it without him."

"I'm afraid he couldn't stay as he needed to get back to barracks. He sends his regards, though."

"No doubt there'll be other times. Now — regarding your situation. You get yourself off to Mair and don't give the show another thought. Just you take good care of her."

"Thank you, Adam. This time, taking good care of her is what I intend to do — if she'll let me, that is."

"And why wouldn't she?"

"Well, I've not always done so in the past, have I? Too busy putting myself, my career, my life and even Gus before her."

"My Gus turned your head. He made you —"

Rhiannon raised her hand, cutting him short. "Adam, when are you going to stop blaming Gus? How many times do I have to tell you that what happened between us was as much my fault as his? It's time to face the truth; I wanted him as much as he wanted me. You have to stop putting me on some sort of pedestal — I'm a big girl now."

"So I can see. I consider myself well and truly told off! And maybe you're right. After all, everyone knows — it takes two, eh? But it doesn't stop me wanting to protect you. After all, you were my protégée; I was the one who first encouraged you to go on the stage, so in lots of ways I still feel responsible for you."

"And I wouldn't want to change that. Knowing you're there looking out for me has always made me feel special . . . the way my dad used to make me feel."

"I'm honoured. Now, go on, be off with you and start packing. You have until the February auditions to sort your family commitments out. On your way you can tell Clara I want to see her. When she finds out that she's to be your understudy for the rest of the tour — it'll be akin to my lighting touchpaper; her screams of excitement will no doubt be heard for miles, so cover your ears."

Rhiannon laughed. "I'll do that. And Adam, thanks again."

306

Back at the digs, in the small bedroom she shared with Clara, as Rhiannon packed her belongings into her valise, she felt as if a huge weight had been lifted from her; leaving the tour was the right thing to do. And now that the decision had been made she couldn't wait to be on her way. Luckily, its being Sunday and no show that night, there'd be no goodbyes. She'd leave Adam to come up with a plausible excuse; "family commitments" would more than cover it.

A few hours later an exhausted Clara, having been put through the paces of a long rehearsal by Adam, entered the room.

"Rhi, what's happened? Why have you got to leave? Does it have anything to do with Frank's visit earlier today?"

"Yes. He brought news from home. I can't say too much; let me just say it's a family problem and I'm needed back in Ponty."

"I'm sorry to hear that. Pleased as I am to be getting the chance to understudy you, I really don't want to see you go. But if you have to . . . Is there anything I can do to help?"

"No thanks. I'm almost packed. In the morning I plan to catch an early train to Cardiff, then another from Bridgend to Pontrhyl and then a charabanc up the valley. It'll be a long trip but I can't wait to get home."

Clara caught around her. "I'm going to miss you. I only hope I can do your song justice. I know I've practised it with you often enough and I've my own costume; the one Mrs Gordon made me before we left, but you're a hard act to follow."

"You'll do fine. I've every confidence in you and, who knows? If you do as well as I know you can, Adam may give you your own slot in his new show."

"Yes, and pigs might fly."

They both laughed.

Rhiannon reached into her valise for a pencil and quickly scribbled Ethel's address on the back of an old theatre programme. "Look, this is where I'll be staying. If you like, you could write to me — let me know how you get on. With everyone going their separate ways for Christmas, it'll be nice for us two to keep in touch."

"That's a great idea. When I write to you, I'll send you my mother's address in Oxford. Whatever happens I intend to be in Cardiff for Adam's February auditions. I really enjoy working for him — I'd settle for any part in the show, really."

CHAPTER
TWENTY-SEVEN

At 7.30 after a long day's travelling, Rhiannon eventually arrived at Ponty Square. The trip up from Pontrhyl station had seemed to take ages; the horse-drawn charabanc had stopped at regular intervals to let valley folk on and off along the way. Rhiannon recognized some of the older travellers but, apart from inquisitive looks, they didn't seem to recognize her. And why should they? Dressed in all her finery — dark-blue long coat, fur hat and muffler — she looked considerably older than her age, and so different from the sixteen-year-old who'd left the valley nearly a year ago.

The horses drew the charabanc to a stop. Rhiannon picked up her valise and, after politely thanking the driver, stepped off. For a moment she didn't move, taking in the familiar surroundings. She was home at last.

She took a deep breath and made her way along Oxford Street, passing Peglers' store and Oliver's shoe shop. Across the road she could see John Jenkins's butcher's shop; it was closed now and in complete darkness, but his house next door, with the glow of the gaslight filtering through the curtain, looked so welcoming, it made Rhiannon feel very warm inside.

She crossed the rough stone road and knocked on the door. From inside the house she heard Aunt Ethel's familiar voice call out.

"Sadie, Martha, there's someone at the door. I'm busy washing the dishes, so can one of you please answer it?"

"I'll go, Mam," one of them called back. Rhiannon couldn't tell whether it was Sadie or Martha.

Seconds later the door opened and Sadie stood there, her eyes startled as a rabbit's in headlights. "Rhi? Is it really you? But you're not due until Christmas."

"Sadie, love, I assure you it is me. I came home early to surprise you all."

Sadie flung her arms around Rhiannon. "Welcome back — we've missed you so much."

"What's all the commotion?" Ethel demanded as she came to the door.

Releasing her stranglehold on Rhiannon, Sadie turned to her mother, "Look Mam, it's Rhiannon. Rhiannon's back!"

"Well, my good God! Sadie, move aside, don't leave her standing on the doorstep, she'll catch her death. Rhi, come on in," Ethel gushed.

"I'll go and find Martha, I can't wait to give her the news," Sadie enthused.

"It really is so lovely to see you, Rhi, we weren't expecting you so soon," Ethel said, leading the way down the hall.

"I know. I wanted to surprise you all. Where's Mair?"

310

"She's having a bit of a lie down. You know she's . . .?" Ethel stopped and turned to face Rhiannon.

"Pregnant? Yes. Frank called to see me. That's why I'm here. How is she?"

"She's fine — as big as a house, mind. You'll not recognize her. She'll be that pleased to see you. I'll go up and call her, shall I?"

"Aunt Ethel, if it's all right with you, I'll go up to see her. I'd like some time alone with her."

"Of course you would. Here give me your lovely coat, I'll hang it up for you."

"Thank you," Rhiannon said, removing her coat, hat and muffler.

"You take your suitcase up to Mair's room, the room you shared with her after my wedding. It's a big room with a large double bed, so I hope you'll be all right?"

"We'll be fine." Rhiannon smiled. "Aunt Ethel, it's so good to be back home."

Ethel sniffled into her handkerchief. "Now look what you've made me do. You go on up and see your sister and when you're both done catching up, come on down to the kitchen and I'll make you both a brew and a light supper. Uncle John is at the church choir rehearsals, but he'll not be gone long. Why, he's going to be that made-up to see you."

"Will he? I'm sure he wasn't best pleased to find out I'd left you to care for a pregnant young girl — that was never part of the bargain. I bet she's been the talk of the valley."

"He, like me, never gave a fig what malicious gossips had to say. What they don't know they make up. But we know the truth. We know that Mair's condition was through no fault of her own. Anyways, the gossips soon found someone else's misfortune to get their teeth into."

"We're so lucky to have the likes of you and John Jenkins on our side."

"All you have to believe is that, working together as a family, we can get through anything. Now, get yourself up to see Mair."

Before making her way upstairs Rhiannon stopped to give Ethel a hug and, placing a kiss on her aunt's forehead, whispered, "You're a real treasure."

Rhiannon gave a gentle tap on Mair's bedroom door.

"Come in, Aunt Ethel, I'm not sleeping."

Rhiannon reached for the decorative china doorknob and slowly opened the door. "Mair, love, it's me," she croaked, as she welled up with emotion.

"Rhi! Rhi! What are you doing here?" Mair cried as she attempted to raise her heavy body off the bed.

"Stay where you are, I'll come over to you. Auntie Ethel was right. I can't believe the size of you. Frank told me you were six months gone, but I never imagined that the skinny waif I left behind could ever get this big."

Mair muffled a nervous laugh. "Yes, I knew that Frank intended calling on you. But I didn't expect you to come see me. Rhi, I'm sorry you had to find out like that. It wasn't that I didn't want to tell you. I thought something was amiss when we were in Cardiff, but I didn't want to believe. I thought if I ignored it, then it might go away."

"You daft ha'peth. You shouldn't have had to go through the worry of it on your own."

"To be honest, when Aunt Ethel guessed at last, it was such a relief. Everyone has been so kind — especially Frank. He writes to me every week. He'll be home for Christmas and New Year. Uncle John Jenkins made me the most fantastic cot and Aunt Ethel has been busy knitting baby clothes. Frank insists that he's buying me a baby-carriage. He's seen one in Howells in Cardiff. He's been saving up for it for months. Rhi? About Frank and . . ."

"Yes. What about Frank?"

"Well, Frank and me . . . we're sort of . . . courting." Mair blushed.

Rhiannon saw it as the blush of a young girl in love. It seemed so natural and yet, at the same time, considering her condition, so out of place. Rhiannon felt a lump rise in her throat.

"Rhi, you don't mind do you?"

Rhiannon swallowed hard in an effort to regain her composure. It worked. "Of course I don't mind. I think it's great news. I always knew that lad had sense."

"It's early days yet. And I am only fourteen, but Frank says, that only gives us more time to really get to know each other. And Rhi, he also says that, even though the baby's not his, we're going to manage just fine."

"And I believe him. If anyone has the strength of character to deal with it, then Frank has. I'm so pleased for you both but, tell me, how did Ethel take the news?"

"As always, she said she knew before we did, and said she couldn't be happier. Secretly, I think she was worried that his career in the army might distance him from her and the valley. As it is, he's back home every chance he gets."

Rhiannon laughed, "And there was I thinking you might be in need of a big sister. I even left the tour to be with you."

"Oh, but I do. I really do! You can't believe what it means to me to have you put me before the tour, it makes me feel so . . . loved."

"Mair. I really do love you. I may not have always shown it but I do."

Rhiannon sat on the bed and caught her sister in her arms. They embraced for what seemed like ages, happy to have restored the bond they had thought they'd lost for ever.

Eventually it was Mair who spoke first. "Well then, sis, are you going to help me off this bed? I think it's time we put Auntie Ethel out of her misery. I bet she wishes she could have been a fly on the wall, eh?"

They both laughed aloud.

With Rhiannon leading the way they headed downstairs to give Ethel the good news, united as sisters and as friends. As they entered the kitchen the look on their faces spoke volumes.

Ethel smiled. "I can see we're going to have such a great Christmas!"

CHAPTER
TWENTY-EIGHT

Gus Davenport, still nursing a hangover, the result of his having over-indulged the night before, stared at the pint of ale in front of him; maybe a hair of the dog, a livener, would set him straight for the day. But as he picked up the tankard he couldn't help but notice how his hand visibly shook. He raised the ale gingerly to his lips and took a small sip; it tasted good. He took a bigger swig. He knew he was drinking too much, but what the hell? Drink deadened his senses, stopped him thinking of what he'd done — of what he'd become: a liar, a coward — an excuse for a man.

He reached into the inside pocket of his overcoat for a cigarette and felt *The Stage* newspaper he'd picked up at the newsagent, from force of habit. It was the bible for every aspiring actor, singer or stage performer, holding as it did, information regarding every show in the country and up-to-date news on who was doing what, where and when. He took the newspaper from his pocket and opened it. The first thing he read was "ADAM FLETCHER'S NEW TOURING SHOW A SELL OUT!"

His eyes scanned down to the list of venues and dates the show would be visiting and saw Saturday 12

December, The Swansea Empire. He checked the date again. Adam's show was actually on in Swansea tonight. He quickly read the list of artistes appearing in the show, and, as he read Rhiannon's name his heart missed a beat.

He remembered how Adam had talked to him about taking her exciting new talent on tour with them, *them* being the operative word. If things hadn't turned out the way they had he would be with them. Damn it all . . . he *should* be with them! Surely, there had to be a way to put things right? Suddenly he knew what he had to do. He set the tankard of ale on the bar, stood up and headed for the door.

"Well now, look who's crawled out of the woodwork?"

"Hello, Adam," Gus said.

"What the hell are you doing here? As far as I'm concerned nothing's changed," Adam snapped.

"That's where you're wrong. I've changed." Gus stared into Adam's eyes, willing him to see how he'd changed.

"Is that so? Why do I find that so hard to believe?"

"Adam, I know what you think of me. But, you're still my uncle and whether you like it or not I still regard you as my friend — perhaps my only friend, and I need you to listen to me. I admit that, by not telling you about the depth of my feelings for Rhiannon, I let you down, but what about our working partnership? Now, be honest, have I ever let you down professionally?"

"N-no, when it came to your work in the theatre, I never questioned your professionalism — that's not what is at issue here."

316

"But that's where you're wrong. The night you ordered me out of your house you also ordered me out of the theatre and . . . ultimately, out of the show."

"You didn't have to leave. You could have stood your ground."

"My leaving with my tail between my legs must have proved to you what a weak-willed excuse for a man I'd become."

"You're right there!"

"So why have I come to see you now?"

"No doubt you'll tell me."

"I came to tell you that, you're right. I shouldn't have left. What I should have done then, and what I now want to do is to . . . stand and face the music. I can only imagine, after you told Rhiannon about my past, how hurt and confused she must have felt?"

"She had a right to know. And yes, I told her everything, so, we must hope, she'll now see you for the scoundrel you really are."

"That's as maybe. But I intend to find her and tell her that I truly love her. Adam, don't look at me like that. It's true! Rhiannon Hughes has captured my heart and somehow — I don't care how long it takes — I intend to prove it to her."

"Well, well! At last you've met your match. But after walking away without so much as a by your leave, what makes you think that she'll want to see *you*?"

"Right now, probably she won't. And who could blame her? But I think you owe me —"

"Sorry? I owe you? I can't wait to find out how."

"By your own admission, where my work is concerned, I never let you down . . . so why ruin my career?"

"It was never my intention. I just needed you to leave — for Rhiannon's sake."

"It must have crossed your mind that, if only by implication, my leaving the show so abruptly would give the theatre gossips a field day. Since then I've tried, without success I may say, to join other theatre companies, only to be turned away. We've always known how much weight your name adds to a show's success. Well, apparently, if the great Adam Fletcher can let me, his own nephew, walk away then . . .?"

"I'm sorry. As I said before, that was never my intention."

"So — help me get a job. I don't mean with this show. I wouldn't want to compromise Rhiannon."

"There's no place for an MC in this show anyway."

"I heard about the new format. How's the compère versus MC experiment been going?" Gus asked.

"It's gone down extremely well, although, if I'm honest, I still think music hall lends itself more to having a master of ceremonies rather than a compère run the show."

"I'm glad to hear it. So, about that job?"

"I'm probably mad to even consider it but . . . I don't know if you saw my advert in *The Stage*?"

Gus shook his head. After seeing Rhiannon's name he'd been side-tracked.

"Well, I'm in the process of planning a new music hall show for my return to the Empire in Cardiff —

auditions begin in February. If you're still interested . . . perhaps you could sit in on the auditions?"

"Thanks. I'll be there. It'll be like old times."

"I'm not saying things can ever be as they were between us but I see no reason why we can't work together professionally."

"Neither can I. There's just one more thing . . . I thought I might stay to watch Rhiannon's performance this evening. I promise I'll keep out of the way. I'll not try to see her."

"You don't know?"

"Know what?"

"Rhiannon's no longer with the show."

"But I saw her name in *The Stage* listed as part of the cast."

"You're right, she was in the show. I'm afraid she left last week . . . personal reasons."

Gus couldn't hide his disappointment. "I don't suppose you'd tell me where she's gone. Has she gone back home?"

"I'm sorry, Gus, it really isn't my place to say," Adam said.

"I understand. Anyway thanks for your time. I'll see you for the auditions in February." Gus made to leave.

"Gus, wait," Adam called. "Before you go you'd better take these." Adam handed him a bunch of keys. "They're your keys to my house. If you're planning to return to Cardiff you're going to need somewhere to stay."

Taking the keys, Gus said, "Thanks. I really appreciate it. Although I'm not sure I deserve such kindness."

"Rhiannon always said blood was thicker than water."

"Rhiannon said that?"

"Oh yes. And believe me when I say that she's said a lot more than that. Why, less than a week ago, before she left the tour, she gave me a piece of her mind. She made it clear to me that . . . what happened between the two of you was none of my business. She made me reassess my first reaction, and how quick I'd been to jump to what appears to be the wrong conclusion. If that's what I did, then I'm truly sorry."

"I don't blame you for reacting the way you did. For years I didn't even like myself. When I lost Mum and Dad, I lost the two people I loved the most. It made me afraid to love again, believing that anyone I truly loved would be taken from me."

"I should have helped you more. But, after their death, it seemed the obvious solution for me, your uncle, to take you in. Now, with hindsight, maybe a bachelor with no experience of bringing up children really wasn't the right choice."

"You did the best you could. I'm not blaming you in any way. It was just the way I was. And you were right. I didn't love Helena Biggins. So you can imagine my confusion when she took her own life. I hadn't loved her, yet she'd been taken too."

"I always accused you of not being capable of loving anyone but yourself. Under the circumstances, how cruel was that?"

"Not cruel at all, really. Part of me believed it to be true and then, just when I'd resolved never to fall in love, Rhiannon Hughes walked into my life and I fell hook, line and sinker. But, truth be known, I was

320

terrified of the way I felt about her. In calling me to book, you gave me a way out — and I took it. Since then I've tried everything to erase her from my thoughts and dreams, I even turned to drink, but while dulling my senses, the effects were purely temporary. When the drink wore off the memory of her came flooding back. I don't think I'll ever stop thinking of her and the truth is, I don't want to."

"So what do you intend to do about it?"

"As I told you earlier, I intend to get back to work and sort my life out and then, however long it takes, I shall find her and throw myself upon her mercy."

"If that's what you truly have in mind, I suggest you take yourself straight back to our house in Cardiff. I'll be back in time for Christmas. We'll talk again then. How are you off for money?"

"I'm fine. You always paid me well. At the moment my bank account is looking a lot healthier than I am."

A few days before Christmas Rhiannon read the much awaited letter from Clara.

16 West Road,
Witney,
Oxon.
England

Dear Rhi,
I hope this letter finds you well and that whatever problem you had with the family has been sorted out. As you can tell from the above address, I'm

spending Christmas with my family and, after three months of living out of a suitcase it feels very odd.

I bet you thought I'd never write. The thing is, ever since the tour ended, I've been battling with my conscience, wondering whether I should tell you something or not. Then I decided you'd want to know so . . . here goes.

A few days after you left the tour Adam got a visitor — Gus Davenport. And although I knew I shouldn't, I couldn't resist eavesdropping. Anyway, the upshot was . . . although I couldn't hear everything, I definitely heard Adam invite Gus to sit in on the February auditions. I also heard Gus ask about you and Adam tell him how you left the show.

I don't know if you'll be happy to read all this — I know how you've battled, trying to get over him. I didn't want you turning up in Cardiff and just bumping into him.

I don't know what your plans are. Adam told me he offered you a spot in his new show and, once again, he's asked me to be your understudy — which makes me think that I must have done all right filling in for you at the end of the tour.

I can't wait to see you in Cardiff.

Love from your friend, Clara.

CHAPTER
TWENTY-NINE

January 1910

Back in Cardiff and, once again, settled into the house he called home, Gus appreciated the lifeline Adam had thrown to him. It felt good to be on speaking terms with his uncle again. Gus vowed to prove to Adam how much he'd changed.

When the tour ended and Adam returned they spent a quiet Christmas together and settled back, almost, to how they used to be: living and working together in harmony. They had already begun planning for the forthcoming auditions. It felt almost like old times; Gus being as ever, keen to learn from his uncle's vast knowledge of the nuts and bolts of putting on a successful show.

For the majority of Adam's shows Gus was given the prestigious role of master of ceremonies. This proved to Gus how much his uncle trusted him to take control and create the magic needed to spark off and encourage great performances from each and every artist. And up to now, at least in this, he'd never let Adam down.

During their time together, although Rhiannon's name popped up occasionally concerning her role in the show, Gus felt it prudent not to push his uncle regarding her whereabouts. Gus's instinct told him that the only place she would have gone was back home and, while he knew she was a valley girl, he didn't have a clue which valley, much less the exact address. His only hope was that Adam might decide to back down and tell him.

"Frank, I wish I could come with you," Mair moaned.

"Me too, but I really think a trip to Cardiff would take too much out of you." Frank turned to Rhiannon. "You know the baby-carriage she wants, don't you, Rhi?"

"Yes, Jones the post's wife has the only baby perambulator in the valley; it has a wooden carriage, four spoked wheels and a handle to push it. Very posh it is, too."

"My major concern is how to bring it here from Cardiff. Our only hope is if the station master will let us put it in the goods wagon. I'm not so worried about the last few miles from Pontrhyl railway station up the valley to Ponty. Blodwyn Jones was allowed to put hers on top of the charabanc, so I'm sure we can too."

The girls nodded their approval. Frank seemed to have it all in hand.

"What time shall I expect you back in Ponty?" Mair asked.

"If we leave now, we should be back long before it starts to get dark. Mair, you'll be able to watch for us on the doorstep."

As Gus made his way through the streets of Cardiff, he felt in good spirits. Thanks to Adam his life was back on track. He'd stopped drinking and was helping his uncle with the new show. This gave him the impetus he'd needed; if he could have another chance to get back with Rhiannon life would be fulfilled.

Gus stopped in his tracks and, not believing his eyes, blinked a few times. It was Rhiannon. She was coming out of the large Howells department store, and she wasn't alone. Behind her, a young man dressed in uniform was pushing a baby-carriage. Gus watched as the young man moved alongside Rhiannon. Now they were walking side by side, both pushing the carriage, and looking very pleased with themselves.

Gus ducked into the doorway of the nearby tobacconist. He didn't want to risk her seeing him. She looked so beautiful and so . . . happy. At that moment Gus felt devastated.

"What's up with you? You look as if you've seen a ghost," Adam joked.

"No ghost — just Rhiannon," Gus snapped.

"You saw Rhiannon? Where? Why didn't you bring her back with you?"

"She didn't see me. I was on the other side of the road. I saw her coming out of Howells, with a young soldier in tow. They were pushing a baby-carriage." Gus dropped his head in his hands.

"And you didn't think to cross the road to speak to her?"

"No. What was the point? Come on, Adam. You don't have to be a genius to work it out . . . new, handsome, soldier boyfriend . . . new baby-carriage . . . now I wonder?"

"You mean you thought the baby-carriage was for her?" Adam gave a loud belly laugh. "Now who's jumping to conclusions? I should make you sweat but instead, let me put you out of your misery . . . If I'm not mistaken, the young soldier you saw her with was Frank Lewis. They grew up together and he's like a brother to her. As for the baby-carriage, I'm sure that, under the circumstances Rhiannon wouldn't mind me telling you —"

"What?" Gus urged.

"The baby-carriage was probably for Mair — the poor girl is more than six months gone. It's a long story. I'm afraid our idea of thwarting Harry and Nellie's plan failed. I'll tell you exactly what happened . . ."

While Adam relayed the story Gus sat in silence.

"I can't believe that all this happened after I left. And what was I doing? I was drowning in self-pity. Poor Mair — what she must have gone through! Is that why Rhiannon left the tour?"

"Yes, she wanted to be with her sister."

"To think I saw Rhiannon today — and once again, in my foolishness, I let her slip through my fingers."

As instructed by Frank, in the early afternoon Mair stood eagerly waiting on the doorstep. She didn't have to wait long for, in the distance, she could see her baby-carriage precariously perched on top the charabanc as it went past. She waved furiously to everyone inside.

326

Minutes later, when Frank and Rhi came towards her pushing the carriage, she couldn't contain her excitement a moment longer.

"Oh Frank, thank you, it's so lovely."

"You're worth it, and more," Frank said, and putting an arm around her he gently kissed her cheek.

Mair, her face a picture of happiness, turned to Rhiannon. "Rhi, it's just what I wanted. You chose so well, you clever thing you."

A week later, when Frank had returned to his regiment, Rhiannon and Mair spent time together making a layette for the baby: nappies, vests, nightgowns, cot and pram sheets. With the baby due in March, there was still a lot to do. Normally, while they worked, they chatted furiously, but not today — today Mair couldn't help but notice how unusually quiet Rhiannon was.

"Rhi, what's wrong? You're so quiet."

"I'm all right. Honest. Now don't you go worrying yourself about me. You've enough on your plate, it won't be long before you have a baby to care for."

"You must be joking. What with Aunt Ethel, Sadie and Martha all staking a claim, I doubt if I'll get a look in." Mair chuckled.

Rhiannon didn't respond.

Mair put down her sewing and took her sister's hand. "Rhi, it's Gus isn't it?"

Rhi nodded, "It's always Gus." She swallowed hard. "I go to bed thinking of him. I wake up thinking of him. And, in between, I see him around every corner. Why, the other day when Frank and I were in Cardiff, I

327

even imagined him secretly watching me — of course, it was just wishful thinking on my part."

"My — you *have* got it bad!"

Just then, a loud knock on the front door made them both jump.

"I'll answer it," Ethel called from downstairs.

Not long after they heard voices — men's voices.

"I wonder who's come calling?" Mair said.

"Probably friends of Uncle John's," Rhi offered.

A few minutes later they heard Ethel call up the stairs, "Rhiannon, could you come down. You have visitors. We're in the parlour."

Rhi looked at Mair. "Visitors for me? No one knows I'm here."

"Well, someone obviously does. And for Ethel to have shown them into the parlour, she must think them important. Well, don't just sit there. Get yourself downstairs and see who it is."

"You're not coming?"

"Of course I'm coming. I'm bursting to know who's there. But I'd like to make myself presentable first. I'll follow you down shortly. Now go!"

Rhiannon entered the parlour and nothing or no one could have prepared her for the scene in front of her. Auntie Ethel was pouring tea into her best china tea service, as if it were the most natural thing in the world, for Adam Fletcher and, even more unbelievable . . . Gus.

On seeing her, both men stood up. Rhiannon reached for the back of a chair to steady herself.

328

Adam spoke first. "Rhiannon. I know what a shock our being here must be to you but . . ." he turned to Gus, whose eyes stared adoringly at Rhiannon, "this nephew of mine, since seeing you and Frank in Cardiff the other day, he's been like a dog with a bone, pestering me for your address."

Rhiannon stared back at Gus. "So I didn't imagine it; you were watching me in Cardiff?"

Gus nodded ashamedly.

"Now, that's neither here nor there," Adam insisted. "What I had to consider was how you'd feel if he just turned up on your doorstep. That's when I decided to come with him — to soften the blow. And hope you wouldn't think too badly of me for giving in to him."

"Rhi, they said they were friends of yours." Ethel looked worried.

"It's all right, Aunt Ethel. You haven't done anything wrong. It's a bit of a shock that's all."

"I took the liberty of introducing myself and Gus to your aunt. Although I didn't explain why we were here," Adam said.

"And why are you here?" Rhiannon directed her sharp question to Gus.

"I had to come. I need you to know how sorry I am for walking out on you, like I did. For letting you down, and Mair too. I should have been more help to both of you."

"You ran away!" Rhi cried.

"Mrs Jenkins, what say we leave these two young people alone for a while, eh?"

"Yes — if it's all right with you, Rhi?" Ethel flashed Rhiannon a look that said, *I'll not leave if you don't want me to*.

Rhiannon, forcing a smile, nodded her approval.

"Right then, if you'd like to follow me into the kitchen, Mr Fletcher, I'll make us a fresh brew in there."

For a while after they left Rhiannon and Gus stood in silence. Each was unable to believe the other was truly in the room.

"So you and Adam are back on speaking terms, then?"

"Yes. But only recently. Rhi, I came looking for you on the tour only to find that you'd left. I was devastated. Rhi, I came looking for you to apologize for leaving you."

"The way you left was so cruel. How could you go without saying goodbye? I really thought you cared."

"I did — I do. When Adam threatened to tell you the sordid details of my past, I panicked. I took the coward's way out and ran away; it's what I always used to do. I thought you'd hate me."

"Did you think me so fickle? I loved you."

"Loved? And what about now?"

She didn't answer.

"Rhi, when I saw you and Frank in Cardiff, pushing that baby-carriage . . . I felt the bottom drop from my world."

"You thought that Frank and I were . . .?"

"Yes. You can't imagine how ecstatic I felt when Adam put me straight. Rhi, I truly love you. I can't live

330

without you. Please say you'll give me a chance to prove it?"

At that moment Mair, in her eagerness to find out who the visitors were, barged into the parlour without knocking. Only to find Rhiannon and Gus locked in a passionate embrace.

EPILOGUE

London 1911

Nellie Parsons tightened her grubby shawl around her scrawny shoulders. Although it was mid May, at night there was still a chill in the air. She'd spent the last hour parading along the Embankment looking for punters, but no one seemed interested.

Through the dense fog a man's shadowy figure approached her. As he came closer she could tell by the way he was dressed that he was a toff.

"Looking for a bit of business, eh? Ten bob can buy you a whole lot of fun," she slurred her words, rubbing her body against his.

The man roughly pushed her away, causing her to lose her balance. "Get off me, you filthy wretch, you stink to high heaven. Ten bob? You must be joking."

"Sod off, you cheeky bugger!" she called out as she watched him march off towards Westminster Bridge.

Although Nellie had sounded disgruntled, in truth she knew only too well how she looked and smelled. Since Harry had forced her out of her digs penniless she'd been living rough, sleeping under the arches, forced to live on the streets.

The toff had been right. Who in their right mind would pay her ten bob for a bit of how's-yer-father? Why, the way she looked she'd be lucky to get five bob. Nellie sighed . . . how things had changed.

When she and Harry had first arrived in London, fifty guineas was the going rate. Thing were so very different then; Harry, his pockets bulging with the proceeds of their ill-gotten gains in Cardiff, had rented them a posh apartment — right in the heart of theatreland parties and well-to-do punters, close to Soho.

Harry's promise of making an honest woman of her was soon forgotten. Instead, one night she'd come home to find their apartment emptied of everything they'd possessed and a note to say that he'd moved on "to better things", whatever that meant. Nellie's so-called friends were quick to explain, telling her about the affair he'd been having with some well-to-do French tart — and how they'd left to start a new life in Paris, France.

"Good riddance! That's what I say," Nellie mumbled under her breath as she slowly made the long trek to the Strand.

Nellie stood outside the New Gaiety Theatre, situated on the Strand. It had been her regular patch since things had got hard, where she could watch the toffs in their finery parade themselves as they waited for the theatre doors to open for the evening performance.

Nellie sidled up to an old gent thinking, he'll do. After all, beggars can't be choosers. "Fancy a bit of business, eh?" she brazenly asked.

"No, I most certainly do not. Get away with you!" he growled, pulling a handkerchief from his pocket and raising it to his nose, as if to stanch a nasty smell.

"What! You think you're too good for the likes of me," Nellie slurred, the effect of hitting the gin earlier.

The man didn't answer. He simply turned his back, no doubt hoping she'd go away.

But she was having none of it. "Hey, I'm talking to you — you stuck-up bastard!"

Completely ignoring her, the man moved away.

"I'll have you know that my stepdaughter's appearing here tonight. She's famous, don't you know? A big star of the theatre . . . I only wish my own daughter — the ungrateful bitch, had shown such talent! What? Why are you all looking at me like that? Don't you believe me?"

At that moment the theatre door opened and everyone seemed to be pushing her, jostling her out of the way. She was more than a little tipsy and already unsteady on her feet, so suddenly she lost her balance and fell to the floor.

She struggled to get up and failed. "Harry — Harry, make them believe me," she called out. "Tell them how I've rubbed shoulders . . . and more . . . oh yes, a lot more, with the rich and famous." She gave a raucous laugh. "Go on Harry tell them."

But Harry was nowhere to be seen. After all she'd done for him . . . even helping him to auction off her own daughter. How could he have just upped and left her?

"Good bloody riddance!" she cried out to anyone who cared to listen. That's right she thought, I don't need him . . . Mair . . . Rhiannon or . . . any-bloody-one! All I need right now is a nip of gin! And I'll show them. If I can get myself cleaned up a bit — maybe plead to the mercy of the do-gooders of the Salvation Army — and take a bath, I'd have punters lining up for me . . . forget five or ten bob . . . more like five or ten pounds!

Yes, that's what she'd do — she lay her head on the cobbled street, it felt cold and wet, she was so tired . . . what she needed was a little nap. Yes, things always looked better after a little nap.

The streets were wet, and the night unusually cold and foggy, when minutes later a horse and carriage carrying two gentlemen theatregoers, raced to catch curtain up at the New Gaiety Theatre and, with the lack of visibility, the driver failed to notice the young woman. The carriage ran over her; just another bump in the road — nothing for driver or passengers to concern themselves with.

The carriage pulled to a halt outside the theatre where Rhiannon Hughes's name was up in lights. The two city gents stepped down from the carriage and joined the happy crowd entering the foyer, all oblivious to the lifeless soul that was Nellie Parsons, lying dead in the filthy street.